Endorsements

"*Infiltrator* is a powerful and engrossing book. You cannot escape the power and depth of its message! Though it is a work of fiction, I felt myself drawn into the life of the main character and identifying with many of his questions. I was also blessed by the answers he found! I would highly recommend this book, and look forward to the next offering by Mr. Kingsbury."

-Rev. Bruce D. Yates,
Associate Pastor, Spencer Church of the Nazarene &
Director, Irish Hammer Power

"I appreciate the ability of Kevin Kingsbury to clearly depict what spiritual warfare may look like if we could visually see it in detail. His working of Scripture and narrative has opened the door for the considering of great thoughts made easier to understand through his illustrations and explanations. I can envision using this work to initiate many discussion starters with those in my church about a number of valuable topics like: salvation, temptation, armor of God, demons, angels, the carnal man, and more. Thanks, Kevin, for a work that is meaningful and well-done."

-Rev. Bryan V. Thompson, Sr. Pastor
Houghton Lake Wesleyan Church

"Kevin Kingsbury writes like a man on fire. Detailed, Biblical, yet imaginative wordsmithing that will pull you in and place you right into the story. A classic story of darkness giving way to the light, of good triumphing over evil. Kevin writes with time and life experience on his side. He has, like many of us, experienced the darkness and has emerged with a passion to walk in humble victory with Jesus. This is a phenomenal read and I'm eagerly anticipating the sequel."

-Gene Troyer
Campus Pastor, Granger Community Church

"Intrigue, betrayal, and a manipulation all play a part in this exciting and challenging new novel by Christian writer Kevin Kingsbury. From the idyllic first moments of Eden, through the trauma of deception and disgrace and horrific spiritual warfare, we see the attacks of Satan on humanity firsthand, in narrative form that brings scripture to life. *Infiltrator* is an eye-opening story that is important for anyone who believes and desires to be outfitted to accomplish the battle God has set before them."

-Rev. Bruce E. Lawton
Sr. Pastor, Lapeer Free Methodist Church

INFILTRATOR

INFILTRATOR

KEVIN L. KINGSBURY

TATE PUBLISHING
AND ENTERPRISES, LLC

Infiltrator
Copyright © 2013 by Kevin L. Kingsbury. All rights reserved.

No part of this publication may be reproduced, stored in a retrieval system or transmitted in any way by any means, electronic, mechanical, photocopy, recording or otherwise without the prior permission of the author except as provided by USA copyright law.

Scriptures taken from the *Holy Bible, New International Version*®, NIV®. Copyright © 1973, 1978, 1984 by Biblica, Inc.™ Used by permission of Zondervan. All rights reserved worldwide. www.zondervan.com

The opinions expressed by the author are not necessarily those of Tate Publishing, LLC.

This novel is a work of fiction. Names, descriptions, entities, and incidents included in the story are products of the author's imagination. Any resemblance to actual persons, events, and entities is entirely coincidental.

Published by Tate Publishing & Enterprises, LLC
127 E. Trade Center Terrace | Mustang, Oklahoma 73064 USA
1.888.361.9473 | www.tatepublishing.com

Tate Publishing is committed to excellence in the publishing industry. The company reflects the philosophy established by the founders, based on Psalm 68:11,
"*The Lord gave the word and great was the company of those who published it.*"

Book design copyright © 2013 by Tate Publishing, LLC. All rights reserved.
Cover design by Rtor Maghuyop
Interior design by Jomel Pepito
Author photograph by Jeannine Eubanks

Published in the United States of America
ISBN: 978-1-62510-885-2
1. Fiction / Christian / General
2. Religion / Christian Life / Spiritual Warfare
12.12.17

Acknowledgment

I would like to thank my amazing wife, Andie, for her encouragement, support, wisdom, and prayers, for her love for Jesus, sensitivity to the Holy Spirit, and willingness to sacrifice to obey his voice, and finally, for believing in me and for believing in my call to write for the glory of God. Thank you, Andie. I love you!

CHAPTER ONE

His shape shimmered as he slipped through the transdimensional barrier separating the unseen world from the realm in which the humans lived. It was not completely unlike the dimensional portal referred to in children's cartoons and comic books through which the bad guys could travel instantaneously to any destination they wished to wreak havoc upon the unsuspecting masses and further their plans for world domination. Ironically, this is exactly what the barrier was being used for. In this case, however, the bad guys weren't wearing costumes and makeup, and the good guys didn't necessarily win at the end of the episode or after the last page was turned.

Looking back through the barrier, Manevid, a loyal servant of the prince of darkness, surveyed his handiwork. He uttered his characteristic low, guttural laugh, blowing a wisp of silvery-blue smoke from his nostrils while thick black saliva dripped from his lower lip and fell to the ground between his leathery clawed feet. Had the average human been able to hear the horrific laugh and set his eyes on the being that uttered it, he would have been instantly struck with such terror as to render him immobile, paralyzed in fear, unable even to lift a hand to wipe the cold sweat that beaded up on his forehead or to press down the hairs that were standing straight up on the back of his neck.

Won't be needing this anymore, he chuckled, then closed his eyes in concentration. For a few seconds, nothing happened. Then his form quickly changed from the terrifying demonic monster of medieval lore to the beautiful angelic creature he truly was.

Once satisfied with his transformation, Manevid returned his attention to the events unfolding on the other side of the barrier.

Two of the girls were terrified. They huddled together against the wall, the light from the flickering candles causing eerie shadows to dance across their faces to the wall behind them. Their breath came in short gasps as if their capacity to voluntarily execute the basic function of breathing had been disengaged, thereby rendering them unable to intake the large amount of air required to expel the terrified scream they each held behind quivering lips. Their hearts raced in defiance of whatever had caused their involuntary functions to revert to basic support of life. They would have been crying, but it seemed even their tears were too frightened and stunned to spill.

A third girl was not so violently shocked by the event. "Whoa, that was so cool!" Anna shrieked, standing amid the burning candles that the girls had placed on the living room floor in the shape of a five-pointed star. She was looking at the place near the corner where the ghoulish creature had materialized a few seconds before, seeming to emerge from within the wall itself, as if hoping it would repeat its entrance. "Let's do it again!"

The fourth girl was just plain angry. "Are you out of your mind?" Mel hissed. She was also trembling although her condition was more from the result of shock and intense anger than simply fear alone. "What was that thing? Ugh!" She shivered, trying to shake the memory of the ugly beast off her as though it had not only burned its image into her mind, but had also, somehow, imprinted itself on her body like a tattoo.

"I don't know. That's why we should bring it back and ask it. Maybe it was the ghost of some dead king from long ago or something."

"Or maybe it was the devil, Anna!" Mel retorted. "Whatever it was, I don't ever want to see one again!"

"Oh, come on, you big baby! It was only a ghost—the result of a harmless little séance ritual," Anna giggled, amused by her friends' reactions to the strange, but intriguing apparition. "I found a book at the library about pagan rituals, and I checked it out. This one looked fun, so I thought I'd try it. Besides, I just made up a name for the spirit. It's not like we called up Satan himself or some real demon or something. We probably just got carried away with our imaginations," she offered, attempting to explain away the creature's appearance.

"Well, it didn't seem very harmless to me," Mel growled, her anger not at all concealed by her tone. She flipped on the light switch and began blowing out the candles, seeking a release for her emotion and not knowing what else to do. "This was a stupid idea," she muttered.

"Hey, you didn't have to participate, sissy girl," Anna said defensively. "We were just messing around. Nobody got hurt or anything. Maybe a little shaken up," she said, looking over at Stacy and Tonya, still sitting on the floor and silently clinging to one another. "But no major damage done."

With the lights back on, the candles blown out, and most importantly, the absence of the creature, Stacy and Tonya stopped trembling, at least outwardly, and began to feel a little bit better. But only a little bit. They cautiously stood up and helped clean up the room, replacing the oversized chair and floor lamp where their candles had been arranged in the middle of the room. Even with the room back to its normal arrangement, there was still an eerie, evil feel to the place. They kept looking over their shoulders to all parts of the room, fearing the reappearance of the creature somewhere right behind them. They wanted nothing more than to get as far away from this place as possible.

"Look, uh, I'm taking off," Mel said, the disgust still evident in her voice. "I don't think I want to be in this house any more tonight."

"Aw, come on, Mel," Anna chided. "It wasn't that bad. Just a hallucination. Let's make some popcorn and watch a movie."

"Sorry, Anna, that was way too creepy for me. I'm going home."

"I'm coming with you," Stacy said.

"Good," Mel said, relieved. "I didn't want to go out there in the dark by myself."

"Oh, listen to you two!" Anna said disgustedly. "Fine, go ahead and go. Watch out that the boogeyman doesn't get you!"

Mel and Stacy grabbed their things and walked out the door. The four friends had been meeting at Anna's house a couple of times a month for most of the school year. Typically, they would watch TV or a movie, maybe play games, do whatever it was that teenage girls did when they got together outside of school. Anna had often voiced her interest in spiritual things, reading books on new age psychology and religion and the like. Recently, however, she seemed to be obsessed with the darker side of spiritualism. She would mimic casting a spell on one of the girls if she did something that deserved chiding from another. Her interest in the dark arts and magic and weird stuff like that had also found its way into her conversations of late. Anna would bring up odd, sinister things to talk about—ancient rituals, animal and human sacrifices, talking with the dead. The other girls shrugged it off as merely a phase Anna was going through although they hoped that it would not be a lengthy one.

"What is wrong with her?" Stacy asked rhetorically as she buckled her seat belt.

"I don't know, but I'm getting tired of it," Mel said, shoving the key into the ignition and starting her car. "That whatever-it-was tonight was too much. Over the top. Something has to be done about her. I think she needs some counseling or something. I'm going to talk to my parents about it. They might know what to do about her."

"She won't get in trouble, will she?" asked Stacy.

"Not trouble," Mel concluded. "She hasn't done anything wrong. Sick and freaky, maybe, but I mean, it's not like she broke the law or something like that. At least not human law. It's just… weird. People shouldn't be doing stuff like that, messing around with stuff you don't understand. It's not right. And it's scary! I think we need to pray."

"Tell me about it," Stacy agreed. Silence settled between them as each girl prayed, asking God to protect them from the evil feeling that gripped them like a giant hand. They asked forgiveness for participating in any way with anything supernatural, at least anything supernaturally evil, and prayed for protection for Tonya and Anna, who were still in that house where the evil presence had manifested itself. Each found her own way to deal with the paranormal experience they had just been privy to while Mel carefully maneuvered the vehicle in the direction of Stacy's house.

Manevid watched as she pulled out of the driveway and onto the road leading out of the subdivision. The car turned left, then sped out of town toward Stacy's house. The girls rode in near silence until they got to the road where Stacy lived.

"I don't know what to think about that," Stacy admitted, her mind going back to the appearance of that hideous creature at Anna's place.

"Me either," Mel agreed. "I mean, I understand what happened, but I don't know what to do about it. I'm going to talk to Mom and Dad when I get home. That was just too freaky. See ya at school tomorrow."

"Yeah, see ya." Stacy slammed the car door and quickly walked up the sidewalk to her door. Once she got it opened and stepped inside, Mel put the car into reverse and backed out of the driveway, constantly checking the back seat and looking around in every direction. She drove the quarter mile to the stop sign, then turned right and headed for home, eager to put the events of the evening behind her. "Forgive me, Jesus," she breathed. "Forgive me for getting anywhere near that kind of garbage. I should have stopped it. I should have stood up to Anna when it first began. Father, give me strength to resist anything like that in the future. I will not give the devil a foothold in my life by allowing stuff like that wherever I am or whoever I am with. I am sorry I didn't say anything to Anna. I will talk to her tomorrow after school. Please help me to say the right thing to her. And please take this creepy feeling away. I know you are more powerful, and I know you are with me. I want you to use my life for your glory, whatever that might mean."

Manevid waited until the car picked up speed. Dark county road, lots of trees, no traffic. Perfect. *She'll talk to her parents about it,* he chuckled. *Not tonight, she won't—maybe never again for that matter.* Manevid looked up at the demon beside him. "Do you know how much work I've put into that girl, Anna? And this puny, insignificant little human brat thinks she is going to mess all that up because she got a little scared when she saw me? No way. I cannot allow it. She is bad enough on her own, but add her father to it? No. He is a genuine menace, that one. And I can't allow all that work to be wasted. I have been filling her mind with thoughts of the occult, with witchcraft, with devil worship, with all kinds of wonderful evil things, and she has been getting more receptive all the time. Even to the point of checking that priceless book out of the library—the one that I put there myself—and conning her friends into trying that séance ritual. She is so close to diving in headfirst to spiritual captivity and depravity! I can't allow that other one to ruin it!" Manevid continued to watch Mel's car as she drove down the deserted road.

Suddenly, Manevid felt an evil presence surround him as an ominous figure manifested itself between him and the other demon. The two demons dropped to one knee, bowing before their master. "Great Prince," Manevid said cautiously, not moving and not looking up.

"Rise," the figure commanded, then he nodded down toward the car Manevid was watching, uttered two words and disappeared as silently and mysteriously as he had appeared.

"Kill her," he had ordered.

A characteristic evil grin crept across Manevid's face. *Finally!* he thought to himself.

"Watch this," he said, leaping to his feet and slapping the demon beside him on the shoulder. His appearance instantly changed back to that of the hideous demonic monster as he jumped through the barrier and into the human world, hovering amid the treetops as he watched the approaching vehicle. A small dip in the dirt that purported to be a ditch ran along the shoulders on either side of the road. On the outside of the dip, trees lined both sides of the road before the land gave way to corn fields, soybean fields, and small patches of privately owned wooded land.

She must be in a hurry, Manevid thought to himself as the car approached at a rather high rate of speed. *Here we go. Steady... now!*

Manevid shot down to the road in a flash, landing on his clawed feet and letting out a loud, thunderous growl. He made eye contact with Mel and stretched out his hands as if to grab her. She screamed and swerved the car to avoid hitting the creature that had materialized in the middle the road. Before she could correct the swerve and get the car traveling safely back down the road, there was a loud crunch of metal and the sound of shattering glass.

"Beautiful, Manevid! Top drawer!" the other demon cried.

"All in a day's work," Manevid smiled, stepping back through the barrier and changing back to his natural state. "That'll be a closed casket affair, or I don't know my funerals!" he added with glee, looking back at the mangled scrap of metal that had, until a few seconds ago, been a fully functional automobile containing a live human. The demons laughed as they watched her guardian angel slowly rise up to heaven, his assignment on earth having been prematurely terminated by the opposition.

Chapter Two

The man silently sat on the forward edge of a new black leather office chair. The very position of his body suggested defeat. He was leaning forward with his upper body slumped over the top of his desk, arms crossed, face buried in the crook of his elbow. Although the fancy chair swiveled, rolled, partially reclined, and was filled with the best cushion filling available to afford its occupant maximum comfort in any of half a dozen positions, its features were completely wasted on the Reverend Dr. Marshall J. Pennington, associate pastor of Community Gospel Church. He was much too frustrated, discouraged, and ill at ease for the word *comfort* to apply, in any stretch of the imagination, to his day, his physical state, or even his demeanor.

It isn't supposed to be like this, he thought to himself. *It simply should not be this difficult.*

He paused, lifting his head and looking up at the ceiling. The dusty old ceiling fan creaked as the blades slowly made their endless circular pilgrimage around the base of the unit, sending a nearly imperceptible cool breeze down to where Marshall sat. Several moments passed. Suddenly, he practically leapt to his feet, eyes still on the ceiling. The snapping of his knees sent the fancy chair gliding across the hardwood floor until it bounced off the wall behind him with such force that it came to rest only inches from where its short journey had begun. If he had been sitting perfectly straight at his desk instead of leaning slightly sideways, the chair probably would have crashed into the potted plant on the sill in front of the tall, narrow window, knocking it out of the window sill and scattering potting soil across the floor. Had such an unfortunate event actually taken place, however—noisy though it may have been—Marshall would not have noticed; he was too lost in the world of his own private thoughts. He came out from behind the desk and walked around the room, throwing his hands into the air and gesturing as though delivering a Sunday morning message on the joy of the Lord to a capacity crowd.

But it wasn't Sunday, it wasn't morning, and there surely wasn't a crowd. Had there been a crowd, they probably would not have listened to him anyway. No, that was unfair. His parishioners loved him, and they always listened attentively to his messages. The problem was, once they left the building, they seemed to forget everything that they had just heard. Even the pointed messages aimed at specific people had failed to get through to them. Counseling had appeared promising in several cases at first, but after painstakingly listening to their problems, identifying the root issues behind their problems, and advising a means of improving themselves, the counselees would terminate the sessions, and all progress would be lost.

Why? Why won't they listen? Why can't they understand? How am I supposed to get through to them?

Marshall walked back over to his chair and sat down, huffing out a frustrated breath. He leaned back in the chair and again looked at the ceiling fan. Sometimes he felt just like those poor fan blades—trekking around the same little path day after day, hour after hour, minute after minute, never getting anywhere, never accomplishing anything—merely one insignificant tiny cog in an apparatus whose sole purpose in existence was to run around in a circle and move air from one place to another.

"I know, fan, I know," Marshall said aloud. "I feel your pain, brother fan. But at least you move air when you 'run with perseverance the race marked out for you.'" He paused, shaking his head and grunting. "Maybe we could change places. I could climb up there and move the air, and you could try to get through to these obstinate, stubborn, selfish people." Even as he said the words, he felt a pang of guilt lash out from his conscience to stab at his heart. They weren't bad, evil people; they were simply deceived. Most of them were very polite and respectful, generally good people. They listened intently on Sunday mornings, congratulated him on another splendid message, then simply returned to their homes and neglected to apply their newly gained knowledge to their lives. Attendance had not increased in over two years. The church hadn't lost any members other than due to deaths within the congregation, but it hadn't gained any either other than due to births within the congregation. Very few of those in attendance were maturing in their faith. The church may as well have been aimlessly cruising on autopilot; so little had changed in the past decade or so.

Pushing away from the desk with his foot, Marshall spun himself in a circle, still absently looking up at the ceiling. *How can I get through to them? How can I convince them that the enemy is out there and that he has them in his grasp? They figure if they aren't intentionally bad, they must be good enough. If they keep a few of the Ten Commandments, tithe once in a while, and show up to church every Sunday—okay, most Sundays—then they are fine, and God is pleased with them. How can I show them how wrong they are? How can I convince them that there is a battle going on every minute of every day and that they are part of that battle whether they choose to admit it or not? How can I expose the enemy to them so that they will believe, so that they will see the enemy for what he is and see themselves for what they are and make a determination to change?*

How can I convince them that by refusing to take sides in the battle, they have already taken the wrong side?

Marshall got out of his chair and knelt in front of it. He was silent for a long time, a renegade tear gently winding its way from the corner of his eye down to his upper lip where it got absorbed in his mustache. Up until then, he really hadn't been praying; he was more or less pouring his heart out to God. Now feeling defeated, like an utter failure, he addressed the Father with great humility.

"Father," he sobbed, "this isn't working. I am not helping them. I pray for them, I teach them, I nurture them, I even socialize with them, but nothing is getting through! I have done everything I know to do, but I can't get through to them! There must be something I am missing. There must be something more I can do. Please help me. Show me how to reach them." He stopped for a moment, reaching up onto his desk for a tissue to wipe his nose. He didn't remember opening his Bible to Ephesians 6, but it lay open at the edge of his desk. The word *struggle* caught his eye, so he absently began to read verse 12. "For our struggle is not against flesh and blood, but against the rulers, against the authorities, against the powers of this dark world and against the spiritual forces of evil in the heavenly realms."

"I know that, God," he said, the frustration evident in his voice. "'Therefore, put on the full armor,' and so on and so on. How many times have I taught that to them? We even have pictures of the different pieces of armor hanging beside the bulletin board in the foyer to help them remember." Marshall pulled himself up into his chair and wiped his eyes. He inhaled deeply, then let out a heavy sigh, resigning himself to waiting for another day to gain victory over that issue.

He pulled his CD rack over to the center of his desk and looked through it, selecting his favorite Bible Reference Library CD case. Without looking, he removed the CD from the case and slipped it into the appropriate drive on his computer. Maybe he would look up that Ephesians passage and try to get something new out of it. Perhaps one of the commentaries on the CD would have some clever new insights.

Rapid gunfire broke the heavy silence. Marshall jolted, his heart beating fast and hard. He froze in his chair, his eyes darting around the room in search of the source of the gunfire, subconsciously attempting to determine which way to jump to avoid being hit. As he did so, his eyes focused on the image fading into view on the computer screen. Marshall let out a reassured breath and chuckled. His son had accidentally switched his favorite game CD with Marshall's Reference Library CD. Now words appeared on the screen in front of the image.

"Operatives: Field Personnel of the CIA" flashed across the screen. The loud introduction music softened with the next screen, which read, "Knowledge is power. Know your enemy."

Suddenly it hit Marshall, the realization causing nearly the same reaction as the unexpected gunfire sound had. How well did he really know his enemy? I mean, really? Sure, he knew that the devil used to be an angel and that he had been kicked out of heaven and was now ruining the earth, but how much did he really know about how the enemy worked? He grabbed his Bible. Yep, right there in Ephesians, the previous verse, Paul says to put on the full armor of God—and why, you ask—so that you can take your stand against the devil's schemes! What schemes? Marshall had heard many examples of the ways of the devil, and those "flaming arrows" also mentioned later in Ephesians 6—there was a long list of what those could be. But just because you may know what kind of weapons the enemy has, you still may not realize exactly how he intends to use them. Marshall leapt from his chair again, his pulse now racing from excitement rather than shock. He walked around the room, his pace rivaling any daytime shopping mall speed walker. He praised God for giving him the idea of researching the works of the enemy.

Back at his desk, Marshall dove into his study with purpose. Soon, his desk was covered with commentaries, Bibles of various translations, study Bibles, study guides, Bible dictionaries, articles from Christian magazines, and enough computer software to make virtually all of those books unnecessary. He read all about Ezekiel 28, where Ezekiel writes about Lucifer getting cast out of heaven, and Isaiah 14, where Isaiah also refers to the fall of Satan. He looked up every name he could think of for the devil in his Bible dictionaries and read a couple of articles on spiritual warfare from a small stack of magazines. And after nearly three hours of intensive study, he found that he had learned almost nothing new. He felt like a beachcomber who digs furiously after hearing a loud beep on his metal detector, only to find that the treasure for which he had been so diligently searching was nothing more than a useless piece of pipe or a rusty old butter knife.

He placed his face in his hands again. "God," he cried, "what are you trying to tell me? What does it mean to know the enemy? There isn't anything else on him!" He paused, sitting in the silence for several moments. The senior pastor had once told him that God will never be able to answer your request if you're still talking. Pray for a while, then just sit there and listen.

"Father," Marshall finally whispered, "I trust you. Show me what you have for me. I have exhausted my own resources. I can't figure out what to do about my flock, and I can't find any new or useful information on the devil. Lord, I am at the end of my abilities. Please teach me about the enemy. I want to know more about the ways of the enemy."

Manevid growled and shook his head. The demon assigned to work on this pastor was failing miserably. It was Manevid's own rotten luck that the loser had been assigned to his division. His voice thundered as he shouted out a reprimand to the small demon, who cowered in fear of his superior. He would show this pastor a thing or two, not to mention schooling the incompetent underling who had botched his assignment so badly. Wanted to get to know the enemy, did he? Well, Manevid could get right up close and personal if that's what he really wanted. Maybe scare the life right out of him. Or maybe just kill him and be done with it. Or better yet, get his wife involved with that new guy at the children's center where she volunteered part time. Yes, a sleazy affair—that did it every time. And—bonus—it would provide a good old-fashioned scandal for the church too! Oh, but I am a clever one, Manevid thought to himself. Now let's occupy his attention and get his mind off that ridiculous praying.

The little demon watched in fascination as Manevid's form slowly transformed. His stature became much smaller, nearly the size of the little demon himself. Hair grew out of his head, long and brown, and fell straight across his shoulders until it reached the middle of his back. His clothing also changed. It transformed to blue jeans and a sweater, shrinking until they clung snugly and seductively to a flawless female human body. His indiscernible face became a lovely female human one, its beauty rivaled only by the body of which it was a part.

"Watch and learn!" Manevid sneered as he stepped through the barrier and into the foyer of Community Gospel Church, forcing tears to stream from the young girl's pretty blue eyes. He dabbed at his sniffling nose as he lifted his hand to knock on the office door of associate pastor Dr. Marshall J. Pennington.

The bright white light filled Community Gospel Church with such intensity that it knocked Manevid back through the barrier, sending him rolling head over heels. As he regained his footing, having already instantaneously reverted to his natural form, he cursed and growled and poised himself to rush at the angel of light who had the gall to confront him. Manevid had only taken two steps toward the barrier when his head thumped into the chest of Mugray, a very large and imposing member of the heavenly host. Mugray was flanked by a pair of angels on each side, standing tall and strong and ready for battle.

Meanwhile, a sixth member of the heavenly host stood in Marshall's office, directly in front of his desk. Sensing a presence in the room, Marshall removed his hands from his face and looked up inquisitively. To his amazement, a man stood in his office, right in front of his desk. Apparently, he had been so involved in his praying that he had not even heard the knock or the creaking of the heavy old door as the man had entered. He appeared to be about Marshall's age, possibly a bit older, clean-cut, professional. He wore a charcoal gray suit—which had the appearance of having been professionally tailored—expensive leather shoes, and a neatly pressed, lightly starched white oxford shirt. The silk tie protruding from beneath his shirt collar was cinched and held in place by a perfect double Windsor knot. The man stood perfectly still, hands clasped loosely in front of him, his eyes never leaving Marshall's.

"Uh…sorry, I didn't hear you come in," Marshall stammered. "Please, uh, won't you have a seat?" He directed the man to a pair of high-backed leather chairs sitting a few feet in front of his desk.

"That won't be necessary, Dr. Pennington," the man said formally. "We are going on a voyage."

"Who are?" Marshall asked. "Is. I mean, who is? What voyage? How did you get in here? Who are you?"

The man raised a hand to silence Marshall. "Marshall Pennington," he began, "I am known as Gudan. You have prayed for a most unusual revelation. The Most High is pleased with you and has heard your prayer. I have been chosen to deliver the answer."

"Are…you…an…angel?" Marshall asked incredulously, trying to take hold of what was happening.

"Yes, I am," Gudan answered. "More specifically, I am your guardian angel. Because of the sincerity of your heart, the Most High has given me permission to make myself visible to you so that your prayer can be most effectively answered. I have been instructed to take you on a journey into what you call the spiritual realm, the world beyond your world. There you will be able to witness firsthand the workings of the prince of darkness and those who serve him.

"Neither of us will be visible to them, nor will they be able to hear anything we say. We will be unable to interfere or interact in any way with the scenes before us, either in the spiritual realm or in the human realm. We will be permitted only to observe.

"No human has ever made this journey before, save the Redeemer himself, and no one ever will again. Be watchful and alert, Marshall Pennington. You have been granted a rare and terrifying opportunity, the acceptance of which presents you with an equally rare and terrifying responsibility. You must teach the people of the Most High. Teach them what you see and make them understand."

Marshall took a deep breath. "As God wills," he said, walking from behind his desk to stand beside Gudan. "I am ready."

"Very well," Gudan said. "Then it begins." He placed his hand on Marshall's arm, and the eggshell white walls of Marshall's office began to shrink before his eyes.

Chapter Three

Marshall could still see his office walls, but they weren't really there. In fact, they were sinking. No, that wasn't it either. Odd…he was rising! With Gudan's hand still on his arm, they were rising up through the building, and then through the sky. The large steeple on the top of Community Gospel Church quickly faded from view.

Marshall's mind raced. It was so full of questions; he didn't know which one to ask first. He decided to establish a modicum of rapport with Gudan first since he anticipated that their time together would not particularly lend itself to casual conversation. He looked over at Gudan. "Not your usual attire, I presume?" he asked, indicating the suit and tie.

"Of course not, Marshall. I merely thought that perhaps you would be more comfortable if I assumed a human form with fashionably suitable adornments. What you are about to witness will provide sufficient shock to your soul without my appearance complicating matters."

"May I ask what you normally look like? Of course, I've read the biblical descriptions of angels and have seen the artistic interpretations in paintings and pictures, but will I get to see your true form at some point?"

Gudan smiled. Truly, the Most High did frustrate the intelligence of the intelligent. Marshall Pennington had a bachelor's degree in religion, a master's degree in divinity, and a doctorate degree in Christian ministries. He had preached hundreds of sermons and had spent the majority of his life studying the Bible. However, when presented with an opportunity to learn firsthand the greatest mysteries of the universe and what lies beyond, his first question was about the true form of an angel. Gudan smiled the smile of a father watching his child reason out the workings of a Christmas toy. He looked over at Marshall. "If you wish," he replied. "Later."

Moments passed. Marshall looked down and realized that he could no longer see the earth. Beneath them was darkness, but all around them was light. There was nothing his eyes could see, just light. He couldn't identify the source of it, but everything was light. Well, not everything, because there was nothing there. No shapes, no forms, nothing. His eyes could only see light. Not blinding or painful in any way, but that was simply all there was: light.

But then, as if far away but coming closer, Marshall could hear sound. It was the most beautiful sound he had ever heard. Again, he couldn't identify it. It wasn't really singing, and it wasn't really instrumental. As a matter of fact, it wasn't really music although it did have cadence and rhythm. But wouldn't that make it music? It grew louder. The sound was all around him, encompassing his whole being. The odd musical sound didn't register only in his ears; he seemed to hear it with his entire being. It penetrated him. It was as though he was in a pool of water, and he had dissolved and become an integral part of the water; so thoroughly did the sound penetrate his soul. Yet it was a good thing. He felt complete peace. There was no fear, no apprehension. Only peace.

Marshall had a thought. He looked over at Gudan, who stood beside him silently. Gudan nodded. "Yes," he answered before the question could even be presented. "Your ears are capable of this depth of hearing on earth as well. However, there is nothing on earth capable of making this sound. Only in the perfection of heaven can such beauty exist."

Marshall nodded his understanding. Tears slowly trickled from his eyes, and he somehow knew that had Gudan not been right there beside him, he would not have been able to handle what he was experiencing. It was beyond all human comprehension.

"And, Marshall," Gudan said quietly, "this is only the music of heaven."

"What do you mean, he's gone?" Supred yelled. Manevid maintained his position, one of disciplined attention though the ground shook from the booming of Supred's voice. "How could you lose a human? Go find him!"

"But, sir," Manevid replied, "where would I look? Humans don't just disappear, yet he is gone. As soon as the angels of light departed, I searched everywhere, but he is nowhere to be found. His jacket, his notebook computer, his keys, and his car—all are still at the church, but he is gone. I believe the angels of light took him."

"What do you mean 'took him'? They don't just take humans! They hide them from time to time, but they don't take them. Go back to the church and wait. Whatever they are doing with him can be undone when he reappears. We'll attack in full force then. For now, go back and wait for him to reappear."

Manevid nodded in obedience and darted from the room, growling to himself and threatening Marshall J. Pennington with all manner of evil when he would return from wherever it was that he had been taken. *You have made a fool of me, Mr. Pennington. For this you will pay dearly.*

"Come, Marshall. We must go now." Gudan led them further into heaven, the music still echoing in Marshall's head. They floated through the air, watching the inhabitants of heaven milling about, tending to their business. Presently Marshall saw in the distance a great mountain, upon which sat a great structure. The entire structure was glowing; light was emanating in all directions as if the sun itself had set right on the crest of that mountain. Marshall knew that had he not been under the protection of Gudan, he would have been blinded by the mere sight of it, even this great distance away from the source of the light. In earth measurements, the top of mountain must have been miles away, for the multitude of beings between it and Marshall was without number. Even so, Marshall could see the great structure as if he were only a few feet away from it.

The top of the mountain consisted of a rectangular plateau whose earth dimensions would be measured in units of miles. Upon this flat area stood a remarkable structure, the magnificence of which would serve to humble the most ingenious architect on earth. This had to be the temple area where the Most High himself dwelt, Marshall deduced. He tried his best to take in the physical attributes of the structure. From his vantage point and certainly due to the presence of Gudan, he could see the entire structure inside and out as though he were taking a virtual tour of it using another of his son's computer programs.

It had the appearance of the ruins of an ancient building unearthed at an archeological dig in that there was no roof and only the bottom fraction of the walls was in evidence. But that was where the similarity ended. The temple area itself was constructed as rooms within rooms, similar to the temple diagrams pictured in the back of study Bibles, except that there was no need for walls and a roof. Those had been added to the earthly temple of biblical times partially in consideration of the weather, but mostly because the glory of God was so awesome that the human beings would not have been able to survive being exposed to it. They had to have walls and ceilings and even a thick tapestry between them and the presence of God so that their lives might be preserved. But in heaven, the dwelling place of the Most High, he could be present in all his glory without the risk of wiping out all its inhabitants.

The base of the structure consisted of a slab of glistening white marble accented with swirls of pure gold. It was perfectly square in shape, with exterior dimensions of perhaps ten city blocks on each side and a thickness of nearly two hundred feet. Covering the surface of the marble slab was the structure's floor, which consisted of diamonds cut in the shape of bricks, each one roughly the size of the refrigerator in Marshall's kitchen. The mortar used to hold the bricks together was a mixture of gold grindings and a potpourri of crushed precious gemstones. The light that was reflected from these particles caused a kaleidoscope of brilliant colors to explode from the floor and shoot up into the sky above the mountain as if they were a billion colored spotlights shooting up into the sky to announce the beginning of every county fair, rock concert, and Super Bowl half-time show the world had ever known.

Great pillars made of the same gold-swirled marble stood at the four corners of the temple slab, each having the diameter of a city water tower and extending up into the sky as high as an unassisted human eye would be able to see. At the top of each pillar was a gigantic golden cherub, facing out from the temple with his wings spread. Along each side of the temple slab, two more pillars stood equidistant from the corners. They were half as tall as the others and were connected at the top by a huge beam of white and gold marble, creating an entryway like a Texas rancher might have at the entrance to his ranch. Webs of strung gold dotted with precious jewels adorned the corners of the entryways, glittering in the light from within. Walls connected the great pillars form the perimeter of the temple area except at the entryways to the temple. These walls formed the perimeter of the courtyard proper. Inside the courtyard proper were twelve hundred seraphim, three hundred along each wall, chanting and shouting praises to the Most High.

The walls, however, were not really walls. They began at the floor like a good wall should, but they only extended a mere fraction of the distance between the floor and the top of the structure. More like parapets than walls, Marshall supposed, albeit very large and extravagant parapets. The temple rooms were separated by these parapets like the backyards of a ritzy subdivided housing community are separated by privacy fences. Each parapet consisted of a horizontal slab of gold dotted with precious gemstones and was supported underneath by intricately carved golden spindles the size of a pickup truck standing on end.

In the center of the courtyard proper was another room, similar in construction but approximately half the size, called the inner court. The inner court was also was enclosed by a golden parapet, but its corner pillars were shorter, like those of the courtyard proper entryways, and there were no pillars along the sides. Stationed along each of the inner court parapets were cherubim, thirty on each side, also shouting a thunderous chorus of praises to the Most High. The cherubim were extravagantly adorned and armed with swords, standing guard before the throne room of the Most High.

In the center of the inner court, high above the inner court floor, was the throne room of the Most High. Consecutively smaller square slabs of gold-swirled marble placed on top of one another formed the staircase that surrounded the throne room on all sides. The floor of the throne room was the same as that of the rest of the temple, but there were no parapets to mark its perimeter. The pillars were much smaller than the others, only extending a few hundred feet into the air and having a proportionately smaller diameter. They were made of gold rather than marble and adorned atop with a cherub carved out of a single-cut diamond, its brilliance defying description.

In the center of this smallest room stood a great golden throne. Its size rivaled the largest, tallest structure man had ever created, its grandeur far surpassing the wildest imagination of the most exotic architect in the history of the world. No earthly king had ever conceived of such a majestic and extravagant throne room, nor would he have had the resources to create it had his mind been able to conceive it. Marshall could not even speculate at how large it must be. He himself felt larger simply from looking at it as though in his mere humanness he was too small to take it in and thus needed to become larger just to grasp its vastness. Adding to its majestic beauty was the fact that nearly the entire surface of the throne was covered in precious gemstones like chopped nuts covering the outside of a giant celestial cheese ball.

The throne itself was atypical in that it didn't have a definite front or back. Its appearance did not at all suggest that it was indeed a throne, yet Marshall knew that this is what it must be. The odd construction of the throne was partially explained by the way that the multitude had gathered around it equally on every side as though they had been poured out from the throne and slid down the slope like hot fudge running down the sides of an ice cream sundae and gathering around the edges of the bowl. Marshall knew that every being there, like himself, would be able to see whatever was happening in the temple as though they were standing right inside the throne room itself.

As captivated as Marshall was with the architectural wonder of the temple and particularly with the throne room itself, nothing he had seen thus far could have prepared him for what he saw next. And once he did glimpse it, slowly drifting into the throne room from the sky above it and alighting on the floor like a snowflake landing on a child's tongue, he couldn't take his eyes off it. Forget trying to explain what he felt to Gudan, Marshall couldn't even make his own mind grasp what he was seeing. There were no words. Human expression was completely incapable of describing what he was seeing. No, not merely seeing—more like experiencing. All the sunsets on all the tropical islands, palm trees gently swaying with the warm tropical breeze, all the majestic mountain ranges with snowy peaks reflected in mirrors of crystal clear lakes, all the perfectly shaped flowers with delicate petals holding droplets of rain, and all the newborn babies taking in their first gasps of air and screaming out the announcement of a new life—all of it was like a cardboard box of frozen garbanzo beans compared to what Marshall was seeing. The wonders of his world, he could describe. The emotions elicited by exposure to those things, he could write in a song or in a poem or elucidate with an eloquent speech. But trying to either understand or explain the magnificence he saw before him would be like a chicken trying to explain the intricacies of quantum physics to a bucket of lard.

Marshall's mind struggled to comprehend; his intellect failed him. His senses were on overload. His soul felt like it had swollen like the fabled Grinch's heart to three times its normal size. Struggling, he found his voice.

"Gudan," he whispered, "that is the most wondrous thing I have ever seen. I have no words. Please, tell me, what is it?"

"That, my friend, is Lucifer."

Chapter Four

Marshall's jaw dropped. He felt as though he had been punched in the stomach. That thing could not be Lucifer! Lucifer, the epitome of evil on the earth? Lucifer, the culmination of all things horrible and contrary to God? It simply could not be! The creature before him was so beautiful! So majestic! So awesome! Then he remembered what he had read in Isaiah and Ezekiel right before Gudan had visited him.

> How you have fallen from heaven, O morning star, son of the dawn! You have been cast down to the earth, you who once laid low the nations! You said in your heart, "I will ascend to heaven; I will raise my throne above the stars of God; I will sit enthroned on the mount of assembly, on the utmost heights of the sacred mountain. I will ascend above the tops of the clouds; I will make myself like the Most High." But you are brought down to the grave, to the depths of the pit.
>
> Isaiah 14:12–15 (NIV)

This is what the Sovereign LORD says: 'You were the model of perfection, full of wisdom and perfect in beauty. You were in Eden, the garden of God; every precious stone adorned you: ruby, topaz and emerald, chrysolite, onyx and jasper, sapphire, turquoise and beryl. Your settings and mountings were made of gold; on the day you were created they were prepared. You were anointed as a guardian cherub, for so I ordained you. You were on the holy mount of God; you walked among the fiery stones. You were blameless in your ways from the day you were created till wickedness was found in you. Through your widespread trade you were filled with violence, and you sinned. So I drove you in disgrace from the mount of God, and I expelled you, O guardian cherub, from among the fiery stones. Your heart became proud on account of your beauty, and you corrupted your wisdom because of your splendor. So I threw you to the earth; I made a spectacle of you before kings.'

Ezekiel 28:12b–17 (NIV)

Gudan looked at Marshall, a sad, forlorn smile on his face. "You see, Marshall, things were not always like they are in your world today. When Lucifer was created, he was the crown jewel of all creation. He was second in glory and honor only to the Most High himself." Gudan paused for a moment. "Time is different here than it is on earth, Marshall. What we are now seeing is long before Lucifer's fall from glory, when he was still fulfilling the purpose for which he had been especially created."

The music started again. That incredible sound that could never be reproduced on the earth regardless of the advances of science and technology. Marshall's head instinctively turned in the direction of the source of the sound. Indeed, it was coming from Lucifer.

"Are you telling me that all that beautiful music we heard before was made by Lucifer?"

"Yes, it was," Gudan answered. "Lucifer was the ultimate instrument of praise. To put it in your terminology, he was the worship leader for the whole of heaven. Except he didn't only make the music. He was the music."

Marshall thought for a long moment, processing what Gudan had said. "So what was it like to worship under Lucifer's direction?" he asked.

"See for yourself. Let's move closer."

Marshall and Gudan floated up over the infinite crowd, hovering like birds, but listening to the songs instead of making them. As he perused the throng, the only word Marshall could think of was *joy*. The beings were the physical embodiment of joy. Each being might as well have been the only one present; so focused were they on their worship. It was as though each and every one of them was sitting alone at the feet of the Most High, praising him with everything that was in them. Even if he had not been invisible to them, he doubted that he could have distracted any of them. Were Gudan to let go of him and let him fall right onto their heads, Marshall suspected they would not even have noticed. They would have gone right on worshipping as if nothing at all had happened. *Oh God, if only the people in Community Gospel Church could learn to worship you like this! God, if only I could learn to worship you like this!*

As they slowly drew closer to the temple, Marshall's mind was reeling. It was so difficult for him to imagine Lucifer worshiping God. *Lucifer!* His arch enemy on earth! The source of most of Marshall's frustration, the evil one he preached against every time it was his turn to stand behind the pulpit on a Sunday morning or behind the lectern in Sunday school class, the one who caused sickness and disease, encouraged infidelity, deceit, and selfishness, the one who "made me do it," as the children say, the roaring lion, prowling over the earth looking for someone to devour. And there he was, *worshipping God!* And it didn't seem fake. He really seemed to be worshipping just like all the others. He seemed focused on God, content only to praise his name for all eternity.

But then Marshall's face became sad. The joy and wonder of the moment faded to be replaced by knowledge of what to this time would be the future. He looked over at Gudan.

"When did he change?" he asked. "How did he become what he is in my world?"

"Before that question can be answered, you must have more knowledge of Lucifer and of his position. Not only was he the music of worship, he was also the most trusted servant of the Most High. Therefore, just as the vessels of a king are fashioned from gold and silver, the best materials available on earth, to make them fit for use by the king, so Lucifer was created to be the very best of all creation so he would be fit to attend to the Most High.

"As the most trusted servant of the Most High, Lucifer was also tasked with guarding the throne room. That is why he leads worship from there. The throne room is a most holy place—the seat from which the Most High rules—and it must never be desecrated by coming into contact with anything that is not holy. Lucifer guards the throne to prevent that from happening. Unfortunately, his task of guarding the throne room ultimately led to his rebellion." Another pause. "We begin to covet that which we see every day. Come, Marshall, let us proceed. Lucifer himself will answer your question."

Marshall and Gudan drifted over to the sky directly above the throne room. As they moved, time became the future. Days, weeks, months, years—Marshall didn't know, but somehow he knew that they were at a completely different time by the time they reached the throne room. The multitude was no longer present. The music had become quiet. Lucifer stood there alone, looking longingly at the throne, wondering what it would be like to sit in it and revel in the praise of the heavenly host. He seemed lost in thought, yet Marshall could hear faint mumbling. Lucifer was talking to himself.

"Why must I only be a servant of the Most High? Does any other being compare with me? Am I not the most beautiful of all creation? Does anyone's wisdom compare to mine? Shouldn't I have a throne from which to govern? After all, does not the whole of heaven adore me? Do they not sing and dance at my beckoning? Does my wisdom not inspire them? Do they not praise me for my music and all but bow to me for my position as guardian of the throne? Do they not marvel at my presence, my magnificence, my power? There should be two thrones here: one for the Most High and one for me."

Marshall looked over at Gudan. The mighty angel's face was masked in sadness.

"Look, Marshall," he said ruefully. "Look at all he had. Look at what the Most High had given him. Beauty, wisdom, status, power, glory, magnificence. Yet it wasn't enough." Gudan seemed angry, but it didn't seem to be solely righteous anger at Lucifer's rebellion against the Most High. It seemed to be something more.

Marshall looked up into Gudan's eyes. "You knew him, didn't you? Lucifer, I mean. You knew him."

"You are very perceptive, Marshall. Yes, I knew him. I am a cherub, Marshall, like Lucifer. I served the Most High in the capacity of inner court guard, right outside the throne room, under the direction of Lucifer himself. I was there the terrible day the rebellion took place. I remained behind when four of the other inner court guards rallied behind Lucifer in opposition to the Most High. We were forced to take up arms against our brothers in defense of the Most High—not that he really needed defending, but we couldn't stand by idly and watch Lucifer blaspheme his name and desecrate the sacred throne room." Gudan stopped. Clearly there was much more, but he had apparently decided that his explanation was sufficient for the time being.

Marshall nodded but didn't speak. He too was deep in thought. How difficult this must be for Gudan, watching this all happen again. His thoughts went from empathy for Gudan to confused sorrow for Lucifer. He truly was an amazing creature, greatly to be admired, but he just couldn't handle the fact that there was someone higher. Second wasn't good enough for him. Marshall was reminded of the story of Joseph in Genesis. He had been elevated to the second highest position in the land of Egypt; even the Pharaoh himself had said that only with respect to the throne would the Pharaoh be greater than Joseph. And Joseph was okay with that. Joseph was in charge of pretty much everything in the country, but he still had to bow to the Pharaoh when he sat on his throne. Joseph was content to do God's will and take whatever position he was given, whether it was a slave or a prisoner or the ruler of all Egypt. But Lucifer was not. He was becoming irritated that he had to settle for second best.

Marshall and Gudan took another step forward in time. They peered into the throne room to see Lucifer talking with four of the chief cherubim who stood guard along the parapets of the inner court.

"We will have a glorious future, my brothers. I will rule on high as supreme ruler, and you will be the new elect, each ruling a portion of the heavens as I see fit to delegate. There is no reason why the Most High has to rule everything by himself. We can share the rule, elevating ourselves to the highest and most coveted positions in the heavens.

"Look at them," Lucifer muttered. He motioned to the legions of angels dancing and praising the Most High, contempt on his face. "Look at them, content to remain as they are, never striving for more. No ambition. They will never elevate themselves as I have done. I am the music for the Most High. I am the worship. My beauty is beyond measure, my power infinite. No other thing that the Most High has created compares to me. I will set my own throne above the heavens. I will be worshipped and praised just like the Most High."

"You speak truth, Lucifer," one of them agreed. "There is none in heaven greater than you, save the Most High himself."

"Indeed," Lucifer nodded. "For now, perhaps. But I believe there is room at the top."

Marshall felt Gudan's hand on his arm.

"Let us go ahead to the rebellion," he said.

Marshall stiffened, and his heart began to pound in his chest. He nodded to Gudan that he was ready.

The scene before them flashed forward in time to another gathering of the heavenly host. Lucifer alighted on the throne room floor and positioned himself so that he could be seen from every side of the stage simultaneously. Amid shouts and cheers from the throng, he began the introduction for a new song. Marshall didn't know how he knew it was a new song, but somehow he did; neither could he figure out how the heavenly host was getting the words although they all seemed to know them. It was as though each being had his own personal holographic projector right in front of him that was displaying the words they sang.

But then suddenly, some of them stopped singing. As Marshall looked around him, he could see close-ups of being after being whose mouth had stopped moving and who no longer joined the singing. Somehow, though their faces were indiscernible, Marshall could see contempt on them. No, it was more like he could feel it. They were disgusted. Some merely confused, others downright angry. In Marshall's world, eyebrows would have been wrinkled, jaws set, teeth gritted. Clenched fists would likely flank stiffened legs, whose feet had been resolutely planted on the ground, readying the body for confrontation.

"Why have you stopped singing?" Lucifer's voice thundered from the throne room. "I am the music! You will follow *me*!" he shouted.

"Never!" came the thunderous reply, which rang through the heavens. The shock began to wear off as the heavenly host realized what was transpiring. Lucifer was opposing the Most High! Unbelievable! And there were those who supported him!

Lucifer purposefully sat down on the sacred throne of the Most High. Taking their cue from their new master, forty of the inner court cherubim surrounded him, ten on each side, as he slowly levitated the throne of the Most High into the air. They drew their swords and waved them back and forth, daring anyone to stop them.

In a flash, Gudan and the fifty-nine remaining members of the inner court guard drew their swords and darted through the sky toward the perpetrators of this horrible, unspeakable act of blasphemous rebellion. Several of Lucifer's guards were struck down immediately, while the rest continued to fight. All across the heavens, the heavenly host engaged in civil war. Pockets of angels and even some of the seraphim took up arms against those loyal to the Most High, fighting for Lucifer and his revolution, hoping to find themselves exalted rulers in Lucifer's new heaven. But that was not to be.

Suddenly, the heavens shook like a dirty rug being banged against the railing of a porch. Thunder ripped and crackled. The loudest sound that could ever be produced on earth would be like the soft thud of a cotton swab falling on a carpeted bathroom floor compared to the intensity that rocked the heavens. A blinding light like a thousand suns, a million times greater than even that of Lucifer, filled heaven with such intensity that every being fell to the ground as though dead.

"*Lucifer!*" The sound of his voice overwhelmed the ear-splitting sound of the thunder like the roar of a Super Bowl crowd at the winning touchdown would nullify the shouting of the peanut guy. Instantly, all the heavenly host, including the cherubim and seraphim, were paralyzed. They were conscious and could hear the voice of the Most High, but they could not move. They trembled inside as the voice again shook the heavens. "*Lucifer!*"

Lucifer rose defiantly to meet the Most High in the sky.

"Lucifer, anointed cherub, guardian of the throne, what have you done?"

"I am taking my rightful place, oh Most High," Lucifer said with finality. "The throne should not be yours alone. I deserve the honor and glory as well, as my beauty and wisdom has no rival in all of heaven."

The sad voice of the Most High echoed throughout the heavens. "Lucifer," he began, "I gave you everything. All heaven was yours to enjoy, save the throne itself. I created you to be the exalted cherub, the anointed cherub, the very music of heaven, full of wisdom and beauty. But this was not enough for you. You have coveted my throne, my glory, my worship. The ability I gave you to create praise and worship was not enough for you. You wanted to *receive* the glory and worship as well. Your heart is full of pride. I created you with love and gave you a place of honor above all the others. You were to be the creation most like his creator, but instead, you have rebelled against your Creator. You have become puffed up in your own glory and have forgotten your place. Surely you will rule, Lucifer, but it will not be here, and it will not be from my throne." The Most High turned to face the throng below them. "Arise, defenders of Lucifer!" he commanded.

They arose, not of their own accord, but unwillingly, at the command of the Most High. A full third of the heavenly host filled the sky, lining up in ranks behind Lucifer, trembling in fear of how their rebellion against the Most High might be repaid.

"Be gone," the Most High simply said. "Go to the earth until I make your punishment come to fulfillment." And with a puff of smoke, they were gone. One-third of the heavenly host was banished from heaven for all eternity, sentenced to live with Lucifer outside of the presence of the Most High.

Only the faithful remained. The seraphim began to sing, quietly at first, then more loudly as others of the heavenly host joined in. The Most High allowed his glory to fade somewhat so that the heavenly host regained the ability to move. They bowed in reverence to the Most High, proclaiming in somber worship his holiness and his justice.

Marshall didn't move. He didn't speak. He simply stood there beside Gudan, tears streaming down his cheeks. His heart broke at the sinful rebellion of Lucifer, who, having been given so much, would not be satisfied with anything less than that which belonged only to God himself. Marshall's mind traveled back through his own life. His heart broke time and time again as he realized how many times in his own life he had done just as Lucifer had done. He may not have ever led an outright rebellion in opposition to the Most High, but in the attitude of his heart, he had done the very same thing Lucifer had done. He had ignored the heart and will of God and had put his own wants and desires above those of God himself. His crime was more of a passive resistance to God's will than an aggressive, outright rebellion, but the sin in his heart was the same. He had simply put his own desires above the will of God. He had let pride in himself prevent him from doing what was right in the eyes of God. He thought of the many times he had asked God for things he had no right to ask for, things that would have served no purpose except to satisfy his own selfish desires. And so many times when he did ask for noble things, he did so out of selfish motives, not thinking of others or even of God, but only of how it might serve to satisfy his own agenda. He dropped to his knees and cried out to the Lord, baring his soul in repentance.

Gudan stood silently beside him, his external smile revealing the internal joy he was experiencing at witnessing the tremendous spiritual step Marshall was taking. He waited patiently, basking in the presence of the Most High and allowing Marshall as much time as he needed to conclude his spiritual business. After a few moments, Gudan sensed the relief of concluded business in Marshall's demeanor. He placed his hand on Marshall's shoulder. Feeling the gentle touch of Gudan's strong hand on his shoulder, Marshall looked up.

"Come, Marshall, we must continue," Gudan urged.

Marshall slowly got to his feet, although he was not actually standing on anything anyway, and looked up at Gudan. He opened his mouth and tried to speak, but his voice failed him. Gudan gave him a knowing smile and a nod, and the pair continued their journey without wasting unnecessary words.

Chapter Five

"Are we leaving heaven?" Marshall asked.

"That depends on what you have learned, Marshall," Gudan answered. "You have seen what the Most High wanted you to see in heaven. You have seen how Lucifer, the most perfect and awesome being ever created, blessed of the Most High above any other creature, somehow got it into his mind that the glory of his own magnificence belonged to himself rather than to the One who had created him in the first place. Dwelling on this folly, he allowed himself to become corrupt to the point of outright rebellion against the Most High. You have witnessed the tainting of his heart with selfishness and pride, the scheming of his brilliant mind for purposes contrary to those of the Most High, and the consequences he must now suffer as a result of acting out his rebellion. So tell me, Marshall, what have you learned from all of this?"

Marshall did not even have to think. He immediately applied what had happened to Lucifer to himself, his flock at Community Church, and to all humanity.

"Many things, Gudan. I have learned many things from this journey thus far, but the most important is how Lucifer went from being number one in all of God's creation to being Satan, the number one adversary of God.

"He didn't just wake up one morning and say, 'You know, I think I'll rebel against the Most High today. Yep, seems like a good day for it. Perhaps I'll start my own little heaven right over there, where I can be worshipped and praised just like the Most High is in this one.' No, that is not at all how it happened. The change was gradual. Lucifer slowly lost his reverence for Almighty God. He gradually lost his fear of the Lord of Hosts. His loyalty and allegiance to his creator began to abate. Then finally and worst of all, he lost his love and devotion for his father figure. He no longer wanted to be subject to the rule of God—not even as the most exalted creature under the rule of God.

"But as I said, it appears to have come about slowly. Lucifer, as guardian of the throne of the Most High, was privileged to see firsthand what it was like at the top. When God was sitting upon his throne, Lucifer was the closest one to him. No one else was allowed to be where Lucifer was. But somehow, Lucifer's eyes went to himself instead of to God. He noticed how wondrous he was. He was going about his business, not caught up in his own beauty and majesty, until he began first, to take his eyes off of God and second, to look to what he wanted for himself. Then, once his desire to please himself became stronger than his desire to please God, his fall and rebellion was imminent. He no longer focused his attention on the praise and worship of God or even on the relationship he had previously enjoyed with God. He became consumed with the gratification of his own wants and desires to the point of ignoring and betraying his God, his creator, his father figure. Had his attention remained on God where it belonged, the throne would have held no allure for him. He would have seen it merely as the throne of the Most High—something belonging solely to someone else—rather than something achievable that could be coveted for himself. Lucifer's sin did not begin with him wanting to set his own throne above the stars and be like the Most High. His sin began when he first put the will of the Most High second to his own will. It was not wrong for him to enjoy the shouts of appreciation from his fellow angels, seraphim, and cherubim. It was not wrong for him to take pride in his music and to bask in the glory and the presence of the Most High after a particularly spectacular worship time of which he was the source. But it was wrong for him to want to become the object of worship, rather than being content to be the source of it.

"All sin on earth, and apparently in heaven too, stems from that one single thing: the creation putting its own desires above those of the Creator. Every single sin, whether it be minuscule and seemingly insignificant or enormous and blatant, stems from the creation putting its own desires above those of the Creator."

"You have learned well, Marshall," Gudan said approvingly. "Yes, it is now time to leave heaven."

Marshall nodded his understanding. "Where will we go now?" he asked as they began to move on.

"We are going back to the earth, but not the earth as you know it. We will now observe the status of Lucifer and his angels after their banishment from heaven but before their final judgment and punishment takes place as described in the Revelation, recorded in your Bible by the apostle John. It is also before the creation account detailed in the first chapter of Genesis in your Bible."

"Wait a second," Marshall said, shaking his head. "Are you telling me that Lucifer and his angels were here on the earth before it was even *created* by God?"

"Not exactly," Gudan said. "Let me put it this way. What we shall now see, Marshall, is what happened during the gap between Genesis 1:1 and Genesis 1:2 in your Bible."

"The gap?" Marshall repeated, uncertain he had heard correctly.

"Yes, Marshall, the gap. What does your Bible say in Genesis 1:1 and 2?

Marshall searched his memory for the exact words. "Genesis 1:1 says, 'In the beginning God created the heavens and the earth.' Verse 2 says, 'Now the earth was formless and empty, darkness was over the surface of the deep, and the Spirit of God was hovering over the waters.'"

"You are correct," Gudan said. "But something has been lost in translation. You see, when Moses wrote Genesis, as the Most High instructed him, he used a Hebrew word that means 'became' or 'had become,' but that could also be translated 'was,' which is how most human Bible translators have translated it. This minor difference in translation causes a drastic change in the meaning of the verses. You see, when the Most High created the heavens and the earth, they were perfect. The first time. The earth was not formless and empty when he created it. It was beautiful and full of wonders. A great gap exists between its original creation, Genesis 1:1, and its re-creation, or reconstruction, Genesis 1:2. Genesis 1:2 should read 'Now the earth became formless and empty.' Very soon, you will see how his perfect earth became formless and empty. You see, Marshall, everything that you have witnessed on our journey thus far happened before the creation of the heavens and the earth, which is detailed beginning with Genesis 1:2 in your Bible. That is why the only references to these things are found in the writings of the prophets, rather than in the biblical books of history or law or even wisdom.

"Okay," Marshall conceded. "That will give me something to study when I get back. But considering the issue at hand, what happened after its initial creation that caused the earth to become desolate and void and empty?"

"Patience, Marshall," Gudan replied. "You will see soon enough."

And see it, he did, somewhere on the barely visible, distant horizon of his mind, for once again, he and Gudan seemed to float along from nothingness to nothingness, using the nothingness in between as the medium for travel. Even so, far beneath them,

Marshall could see a small lighted ball. Not a ball of light, but a ball that was lighted. He could see the various colors in evidence across the surface of the ball though he could not discern the shapes that separated those colors from each other. As they moved closer, Marshall gasped in wonder. Before him in space hung what could only be the newly formed earth, with all its mountains and valleys, rivers and streams, woodlands and grasslands, lakes and oceans. Hardly had Marshall taken note of the unspoiled, nonpopulated, perfect beauty of the place when the fireworks began. From somewhere over his left shoulder, a blinding flash of light illuminated the sky as if someone had just tugged the pull chain that turned on the sun. Marshall jerked his head in that direction and saw the immense ball of light plummeting toward the earth as though every star in the universe had been fired from an intergalactic shotgun and was falling toward the earth at the same time. Unfortunately, the stars would have done far less damage than what was really falling toward the earth in that fireball. An astronomer or scientist would have predicted that an object of that magnitude colliding with the earth would cause the desolation of the entire planet upon impact. However, there was no impact; thus, there was no damage caused when the object arrived at the earth. The damage was, in fact, severe—but it occurred shortly after the object arrived on the earth. It was the result of the presence of the object on the earth, not an impact of the object with the earth.

The object in question was the congregation of Lucifer and his followers, driven to the earth against their will by the command of the Most High. As they entered the containment area of the earth's atmosphere, the force driving them forward released them. Like a disobedient child being confined to his bedroom for punishment, so Lucifer and his followers had been confined to the earth for their immediate punishment. Once inside the earth's atmosphere, they regained control of their bodies and were able to move about as they pleased.

Lucifer alighted on the surface of the earth, cautiously taking in his surroundings. He surveyed the beauty of the place—the handiwork of the Most High. He noted the effort with which the Most High designed and created this place and all its wonders. Due to his superior wisdom, there was not a being alive that could understand and appreciate the intricate handiwork of the Most High as fully as Lucifer could. Ironically, there was also at this moment no being alive who hated it more. Fury rose up in his throat. He growled like a caged animal. Gone was the beautiful music. Gone was the peaceful worship of the Most High. Instead, the entire earth shook with the terrifying scream of Lucifer, the anointed cherub, son of the dawn, the supreme wonder of all creation. No longer did he utter the music of heaven; now his music was a scream of anger, rage, frustration, humiliation, defeat. The vehemence with which it was uttered sent a wave of panic through the other fallen angels, sending them cowering up into the sky. No longer was he Lucifer, son of the dawn; he had now become Satan, the adversary of the Most High.

Satan tore through the earth on a frenzied rampage of destruction. Everything he saw reminded him of the Most High, so he destroyed it all. Thunder filled the skies, lightning flashed and lashed out at the surface of the earth, exploding, burning, shattering, crushing everything it came into contact with. Tidal waves and tsunamis caused by the shuddering earthquakes raged across the seas and onto the land, destroying everything in their path. Volcanoes spit and sputtered out their poisonous gases and molten rock, causing the earth to lurch in pain like a patient on the operating table with no anesthesia. The whole planet convulsed and shook until the temper tantrum of Satan subsided. What remained was a desolate wasteland—formless, void, empty.

Marshall stood in silence, watching Lucifer huff and puff and walk around like an angry bear waiting to eat whatever had awakened it from its slumber. *That explains some things*, Marshall said to himself.

Before long, Lucifer rallied from his humiliating defeat at the hands of the Most High. The tantrum had successfully purged the excess anger from within him, like a relief valve on a pressurized system, allowing him to think rationally and to concentrate on what he was going to do next.

He decided that he had better take charge of the situation, particularly of the multitude of angels who had joined him in his exile from heaven, and establish himself as their supreme ruler. He quickly began to organize them into a working force. He was unsure of what his next move would be, but he did realize that organization would be one of the keys to pulling off whatever plan he came up with.

He organized them by rank, placing the cherubim out in front, the seraphim directly behind the cherubim, and the rest of the angels behind the seraphim. He ordered the entire company to stand at attention, then ordered the rest to stand fast while he pulled the cherubim aside.

"You are the elite," he told them. "Assess the company. Take inventory of our assets. I want a list of the name, rank, skills, and abilities of every soldier we have. Divide them into squadrons, battalions, divisions, whatever is appropriate, according to their skills and abilities. Also, find a place to set up a headquarters and choose an appropriate number of them to stand guard around it. Be finished by the time I return. At that point I will address the company."

With that, Lucifer disappeared from their view in a flash of light.

Marshall and Gudan also moved on, stepping forward in time to catch the conclusion of Lucifer's address to his throng of loyal followers.

"Therefore, since the Most High has betrayed me and made me his adversary, I am no longer to be called Lucifer, son of the dawn. I am now to be called Satan, adversary of the Most High. We will have our revenge against the Most High and the host of heaven. We will take our rightful place of leadership in the universe when I, the prince of darkness, overthrow the God of light and claim the heavens for my own dwelling place. Then my throne will not be beside that of the Most High but rather above it! His will be the stool where I rest my feet!"

The crowd cheered as Satan delivered the final line, his blasphemous boast driving the message home.

Marshall and Gudan quickly took another step forward in time. They watched in awe as the spirit of God hovered over the waters of the desolate earth. No human being could conceive of what it must have been like to witness the creation of the earth, yet here Marshall was, looking on as the earth was reconstructed and reformed in obedience to the mere command of God. He saw the first light appear, watched the separation of the waters from above the earth and upon it, watched the dry land appear.

Unfortunately, he could not completely enjoy this experience, for Gudan had allowed him to watch Satan's reaction to the same events out of the corner of his mind's eye.

Satan observed from his perch like an evil prowling cat studying a wounded mouse as it stumbled across a kitchen floor, nearly purring with joy in anticipation of the pounce. He waited patiently for the Most High to finish reconstructing the earth, every minute detail of it, so that he could ravage it again. *But what was this? Evidently there would be some improvements this time. Vegetation, yes. Grass, herbs, trees…right. Now lights—greater for the day, lesser for the night. But wait a minute, what was this? Life in the oceans? And in the skies? Now beasts in the fields? Amazing! What on earth was the Most High up to? Oh, what fun it would be to destroy all of this! Moving targets!* Satan pranced around with glee, anticipating the havoc he would wreak upon his newly restructured prison.

Suddenly, with shock rendering him motionless, he looked onto the final scene of creation taking place before him. The glee slipped away. A deep feeling of anguish took its place. Pain of a magnitude he had never experienced filled his heart. Anger sprouted, quickly growing and giving way to rage. Once again, fury began to boil up within him as he came to a great realization: he was being replaced. The Most High was creating a new race of creatures with whom he could enjoy intimate fellowship, just like he had with Lucifer! The other creatures he had made—the creatures in the sea, in the air and on the land—were interesting and would be very fun to destroy, but they really were nothing special. Far superior to the plants and vegetation, to be sure, but merely animals nonetheless. No soul, no spirit. Intelligent minds in many cases, some capable of a significant degree of learning and growing in intellect, but even so, they were nothing in comparison to this last race. No, these last two were quite different. These two were created in the very image of the Most High! Triune beings, with mind, body, and spirit! In this, they were superior even to the angels. In other ways, however, they were far inferior to even the least of the angelic host. The first one he called a man and named it Adam. The next one, a mate for the first, was called woman, and the man named it Eve. The two were united before the Most High, and the three of them enjoyed inexplicable harmony and unity. But perhaps most infuriating of all was the way that the Most High looked at them. He loved them. He truly loved them, with a love that was nearly beyond the grasp of the very beings to whom it was directed and with whom it was shared! By creating them to so closely resemble himself, the Most High had not only created a new race of beings similar to himself with whom he could enjoy intimate fellowship, but he had also simultaneously created a great mystery. The Almighty God, completely self-sufficient and self-sustaining, had created within himself a longing for union with his creation, and within the creature, a longing for union with the Creator! The basis for this union was the unfathomable love of the Most High, which Satan was aghast to see flowing out of the eyes of the Most High and showering the two humans.

Lucifer staggered in disbelief. This was a slap across the face! The unmitigated gall of the Most High, coming down here to the place of Lucifer's exile to create his replacement! He—Lucifer—had been the Most High's most beloved! He had been the created being most resembling the Creator! But now, these—these *humans*! The Most High was creating these beings solely for the purpose of intimacy and fellowship with him—right in front of the discarded face of Lucifer!

He set his jaw. The despondent, forlorn look of a rejected child crossed his face. Anguish overwhelmed him as his abandonment became complete.

Rejected. Abandoned. Replaced.

Inferior. Substandard. Shamed.

Dishonored. Devalued. Hopeless.

A failure. A misfit. A mistake.

These and many more equally self-deprecating thoughts filled his mind. Then slowly, as the moments passed, his face began to change. The pained look gave way to anger. Fury. Hatred. The intense desire for acceptance and belonging slipped away, an even more intense and consuming desire for revenge taking its place. His jaw clenched. His eyes squinted. Quietly, he exhaled his understanding of what was taking place before him.

"Truly, I am Satan," he spat out. "This act of malice confirms it. The Most High is rubbing it in my face by choosing this place, of all places, to create his beloved race of humans. He can fellowship with them and take care of them without even glancing in my direction, just to make me suffer through watching it all happen. The banishment from heaven was not my punishment; watching myself be replaced by this substandard race of animals is."

A moment passed. Rage continued to build up inside him until once again his face underwent a change. The look of hurt and anger also gradually subsided. And then Satan smiled. He had an idea. Satan smiled as he nodded his head at his wonderful, horrible idea. He wouldn't destroy this place after all. No, no.

That would be much too insignificant of a payback for what the Most High was doing to him. And besides, all the damage he had inflicted upon the earth the first time had been quickly and efficiently restored, taking only a few days and a handful of words spoken by the Most High to accomplish! No, he would not touch the earth itself this time. Instead, he would destroy the humans. But not by killing them—oh no, that would be much too quick and painless for the Most High. He would do much worse than that. He would turn them against the Most High. He would infiltrate their world with the help of his followers, and he would crush the spirits of the humans. He would find some way to keep them from fulfilling the will of the Most High. He would study them and observe their interaction with the Most High, seeking to discover what it was that he wanted most from them, and then he would find a way to prevent him from getting it. These humans were the key to his revenge against the Most High. He would destroy their relationship with him! Rather than simply destroying them, he would find a way to entice them to follow him instead of the Most High. If he could not take heaven and his rightful place of preeminence by force, he would steal it by stealth.

With an intensified resolve, Satan burst into the air. He shouted for his elite. Standing in the headquarters as Satan approached, they snapped to attention at his arrival.

"At ease," he said. "My friends, our victory is made sure. And believe it or not, our pathway to victory has been marked out by none other than the Most High himself."

The elite scrunched their faces in disbelief but dared not turn to look at each other, for fear their hesitancy would be looked upon as disloyalty or lack of faith in Satan, their leader. He continued, "The Most High has recreated the earth. Dispatch soldiers in teams to inspect the new earth. I want to know everything there is to know about this new planet. Scout it out—every mountain, every valley, every stream. I want to know everything. Set up a training regiment so that each team can teach the others about what they have found. All intelligence comes to me first, but get the training regiment in place to begin at my command as soon as I have reviewed the information.

"Do not interfere in the workings of the earth in any way, and leave the humans alone. Do not even let your presence be known to them. Yet." Satan smiled again. "Supred, Candeg, Zulef, stay. The rest of you, you have your orders. Dismissed!"

The company departed in a flurry of wings, leaving Satan and his top three cherubim alone to talk.

"You three will reconnoiter the humans. I want to know every move they make, every word they say, every thought they think. I want to know their schedule—how they spend their days and their nights, where they go, how long they stay, and what they do while they are there. I want to know when they sleep, how long they sleep, and how long it takes them to fall asleep. I want to know what they eat, how much, how often, and where it comes from. I want to know more about them than they know about themselves. I want to know what the Most High does with them, how he interacts with them, and what is expected of them. I want to know everything there is to know about the relationship between the Most High and his new race of beings. And I want to know *now*." Taking their cue, the trio disappeared with three flashes of light.

Satan relived the scene he had witnessed of the formation of the man. The Most High had formed him with his own hands out of the dust of the earth. He had meticulously shaped his body, then breathed his spirit into him. The love in his eyes as he looked at his creation was more than Satan could bear. And then that woman! The Most High had positively beamed when the man had looked upon her, smiling and nodding his approval. But it had made Satan feel like a cigarette butt flicked on the ground, not merely used and discarded, but tossed away, crushed under a shoe, and ground into the dirt.

"I'll get you," he hissed at the humans, hate spewing forth from his heart like blood spurting from the artery of a severed limb. "Just you wait. I'll get you. I'll get all of you."

Chapter Six

"Lucifer felt replaced," Marshall said absently, not really talking to anyone. He and Gudan were again traveling forward in time.

Gudan nodded. "Yes, Marshall. That is exactly what he felt. And not only replaced, but replaced with a decidedly substandard surrogate. The human race is inferior to the angelic race in many ways, yet the Most High has chosen to exalt the humans to a position above the angels in the kingdom of heaven."

"It doesn't really make sense, does it?" Marshall asked.

"Not to me," Gudan replied. "But the wisdom of the Most High far surpasses my own. May his will be done!"

Marshall pondered in silence. He was beginning to understand the motivation behind Satan's work in his world. He was not merely some wild, evil angel bent on opposing God simply for the sake of opposing God. No, he was a hurt child, striking out in anger at the father who had rejected, abandoned, and replaced him. But he was not to be pitied; he was also the second most powerful being in the universe, who had intentionally betrayed the Supreme Being in an attempt to overthrow him and claim leadership of heaven in his stead.

Gudan motioned for Marshall to stop. He looked down, and beneath him was a lush garden, full of all kinds of vegetation. There were trees, bushes, plants bearing countless varieties of fruits and vegetables, grassy meadows, rocky streams, and flowing rivers. The garden was also filled with animals of every kind, the air with a variety of birds, and the waters with a myriad of fish and other aquatic life. This was where the man and his wife lived. This was the garden of Eden, the first home of Adam and Eve. But Marshall knew he hadn't been brought here to look at the beauty of the garden. He wanted to close his eyes so he wouldn't see what he knew was coming. He wanted to tell Gudan that he had seen enough and to take him back to earth, but he knew that his journey was not yet finished. His questions had not yet been fully answered. In fact, Marshall thought, all that he had seen thus far was presumably merely the preface to what he would yet witness on this journey. Consequently, he steeled himself for the tragic scene that he knew would soon come into view. He was relieved, however, to see that in the scene unfolding before him, the three beings present were Adam, Eve and God, not Adam, Eve and a serpent.

What Marshall saw was one of those scenes that, had it been portrayed by professional actors on a movie set, would have taken many attempts to depict accurately; so foreign to the natural way of things were the relationships represented. There were three people, yet no inequality, no envy, no strife. There were subordinates and superiors, yet no resentment or grudging compliance. There were three hearts, three souls, three minds, yet no confusion, no misconception, no animosity of any kind. Instead, there was absolute peace, absolute joy, absolute love. It was as if the three were completely immersed in love—real, honest, unconditional love, not the worthless, self-gratifying facsimile of love commonly depicted in books and movies—so completely that due to the total immersion, there was simply no room left for anything other than love to exist. There was also complete unity;

the three seemed as one. Still three separate entities, yet so utterly unified as to nearly exist in spirit as a single entity.

As Marshall looked on, he was privy to a high-speed review of the interaction between Adam, Eve, and God himself. It was only by the presence of Gudan that he could take in what he was seeing, for not only did he see and hear what was taking place before him, he also was given the ability to comprehend the scenes to such a degree that he experienced the actual feelings and emotions of each person as though he himself were an accomplished actor playing each of their parts. And the feeling was good. It was very good. It was an overwhelming sense of absolute love, absolute peace, and absolute joy; a feeling of contentment such as that was not even remotely possible to achieve on earth. And this was everyday life for Adam and Eve in the garden. This was not the emotional high one may experience after an intense prayer session following a revival service or the winning of the championship title for any given sporting event or the kissing of the bride to complete the marriage ceremony or even the delivering of a perfectly healthy baby after years of waiting and praying for a child. No, what Marshall was witnessing were simply the common, everyday scenes of everyday life—every day, every night—living almost constantly in the presence of Almighty God.

"Marshall, do you truly understand what you are seeing?" Gudan asked without taking his eyes off the scene before them.

Marshall, having become slightly hesitant to respond instantly to Gudan's questions, contemplated for a moment before replying. "I believe so, Gudan. I see that mankind lived in perfect peace in the garden of Eden before they sinned. Everything was wonderful. God was right there with them. Just like the old hymn goes, they walked with him and talked with him. They could interact with God, their creator, any time they wanted to, in person! He was right there with them! Any time they wondered about anything, he was right there to ask questions to. And they shared such a deep and peaceful love and fellowship, and they…they…it is so wonderful, Gudan! I hardly know how to describe it!"

Gudan smiled at Marshall's response. "Look deeper, Marshall," he said. "Interaction with the Most High is certain to be perfect in such a situation. Look rather at the interaction between Adam and Eve."

Marshall reviewed several scenes in his mind, then looked again at those still being unfolded before him. He watched Adam and Eve as they talked. He watched as they worked. He watched as they interacted with each other and with the world around them. With great astonishment, Marshall's mind began to grasp the significance of the interaction of these two humans with each other and with all of God's creation. Their communication was perfect. Their cooperation was perfect. Their generosity, kindness, goodness, humility, and respect for each other were perfect. It was the kind of scene that would make people snort and shake their heads at the wouldn't-it-be-nice impossibility of it actually being real. Yet it was real. Just another day in the life of the first two humans on earth, the pride and joy of the Creator.

And to take it a step further, it was not only their mere existence that was the essence of pleasant, blissful contentment, but also their work. There was no drive to succeed, no ambition to get more, no inherent need to become better than the other. What higher state could possibly exist than perfection and perfect contentment? It was the most wonderful, blissful existence imaginable, far more blissful, in fact, than the human mind was capable of imagining. Yet here it was, happening right before Marshall's eyes, between two humans.

Suddenly, Marshall's chest tightened. He began to realize what Gudan was getting at. Sure, Adam and Eve had a relationship like that, but there were only two of them, and they lived very closely with God. But what if there were millions of them? What if the whole earth were filled with humans? What would it be like then?

"It would have been the same," Marshall said quietly. Gudan looked at him, waiting as the thoughts materialized in his mind and were subsequently formed into words. "Were there at this time millions and millions of humans inhabiting the earth, the state would have been exactly the same. No one would envy another. No one would step on another to get ahead. No one would selfishly choose to seek his own gain rather than look to the needs of another. Even the millions would experience this same absolute selflessness and community."

Marshall's mind went to the book of Matthew where in chapters five through seven Matthew records the Sermon on the Mount, a discourse delivered by Jesus in the Judean countryside to all who would listen. There, Jesus explained how mankind was intended to interact with each other. Marshall thought also of the teaching on love found in the thirteenth chapter of Paul's letter to the Corinthians. Those and many, many other Bible verses were written to specifically admonish people to treat one another exactly as Adam and Eve were treating each other in the scenes Marshall was viewing. It was one thing to read about how God wants humans to treat each other and even to teach on the subject, but it was quite another thing altogether to witness it really happening.

To observe such selfless love and community would bring a tear to the eyes of any conscientious observer. To Marshall, however, it was a bittersweet experience—and even that, much more bitter than sweet. The tears not only praised the wonder of it, but also mourned the death of it, for Marshall knew what the next scene would hold. He knew that sin would destroy the perfect existence enjoyed by the only two perfect humans ever created. As if on cue, Gudan tightened his grip on Marshall's arm and led him forward.

Then Marshall, standing in the unseen world where spirits are visible, could see what Eve could not, for she stood in the human world where spirits were invisible. She may have seen the serpent twitch, she may have seen his eyes blink or his lip quiver, or she may have even noticed a distinct change in his countenance, but she would have had no way of knowing what was actually taking place right in front of her in a parallel realm.

Marshall, however, saw everything. He saw Satan approach the serpent, slowly move in closer and closer, then dissolve right into him. It was as though Satan were a wisp of smoke that fell on the serpent and disappeared. He was there, and then he wasn't, but his presence remained. The new twinkle in the eye of the serpent was nearly imperceptible, but Marshall could see it. He could see it, and he understood what it meant. Satan had entered the serpent—just like he later entered Judas Iscariot and would eventually enter the Antichrist. A throng of demons watched from above like spectators at a sporting event. For them, however, this was no leisure activity. They were in training. Their master was at work, and they would either learn his tactics or suffer his wrath.

Gudan led Marshall closer. They stood right in front of Adam, Eve, and the serpent. Had they crossed through the barrier, they could have reached out and touched them. It was all Marshall could do not to scream at Adam and Eve, warning them of the danger, of what they were about to do to the entire human race, of the terrible price that would have to be paid to put right the terrible wrong that they were about to do. His body was tense, but he said nothing. He simply watched and listened.

"Yes, we had some from that bush yesterday," Eve answered. "It was the best one so far."

"Well, that's only because you haven't tried this one yet," the serpent said, pointing at the tree of the knowledge of good and evil.

"The big one in the middle? Oh, we can't have any from that tree."

"You can't? But why not? Look at how beautiful the fruit is! It looks much better than the fruit from that little bush you ate from yesterday! Plump and juicy—why, I bet it is sweeter too! It must be simply wonderful."

"That may be," Eve said. "But we can't eat it. God said so."

"Are you sure?" the serpent questioned. "Did God really say, 'you must not eat from any tree in the garden'?"

"Of course not! We eat from trees all the time! He said we can eat from all the trees in the garden, except that big one in the middle of the garden. We can't even touch it, or we'll die."

"You will not surely die," the serpent said. "You see, God knows that when you eat of it, your eyes will be opened, and you will be like God, knowing good and evil."

Again tears slowly fell from Marshall's eyes. He didn't watch the rest of the scene. He had seen enough. Satan was indeed a formidable opponent. He was so wise and clever in his deception. He had known God's words better than Eve did! When she said that they would die if the ate the fruit, she hadn't even quoted God correctly, but Satan had. She had simply said, "Or you will die." Satan had quoted God verbatim when he countered her statement with "You will not surely die."

Marshall's mind began to race as the spirit of God filled it with new insights about his enemy. Satan, although he is the father of lies, doesn't make up lies all the time. He doesn't need to. He doesn't even need to come up with things on his own all the time. Much of the time, he simply twists the word of God, thereby taking away its effectiveness. He stretches and bends the words of God in such a way as to make them only partially true, which is basically the same as untrue, except that it is usually much more damaging. He still keeps the truth in there in small doses but dilutes it enough to render it ineffective and useless. He deceives people by "reinterpreting" what God has said. He makes it sound as though he is quoting God's words, but he is merely talking like God, not speaking the truth from God. He deceives. His deception causes things which are not of God to appear better and more desirable than the things which are of

God. And then he leaves you alone to allow your desire to please self overcome your desire to please God.

With deception as the primary weapon in his arsenal, Satan clings to this devious and cunning strategy: making humanity think the devil is strong where he is actually weak, and making humanity think that they themselves are weak where they are actually strong. If a person believes that the enemy knows nothing about God or about his ways, he will believe anything that comes his way in a "God wrapper," because "it must be from God since our enemy knows nothing of him." That is one of the keys. Satan doesn't need to preach anti-God. All he needs to do is preach a different god or a slightly modified god. He never told Eve to betray God. He simply said that God didn't really mean what he had said or that he had only told them a partial truth and that it wasn't really as bad as God had made it sound. In fact, Satan convinced Eve that eating the fruit would actually make her more like God, which was what she was striving for anyway. He used her devotion to God against her and deceived her into betraying the very one she was trying to become more like and closer to.

Had Marshall been sitting in a classroom or even in a pew in his church, he would have been furiously writing down these thoughts as they entered his mind. In this case, however, he doubted that he could ever forget anything he was being exposed to even if he tried.

"Marshall, do you realize what has happened here?" Gudan asked.

"Yes, Gudan. The fall of man," Marshall said softly, wiping a tear from his eye and sniffling.

Gudan hesitated. "Yes, Marshall, in its barest form, that is what has happened. Mankind has broken the law of the Most High, allowing evil to enter his perfect world and tarnish it forever. There will be repercussions on various levels for all eternity as a result of the actions of these two.

"For mankind, the repercussions will be immediate and terrible. They have destroyed the perfect fellowship they had previously enjoyed with the Most High and with each other. Never again will mankind on the earth enjoy such an experience of unabashed and unhindered unity with the Most High, much less with his fellow man. Even in the most intimate of human relationships, there will be fear. There will be uncertainty. There will be mistrust to some degree. There will be the knowledge that to be failed by a loved one is not only possible, but nearly guaranteed to one extent or another. That which, in the earthly realm, will be misconstrued as love will be shallow and conditional, resulting in an insatiable striving to be good enough and to maintain the relationship at all costs. This will in no way mirror the comfortable, effortless existence of mutual unconditional love as designed by the Most High and shared between him and mankind. That is what Adam and Eve shared with the Most High. That is what they foolishly rejected by their disobedience. Therefore, for the entirety of their existence on earth, they will have an intense desire to strive for exactly what they sacrificed in a futile attempt to achieve what they gave up to achieve it."

Marshall nodded. "So in order to become more like God and thus able to be closer to him, they sacrificed the very closeness which they already possessed in their attempt to achieve what they had just given up to achieve it," he concluded aloud.

"That is correct, Marshall," Gudan agreed. "But it doesn't end there. They will also be banished from the garden just like Lucifer was banished from heaven. They will now have to work the land for their food and make their own way in a world that can no longer be subdued by them. Everything they need will still be available to them, but it will no longer be freely given to them. Life will become more difficult for them physically. However, infinitely more significant is the devastating effect their betrayal will have on them spiritually. Their relationship with the Most High has been destroyed. They have broken their father's heart.

There was grief in heaven on this day, Marshall. I remember it as vividly as if it had happened today for the first time.

"Mankind will now begin to suffer the most detrimental aspect of his punishment. His soul has become prone to evil. Had Adam never sinned, his children would have been born perfect and sinless, enjoying a perfect relationship and unhindered fellowship with the Most High. But since he did fall, his children will now be born into sin and into a broken relationship with the Most High. Now they will be slaves to sin rather than free men living in perfect fellowship with the Most High. Now, their only access to the Most High will be through the blood sacrifice of a burnt offering."

"How wonderful it must have been, Gudan, to walk and talk with God face-to-face," Marshall thought aloud.

"Yes, they gave up a life of joy and pleasure that defies description," Gudan agreed. "And for what? What could possibly have motivated them to throw away such a wonderful existence? Love of self. They put their own wants and desires above those of the Most High, just like Lucifer did. They are no different from him. Sure, Lucifer led a revolt in heaven, directly opposing the Most High to his face, but do not you do the same when you oppose him and put your own will above his? That is all that Lucifer did. He wanted to rule. He wanted to receive the glory due the Most High. He wanted to be in control and in command. Adam did the same thing. His desire for knowledge was greater than his desire to be obedient to the Most High. When he saw that the fruit was good for making him wise like the Most High, he ate it. When he saw that he had the chance to be in control and to make his own way, he took it. Would not the Most High have given him anything he had asked for? Was there any good thing that the Most High would have kept from him? Had he been content to take the Most High at his word and chosen obedience rather than rebellion, he would have been given knowledge far superior to anything mankind will ever achieve in his fallen state.

But he was ambitious. He put his will above that of the Most High, and their relationship was destroyed."

Marshall didn't speak. He knew that he probably would have done the same thing had he been the one in the garden. In fact, how many times had he put his will above God's in his own life? In his ministry? He was really not that much different from Lucifer, except for the simple fact that his sin was easier to cover up and easier to ignore. However, although the punishment for his sin in the human realm may not have been immediate as it was for Lucifer and for Adam, the ramifications of his sin in the spiritual realm were every bit as immediate—and as severe. His relationship with God was still subverted with comparable severity. And God still wept at his disobedience.

Chapter Seven

The roar from the fallen angels was deafening. All across the earth, their shouts could be heard. They cheered their leader, flying back and forth through the sky with exuberant glee. The humans had fallen! The humans had fallen! All their preparation had paid off. They had been watching and listening to the humans ever since the Most High had placed them in the garden. Now, finally, the humans had been brought down. And it had been so simple! All the evil one had done was to talk to the female human. He steered the conversation around to the forbidden tree, and she took the bait like a hungry fish biting onto a plump, juicy worm.

"Supred! Candeg! Zulef!"

The three fallen angels were at Satan's side in an instant. "How can we serve you, Great Prince?" the three generals said as they bowed in front of their leader.

"Assemble the troops at headquarters. I will address them in one hour's time."

"As you wish, Great Prince," they said in unison, then fluttered off to carry out the order.

Silence fell over the assembled crowd as Satan stepped up to the podium. Without introduction or preamble, he began his address: "The Most High banished us from our home in heaven. He took away everything we knew and cast us out of his presence. Then he humiliated us by creating that race of inferior creatures he calls humans to replace us. He created for them their own little world where they can live and go about their business. He even came down from heaven himself to walk with them and talk with them.

"But today, today is a day of *victory*! Today is the day that we gained the upper hand over the Most High! For today is the day that the humans—his beloved ridiculous creation—betrayed him!"

Another eruption of shouts and cheers filled the spirit world. Satan was thoroughly enjoying this celebration of his victory. The success of his mission caused a satisfied grin to cover his face even though he knew that this success was only the beginning of his torment of the humans. And torment them, he would. He and his evil minions would infiltrate their entire world, driving them further and further away from the Most High and the joyful, peaceful life he had intended for them. He would get back at the Most High by turning his prized creation against him. And those he couldn't influence to betray and abandon the Most High, he would torment all the more, making them suffer in every way he could imagine. Satan gritted his teeth just thinking about it. "Those wretched humans," he growled. "I'll get them. Every last one of them. I'll get them all."

Ironically, this new horrible, evil crusade Satan was obsessed with, while aimed specifically at mankind, in reality had precious little to do with the humans. Although they were the obvious recipients of this intense loathing, they could only be considered the cause of it by the simple fact of their existence. It was not the result of some declaration of war between the humans and the kingdom of darkness, nor was it on account of any broken treaty or other treachery on the part of the humans. No, in this case, the humans were completely innocent of any wrongdoing.

The absolute hatred of their kind existed in and nearly consumed Satan for one simple reason: the Most High loved them so much. How the Most High could care at all for these puny, insignificant creatures was completely beyond him, but the reason why he loved them was not important. What was important was the bottom line fact that, for whatever incomprehensible reason there might be to explain it, it was true. The Most High did care for them. He loved them. And therein lay his weakness.

If one cannot prevail against his true enemy on the field of battle, then he must retreat, regroup, and rethink his plan of attack. Perhaps hand-to-hand combat would not be necessary to defeat the Most High. Perhaps if that which is most dear to him were destroyed—or better yet, convinced to betray him as well—maybe then he would simply lose heart, and victory would be attainable. Satan would show the Most High the true anguish of being betrayed and abandoned. The humans must be defeated. They must be destroyed. They must be corrupted and brought under Satan's rule. Only then could he throw it back into the face of the Most High and have his revenge.

Satan ended his address with a charge to all his angels. "You will infiltrate every facet of human existence and corrupt it. Everything the Most High has established must be destroyed, manipulated, perverted, or abandoned. The humans are to be taught and influenced to rebel against the Most High in every way imaginable. They must be convinced to reject the sovereignty of the Most High, each one doing as he sees fit and as seems good in his own eyes. In this way, we can control them. We can deceive them all, just like I did the first two. The Most High has commanded them to multiply and fill the earth. This command they will obey, and we will be there. We will be there in force! We will turn their hearts away from the Most High, and once their loyalty to him has been broken and they belong to us, we can guide them further and further away from him, deeper and deeper into depravity and corruption. Once they reject the sovereignty and protection of the Most High, we can even enter them and possess them just as I did the serpent! You were there. You all saw how I possessed the serpent and made him deceive the woman. Imagine the possibilities! Once we can enter them, there will be no facet of human existence beyond our reach, our influence, our control! We will be able to make them do terrible, horrible things to themselves and to each other! Things they would never do if left alone, even in the depths of their own degeneracy. We can wound their bodies! Wrack their bodies with illnesses and diseases! Cause them to be lame, deaf, blind, mute! Confuse their minds and cause them to be insane, irrational, delusional! It will be utter mayhem beyond our wildest dreams! Death! Destruction! Corruption! Depravity! Betrayal! Unbridled evil! Unrestricted perversion! Uncontrolled wickedness!" Satan laughed a chilling evil laugh. "Now go!" he shouted to his soldiers. "Go and destroy them from the inside out! Before they are even born, begin their destruction. Attack them in their mother's womb. As soon as they are born, intensify your assault. Attack the babies in their mother's arms. Wound them. Break them. Warp them. Let no human child grow up unscathed."

And so it was that the war between Satan and God was brought to earth, and mankind became the soldiers through which the war was fought. It was like a live chess match played with game pieces that not only had been equipped with intelligence and the capacity to reason but also possessed the free will to choose for themselves how they would play the game. They could not be manifestly controlled, but rather had to be influenced to go this way or that by whichever power held their allegiance. Not only were the opponents required to have a plan and a strategy for defeating their enemy, but they would also have to be able to convince their game pieces to carry out their wishes against the opposing team.

Gudan turned to leave, followed closely by Marshall. They walked in silence, pondering what they had just witnessed. Marshall's mind drifted from the fall of mankind to the redemption that God had provided through the Old Testament system of animal sacrifices, not so much a redemption in terms of removing the sin completely, but rather providing a covering of the sin to permit the barest resumption of fellowship between creation and Creator. He thought of all the rituals and rules that mankind had brought upon himself by yielding to the temptation of Satan and sinning against the Father. The same prideful desire to be better than they were had caused the humans to make the same mistake Lucifer had made—first, that of putting their own will above God's will and second, of sealing their fate by foolishly acting out their rebellious attitude. Because of that, God, who is abounding in love and mercy, devised a way for them to reestablish fellowship with him and repair the fractured relationship to a certain degree. Through a series of animal sacrifices and offerings to God, they were permitted to have fellowship with him again although only a fraction of them decided it was worth the effort. The rest were so deceived by Satan that they preferred to live in darkness without the presence of God in their lives. In fact, at one point, Satan and his followers had so deceived the world into living apart from God that God granted them their desire of separation from him by wiping them all off the face of the earth. He had spared only the family of Noah—the only ones who had remained true to him and kept his laws.

Then later, because most of mankind had become corrupt again, God chose one man to begin a race of special people who would be like a trophy to him forever. He would take care of them and be their God, and they would be his chosen people. Unfortunately, even these people rebelled against God and were unfaithful.

Finally, God put into action the ultimate plan of redemption. He would create a bridge between mankind and himself. This time, he would make it more personal. He would bridge the gap by providing one perfect sacrifice that would once for all redeem all mankind forever to himself.

Chapter Eight

"He told her what?" Satan stormed across the floor to stand face-to-face with the frightened little demon. Froape cowered, shrinking back until he bumped into the legs of Eurad, the fallen angel designated as the prince of Nazareth. Eurad himself stood significantly less erect than he typically did because of both the demeanor and the proximity of the prince of darkness. Froape and Eurad stood behind Candeg, one of Satan's generals. Candeg turned to face Froape and Eurad as Satan stomped past him to approached them.

"Great Prince," Candeg began, "Eurad came to me as soon as he heard from Froape, and I—"

"Silence!" Satan shouted, pointing a finger at Candeg without turning to face him. His gaze was still fixed on Froape. He moved a step closer to Froape, slowly drawing the outstretched finger around to level it at him and lowering his voice to a forceful, gravely whisper. "I want to hear it from you," he said with an intensity that shrouded Froape in fear like a wet blanket. "Tell me everything you saw and heard down to the very last detail."

"As you c-command, Great P-P-Prince," Froape stammered, trembling.

"Relax, little one," Satan soothed, placing a hand on his shoulder and directing him to several chairs arranged on the other side of the chamber. Although seething within, he forced himself to exude a relaxed placidity, thereby putting his frightened subordinate at ease, all the better to obtain the information he needed. "Just tell me what happened. Everything you saw and every word you heard. Don't leave out the slightest detail. Allow me to determine what I do and do not need to know. Fair enough?" He turned to the others without waiting for an answer. "Candeg, Eurad, would you please wait in the outer chamber?"

The general and the prince of Nazareth silently walked through the door, closing it behind them. Satan ushered Froape to one of the chairs and turned another so that they could sit facing each other.

"Now, demon Froape, you were saying?" Satan prompted. "Candeg tells me you are assigned to the Nazareth detail."

Froape responded to Satan's altered disposition with a commensurate change in his own. No longer fearing that his existence would soon be snuffed out for reasons beyond his comprehension, he began to excitedly relay his story to the prince of darkness.

"Yes, I was assigned to a peasant girl living in Nazareth. Until today, she seemed to be just another Jewish peasant girl going about her daily business. Since she has reached the common age where young girls are given in marriage, her training around the house is basically complete. Therefore, she spends her time going about the household tasks such as grinding wheat for flour, baking, cooking and preparing food, weaving thread, and making clothing for the family. Her father is a regular attendee of the local synagogue, and Mary herself is a rather devout follower of the Most High. I have spent much time and effort trying to dissuade her in any way possible, but she seldom yields. She spends too much time praying to the Most High and meditating on the law of Moses and the words of the psalmists and the prophets."

"I understand, Froape. Now tell me about the visitor," Satan said calmly.

"Of course, Great Prince. It was near the end of the day in Nazareth when the men were typically gathered at the meeting place in the middle of the village and the women were cleaning up from the family supper. After helping her mother clean up the eating area, Mary had gone into her room to relax and to prepare to retire for the evening. I was trying to convince her that she was too tired to pray and that she should just go to bed when suddenly a messenger of the Most High appeared. It was Gabriel, and he had a message for Mary. I was as shocked as she was—I mean, what business could the Most High have with an insignificant little peasant girl anyway? And Gabriel? Such a high-ranking angel to visit such a nobody!

"Anyway, Gabriel was the first to speak. He said, 'Greetings, you who are highly favored! The Lord is with you!' I tried to scare her, telling her that the angel was an enemy and that she should be afraid. And she was afraid too until Gabriel told her not to be afraid since she had found favor with God. Jerk. Well, I didn't even know what he was there for until he started talking again. Then it all made sense to me. He told her that she would become pregnant and give birth to a son and that she should call him Jesus and that he would be great and would be called the son of the Most High. He even said that the kid would inherit the throne of David and that he would reign over the house of Jacob forever.

"Well, she was nervous enough, so I didn't even say anything then. Mary asked Gabriel how this could be since she was a virgin, and let me tell you, she was very strict on that point. It certainly isn't my fault that she is still a virgin. Anyway, Gabriel told her that the Holy Spirit would come upon her and make her pregnant, and that's why he would be called the son of the Most High.

"I reminded her that she was engaged to Joseph and that he might not think too highly of marrying a pregnant woman. After all, how could she convince him that she hadn't been unfaithful to her pledge to him if she turned out to be pregnant? Joseph probably wouldn't even want to marry her anymore. After all, it is against the law for an unmarried woman to have sexual relations, under penalty of death. If Joseph could prove that she was not a virgin and the state of pregnancy would be rather convincing evidence, then the men of the city would take her to the door of her father's house and stone her to death, thereby dishonoring her entire family for generations. Not only would she lose the man she is to marry, she would disgrace her family and get herself killed for her trouble. No, I told her, this is not a good idea. You should tell him you can't do it, at least not until you and Joseph are properly wed. But do you know what she did? She just bowed her head and said, 'I am the Lord's servant. May it be unto me as you have said.' What kind of response is that? See, she doesn't even listen to me! She has always been obstinate like this! I have tried every trick I know to get her to—"

"All right, Froape," Satan interrupted. "I understand. Is there anything else you can tell me about it? Did Gabriel say anything else?"

"No, Great Prince, nothing else. He just left."

"Thank you, Froape. You have done well. You may now return to your post."

"As you command, Great Prince," Froape said as he bowed and backed toward the door.

Satan paced the room, hatred and anger filling him until it overflowed in the form of curses against the Most High and against Mary and against Gabriel and against everything that had anything to do with the Most High. Finally, Satan became quiet and flopped down into his chair. *And so it happens,* he muttered to himself. *The prophesied virgin birth of the Messiah. The next slap in the face from the Most High. Well, this time things will be different. This time, I will get the upper hand. I will destroy this virgin and the spawn of the Most High that lives within her. Mankind belongs to me, and I will not let this ridiculous plan of redeeming them come to pass. After all, was I ever redeemed? Did the Most High ever devise a plan to reinstate me after he banished me from my home? But now he is going to send a redeemer for these insignificant little nothings he has created to humiliate me. No, there must be some way to stop it. This plan has to be stopped.*

"Candeg! Eurad!" Satan bellowed at the closed door. Sensing that their master's mood had not improved with Froape's telling of the story, Candeg and Eurad wasted no time getting through the door and presenting themselves to Satan.

"I want that baby dead," Satan said bluntly. "Beginning right now, the only thing that matters to either one of you is the destruction of that child. Under no circumstances is this birth to be permitted. I don't care if you have to bury the entire city in molten lava or bring in a tidal wave or poison the well where they all get their drinking water or even if you have to kill every living being on the face of this planet. Do what you must, but that child is never to take its first breath! Understood? Go!"

Candeg and Eurad nodded and bolted through the door and out of the headquarters.

→ ✢ ←

While it was quite fascinating to experience Gabriel's visit with Mary firsthand, it was a scene that Marshall had heard, taught, acted out in dramas, and preached many times before. What was new to him, however, was gaining firsthand knowledge of Satan's reaction to the same event. Even knowing what the outcome of the situation would be did not prevent him from becoming tense as he watched Satan turn two of his generals loose on the baby Jesus. Not to worry, of course, because the protective force on baby Jesus was absolutely impenetrable to anything the kingdom of darkness could come up with to pit against it. Marshall watched

Satan fume and pace, rant and rave about his failed attempts to destroy the baby Jesus before he could even be born.

"We will now travel to a time approximately one year after the birth of the Messiah," Gudan explained, "while Joseph, Mary, and the baby are still in Bethlehem. Not wanting to make the journey back to Nazareth with a very young child, Joseph and Mary settled temporarily in Bethlehem. Joseph found an opportunity to ply his trade as a carpenter, which allowed him to acquire adequate housing for his family for the duration of their stay in Bethlehem."

Time became the future as Marshall looked through the barrier, expecting to see a very small boy sleeping peacefully in his mother's arms. Instead, he was surprised to see a tortured, paranoid man in the master bedroom suite of a palace. The man was tossing and turning in his huge fancy bed, fitfully attempting to rest in spite of the inner turmoil he was obviously enduring. Marshall was fairly certain that the source of the torment could be explained by the presence of Sodyem, a high-ranking fallen angel designated as the prince of Jerusalem, and Alstes, the man's assigned demon, hovering near the ceiling in the man's bedroom. Sodyem was hovering right over the bed, talking to the man as he grasped desperately at the elusive peacefulness of sleep. Marshall stepped forward and strained to hear the words Sodyem whispered into the ear of the king of Judea.

"They say this baby is a king. They say his kingdom will last forever. Then what will happen to you, Herod? If this baby is to be king, where will that leave you? And how will he come to power? Will he lead a revolt? Will he have you assassinated and usurp your throne? Regardless, he must be stopped. For the good of the monarchy and the Roman Empire, he must be stopped. And you must stop him. You must stop him. Find the baby and stop him!"

Herod threw off his blanket and bounded out of his bed. "Leave me alone!" he shouted. A layer of cold sweat covered his body and threatened to drip from his forehead. His muscles were taught, his body rigid. He looked around the room as if expecting to see someone standing there beside him. He walked briskly around the large bed, over to the window, back to the other side of the bed. Nothing.

"What baby?" he yelled to the empty room. "What baby? Where?"

His questions hung in the silent room unanswered. He knew no one was there, yet he could feel a presence. He also knew that something had spoken to him although he could not see the prince of Jerusalem hovering right above him. Sodyem chuckled with amusement.

"The master is right," he remarked to Alstes. "These humans are pathetic. Such a powerful man by their standards, yet just a few words whispered into his ear, and he is so upset and flustered that he can't even sleep. He's sweating and nervous, jumping at shadows. I wish I could toy with him some more, just to watch him fumble about, but I do have my orders." Turning back to Herod, he added, "That is enough for tonight, 'Your Majesty.'" Sodyem motioned a mock bow dripping with sarcasm and disdain as he and Alstes left Herod's private quarters and passed back through the barrier.

His official title was Herod the Great, son of Antipater, king of Judea and ruler of the surrounding territories. He had been appointed king of Judea by the Roman emperor after his father's death. He was a harsh ruler, ruthless, cunning, intensely loyal to the emperor of Rome, and fiercely protective of his position and of his throne. He had once slaughtered every male member of his family that may have had a legal claim to the throne, just to ensure that no one would try to take it from him. He had also murdered one of his wives to protect his throne and later her two sons when they found out that their father had taken their mother away from them. He had no conscience. He showed no mercy. He was the perfect candidate for Satan to use to get rid of the Messiah.

The next morning, Herod awoke tired, grouchy, and meaner than usual. Although he did eventually get a small amount of sleep the previous night, he got very little in the way of actual rest. His sleep was fitful and light. And if that weren't enough, the nightmares were back. He had been experiencing them off and on for almost a year now. He was stubbornly reluctant to call in his advisors or his wise men to assist him for fear that they might see his nightly torment as a sign of weakness and plot against him. No—not Herod. There could be no sign of weakness of any kind. He could handle this by himself. They were just dreams after all, not something to become overly concerned about. Besides, enduring the dreams through the night was difficult enough without the added anguish of bringing them to his own mind on purpose during the day. The problem was, they were occurring more frequently now. And although the underlying theme was always the same—the loss of his kingdom—the dreams were becoming more and more vivid and forceful. Sometimes he would see himself killed by his own cabinet officials; other times he would meet his untimely demise by more or less natural causes, such as falling from the turrets of one of the palace towers. Sometimes he would be poisoned by his cook or by his cupbearer, and other times he would be kept alive but locked in the dungeon of his own palace. Here he would be tortured both physically by the prison guards and mentally by the knowledge that someone else was ruling his kingdom in his stead while he was chained to the wall in the very same dungeon where he had ordered the torture and execution of many men. Most of those men had not even been guilty of a crime thus deserving imprisonment, to say nothing of torture or death. As unsettling as these images were to him, he was tormented more than anything else by the face of the male child. The face would appear in the sky, in his wine, in his bowl of soup. It would appear and point at him, laughing.

It's eyes would bore into his mind like a sharpened sword boring into the soft tissue of his belly. It would dance around and shout at him, laughing all the while. Herod knew that the male child was the one stealing his throne, but he didn't know how or when. It simply didn't make sense. Hadn't he already taken care of that problem? Hadn't he killed every possible male heir to his throne years ago? How could there be another one out there waiting to tear his kingdom apart and relieve him of his life? Where would he come from? Who could he be?

Herod put the thoughts from his mind. Worrying would certainly not solve the problem anyway. Probably what he needed was simply a change of activity right before retiring for the day. Perhaps if he had more wine, he would be able to sleep more soundly. Or perhaps less wine. Maybe he could wear himself out with female companionship as he turned in for the night, then maybe the horrible dreams would find his body and mind too exhausted to concentrate on them, resulting in a period of restful sleep. Either way, he could beat this inconvenience. He was, after all, Herod the Great.

As his luck would have it, however, Herod the Great found himself weak in the knees later that same day when news came to him of some magi from the east who had recently arrived in the city of Jerusalem. Apparently, they were asking people where to find 'him who was born king of the Jews.' They were astronomers from the distant kingdoms of the east who claimed they had seen his star—a new star indicating the birth of a king—in the western sky and were coming to worship the new king. They had followed the new star as far as the region of Jerusalem, but upon arrival, their destination had become unclear. It was, after all, a star, which would be able to direct them to a particular region of the planet easily enough but which would be quite incapable of pointing them to a particular street or even a particular city.

This was all well and good for Herod. They could follow whatever star they wanted to forever for all he cared, but the part that bothered him was the claim that the new star they had seen announced the birth of the new king of the Jews. Herod was the king of the Jews. He had already slaughtered all his own sons, so who else could have been born king of the Jews without his knowledge? His horrible dreams were becoming an equally horrible reality right before his eyes!

But then he remembered something, something from his training in Jewish law. Becoming a convert to Judaism had more or less been a political move for Herod as opposed to an attempt to find and serve God. He believed that knowing more about the religiosity that dominated the Jewish culture would assist him in ruling them more effectively. Not that his concern for ruling them effectively had anything to do with fairness or concern for the Jews; rather, in Herod's mind, ruling them effectively meant subduing them effectively so that his authority would never be questioned even to the slightest degree by any of the Jews under his rule. However, even though he didn't take his conversion seriously or change his lifestyle accordingly, he did remember from his indoctrination that central to their culture were the many prophecies concerning the Messiah, the promised one who would bring deliverance to the Jews and set up an everlasting kingdom. Another twinge of fear shot up Herod's spine. Immediately he called together the chief priests and the teachers of the law, the religious leaders of the Jews. He asked them where their Messiah was supposed to be born according to the prophecies. Without hesitation, they recited Micah 5:2, where the prophet had predicted that the Messiah's birthplace would be in the city of Bethlehem in Judea.

Now Herod understood. For the past year, he had been tormented because of the presence of this Messiah. His dreams, those terrible dreams, had been telling him that the Messiah had already been born!

"You must stop him! The baby must be killed! He is a nuisance that has to be stopped! He is a threat to the throne! Killing the child is the only way to secure the throne! The child must be stopped!" the voice had repeated over and over and over. And now, finally, Herod understood. And he also understood what had to be done about it. Not even a prophesied Messiah was going to take over his throne. Not if he could help it. And help it, he would!

Herod dismissed the religious leaders and thought about what to do. This baby was a nuisance that had to be stopped. He was a threat to Herod's throne, and no such person was allowed to live. He would find this baby and have him killed. That was the only way. It was the only way to stop this child-king and secure his own throne. He summoned the magi from the east and had a secret meeting with them.

"Gentlemen, I have discovered the whereabouts of the child you are searching for. Now that I know who he is, I also wish to go to him and to worship him. Go, then, to Bethlehem of Judea, and when you have found the child, report back to me immediately so that I may come straightaway and join you at his side and worship him."

The magi joyfully agreed, thanking the king profusely as they bowed and scurried out of the palace. They continued their journey with renewed vigor. Finally, after all this time, they would be able to see the promised Messiah! How wonderful that would be!

Marshall looked up at Gudan. Even though he had known the story since childhood and had even studied it in depth as an adult, seeing it happen right before his eyes brought a whole new depth of reality to it. Gudan nodded his understanding of what Marshall was feeling and motioned back to the scene before them. Time had again passed. Marshall looked down to see Satan berating one of his princes—the prince of Jerusalem.

"They're not coming back, Sodyem!" the prince of darkness screamed. "The magi are not coming back, and the child still lives! Do I have to handle this myself? Can you do nothing on your own?" Sodyem stood stock still, knowing that any answer he gave would be the wrong one and would get him punished further. "Out of my way!" Satan bellowed. He backhanded Sodyem, sending him flying through the air head over heels like a couch pillow tossed across a living room. He thundered toward Herod's palace, threats and curses pouring out of his mouth with every step like fertilizer spraying out of a farmer's spreader.

Herod was walking through the courtyard, trying to figure out what to do about the magi and their treachery. Well, forget the magi, what about that child-king? How would he stop him now? Even if he went down to Bethlehem himself, how would he know the child-king even if he saw him?

Birds, rodents, and even insects fled from the courtyard as the presence of Satan filled the place with evil.

"Herod! Herod, will you not preserve your throne? The throne is threatened by the child-king. The child-king must be stopped! Even now he is being groomed to take over your kingdom, to live in your palace and enjoy the luxuries that your hands have acquired. Will you sit idly by and watch it happen? What will you do? How will you destroy this usurper? How will you make sure to get the right one? How could you possibly know which one to kill? Sometimes one must sacrifice a few sheep to get the wolf. Find that child and kill him!"

Satan shot a look at Sodyem, then at Alstes, then back at Herod. He reached through the barrier, grabbed Alstes securely by the throat, and pulled him back through the barrier. Pointing at Herod with one hand, he suspended Alstes in front of him with the other, their faces mere inches apart.

"He is your charge, demon!" Satan growled menacingly through clenched teeth. He pulled him closer so that their faces nearly touched. "You take care of it."

His grip tightened, his glare intensified. He spoke slowly, pausing between each word. "Now…find…that…child…and…*kill…him!*" He reared back and threw the demon at Herod like a baseball pitcher letting loose his best fastball.

Alstes flew to the air, through Herod, and slammed onto the ground on his back. Quickly righting himself, he glared at Satan then strode resolutely toward Herod, dissolving from sight as he entered the body of the king of Judea.

Suddenly, Herod had an idea. A hideous smile covered his face. Yes, this plan would work perfectly. He would kill the child-king, and he would make sure that he got him because he would kill them all. All of them. Every male child born within the past year, ever since he had started having those dreams. No, wait, wouldn't want to miss him by a few months, just in case the dreams didn't begin exactly when the child was born. Well, two years, then. Every male child two years of age or less. Yes, that would work. He would kill every one of them throughout the entire region of Bethlehem. That will purge the usurper from his land. An evil chuckle accompanied the hideous grin. Yes, that would definitely take care of that little usurper. Long live King Herod the Great!

"Yes, that should take care of the little usurper," Satan agreed. "Long live King Herod the Great!" Satan also uttered an evil chuckle to accompany a hideous grin as he walked back through the barrier to face Sodyem. Without a word, Satan brushed past Sodyem and vanished in a flash of light.

Chapter Nine

The demons were gathered around the city like a frenzied mob of sports fans watching their favorite team completely dominate and soundly defeat their biggest rival. Whoops and hollers and cheers filled the air with venomous glee. They laughed and pointed, yelling to each other, neither wanting to miss the part they were seeing nor wanting to miss what anyone else was seeing.

Marshall also tried to see the events unfolding in the middle of the crowd, but he couldn't. The crowd was so thick, all he could see was line after line of demons jumping and cheering in victory. Gudan took Marshall's arm and moved them forward in time. "No, Marshall," he said. "You do not need to see that. Look instead at this scene."

"But what was it, Gudan? What were all those demons so excited about?"

"You will see, Marshall. Look." Gudan pointed to the scene before them.

Marshall looked and saw what he thought was a graveyard. "Oh my," Marshall exclaimed. "A graveyard? This is a graveyard? Those hideous creatures were cheering over someone's death? They were that excited over someone dying?"

"Not someone, Marshall. And it is not a graveyard. It is the city of Bethlehem."

Marshall opened his mouth to speak, then closed it silently as the realization of what he was seeing gripped his heart tight enough to nearly cease its beating. "Bethlehem," he whispered to himself. "Bethlehem…after. . .after. . ." Marshall again stopped. The lump he felt in his throat prevented even the whisper. He closed his eyes. Tears escaped from the corners. Without opening them, he addressed Gudan. "Thank you," he said. "That was a crowd of demons cheering the slaughter of all of Bethlehem's male babies, wasn't it? Thank you, Gudan, for not making me watch it."

Gudan nodded. "Yes, Marshall. It was indeed. It was important for you to witness the reaction of the forces of darkness to that terrible holocaust. Witnessing also the deep sorrow you see before you will paint a sufficient picture for you."

Marshall opened his eyes and, wiping the tears away, looked again at the city. Yes, it was a city, not a graveyard. However, there were so many open graves, piles of dirt, and weeping, mourning people that he hadn't recognized it for what it was. "All those babies," he whispered quietly to himself. All those precious babies." More tears joined the others, this time rolling unashamedly down his face.

He felt Gudan's hand on his arm. "Come, Marshall. Now," Gudan explained, "you are going to see something that not even the forces of darkness were allowed to see. It is a scene that has never been witnessed by anyone outside the heavenly host until now. We will go back again to the night of the terrible holocaust, but we will see the handiwork of the Most High instead of the handiwork of Satan."

Marshall was eager to see, but all he could see was light. Slowly, his eyes became accustomed to the scene before him, and he began to be able to discern shapes. It was a legion or more of the heavenly host, gathered around Jesus, Joseph, and Mary in such a way as to render them all completely invisible, both to the human eye and to the eyes of the forces of darkness.

"Be still, Marshall," Gudan commanded. He brushed his hand down across Marshall's eyes, gently touching his eyelids and closing his eyes. "Now look off to your left."

When Marshall opened his eyes, he could see Joseph, Mary, and Jesus being led away from Bethlehem by a detail of the heavenly host. Marshall could tell by their appearance that, as they surrounded the trio, they and the humans were completely invisible to the forces of darkness and to any other humans. Only because of Gudan was Marshall able to see them. He looked back at Bethlehem. Yes, the house of Joseph, Mary, and Jesus was still shrouded in light from the presence of the guarding force of the heavenly host, confirming for all appearances that Jesus was still there! "The original sleight of hand!" Marshall grinned to himself.

The prince of darkness, on the other hand, was not quite so amused. Rader, the prince of Bethlehem, and Sodyem, the prince of Jerusalem, were suspended several feet above the ground, their breaths coming in short, shallow gasps as the prince of darkness tightened his grip on their throats. In a fierce but low, menacing growl, he spoke through gritted teeth slowly as if addressing someone unfamiliar with the language. "What did you say? What do you mean he wasn't there?" Satan paused, then shrieked as he flung them to the ground, watching them bounce and roll like stuffed dolls, crashing out of the master's chambers and flipping end over end until they finally came to rest on the other side of the headquarters. "Get back in here!" Satan commanded. Rader and Sodyem scrambled back into the master's chambers, standing at attention before him, breathing heavily and wincing in pain. Satan repeated his question, venom dripping from his lips, "What do you mean, he wasn't there?"

"The Messiah wasn't there!" Rader began. "We were at the slaughter, watching with the rest of the soldiers. After, we stayed on to watch the burials and see the families cry. The pain and anguish of the survivors makes the killing so worthwhile."

"Then we decided to go and see the family of the Messiah," Sodyem took over. We really wanted to see them suffering. We wanted to bask in the destruction of all their hopes and dreams, but we couldn't find them! Anywhere!"

"So we immediately called in a search detail to find them. We checked every grave, Great Prince. Every one. We looked at every single person in the entire city, and they were not there! We expanded our search to the surrounding countryside, remote villages, everywhere. But they were simply not there!"

Satan's roar shook the earth. In unabated fury, he stomped back and forth across the earth, cursing the humans, cursing his subordinates, cursing the host of heaven, cursing the Most High.

Marshall looked at Gudan. "Satan wanted to kill Jesus before he could even grow up," he observed, stating the obvious more to himself than to Gudan. He was thinking aloud as the processes of his mind caught up to the stimulus presented to his eyes, thereby filling his mind with the enlightenment of the word of God.

"Yes, Marshall, that is correct. Satan did everything in his power to prevent the birth of the Messiah. All the forces of evil were working together to thwart the redemptive plan of the Most High, which was essentially set in motion with the birth of the Messiah. You see, because Jesus was the Son of the Most High, he was all God and was endowed with all the attributes and characteristics of God. When he humbled himself to become a man, then he became all man and was therefore subject to all the desires and limitations of mankind. He felt emotional and physical pain, mental and spiritual fatigue, temptation of all varieties, and relational confrontation. It was this dual nature that allowed him to become the perfect example of what the Most High had originally intended for all his creation—mankind as well as the angelic beings—to be: intelligent, fully mature beings exercising their free will by choosing complete obedience to himself. Jesus was not merely the perfect example of how humanity can have a right relationship with the Most High. He was also the perfect example of the relationship the Most High had intended to have with his first love, the created angelic beings, all along."

Gudan paused, allowing Marshall to ponder what he had said. Sensing that Marshall had caught up with him, he continued, "Upon ascertaining that he had utterly failed to accomplish his task of eliminating the prebirth of the Messiah, Satan was forced to alter his strategy from preventative to manipulative. He realized that not only was he powerless to destroy the Messiah, but just as he had been powerless to force his will upon Adam and Eve, he was also powerless to force his will upon the Messiah. He could not force the Messiah to do anything. Rather, he would have to rely on his own cunning powers of persuasion, manipulation, deceit, and coercion to influence the Messiah. Realizing the futility of an obvious frontal attack, Satan began to formulate a plan, not to simply destroy the Messiah, but rather to render him powerless and therefore useless to the Most High and his plan of redemption."

Satan was still seething with fury. He paced back and forth in his private chambers, growling and cursing the Most High and those stupid angels who had refused to join his rebellion. "Okay, so the child can't be destroyed," he admitted with a growl to the otherwise empty room. "The Most High has placed an impenetrable shield of protection around him so that even I can't get to him to relieve him of his life and put a stop to this ridiculous plan of redeeming that pathetic race of creatures he calls the humans. Then I will find another way."

Satan worked it over in his mind. He went back to his first dealings with the humans. "They had been so easy to manipulate and deceive!" he bellowed. "So willingly and foolishly they had accepted my words and followed my leading, right down the path of their own destruction!" Suddenly, Satan stopped pacing. "That's it!" he whispered to himself. "Yes, that's it! If Jesus has become a man and is not controlled by the Most High but rather is merely subject to him by his own choosing, then he can be influenced. He can be manipulated. His will is his own, as is the option to choose between his own will and that of the Most High. Victory has once again been handed to me by the Most High himself! I will convince Jesus that to follow the plan of the Most High is not in his best interest. The Most High may have prevented me from destroying him outright, but he cannot prevent me from getting into his head and doing what I do best!" Satan howled with laughter. This would be his greatest achievement, even greater than turning a full third of the heavenly host and an entire race of those pathetic humans against the Most High. Now he would have a chance to attack and destroy his enemy from within his own mind. And he could do it himself! He didn't have to rely on that idiot Herod or any other human. He, Satan, the adversary himself, would be able to get to the Messiah and destroy him. Satan again chuckled with glee. "He has made himself vulnerable. By becoming a human and giving up free use of his godly power, he has made himself vulnerable to my attack. Now he must choose, like any other human, whether to obey the will of the Most High or to follow his own ideas and make choices that seem best to his human mind. Yes, by requiring for his plan of redemption that a perfect human live a sinless life and ultimately sacrifice himself to pay the debt of sin for all mankind, the Most High has also provided the access and opportunity by which that plan might be circumvented and instead plunge mankind into eternal punishment and separation from himself with no means of escape or redemption!" Impending victory and sweet vengeance filled Satan's mind. "And not only will this plan work on the Messiah, it will also be effective for every human being on the face of the earth. This plan will be universal as will their destruction. This, the greatest and most delicate of all missions, must begin immediately. What was the child now—two years old? Perfect. What better time to begin his corruption and ultimate demise!" Satan bolted from his chambers in a blazing trail of light.

His voice shook the heavens. The music that emanated from him reached the ear of every demon everywhere in the containment area of planet earth. But it was not the music he had been created to produce. No, this was the music used to summon his underlings to an assembly. Every demon under Satan's charge immediately stopped what they were doing and raced back to Satan's headquarters, no one wanting to be the last one to arrive and definitely not the one to arrive after the master was ready to address the company. Making the prince of darkness wait was not a wise career move.

"The Messiah has eluded us," Satan began. "The Most High has hidden him from our sight and protected him from destruction by our hand. He must be found. I have called back every soldier in our ranks to hear this address because this is of the utmost importance to our success against the Most High and the heavenly host. The Messiah must be found. You will search everywhere. Not just where you think he could be, but everywhere. Even where there is no possible way that he could be. Especially where there is no possible way that he could be! He is in hiding from us, and he must be located. This is the only mission of every one of you until he is found. At that point, you will be relieved and reassigned. But for now go find him!" Satan shouted, dispatching his troops.

Gudan led Marshall forward in time to a point where Satan was again preparing to address his troops.

"The Most High kept the Messiah hidden from Satan's sight for about three years," Gudan explained. "When Herod died and the child was no longer in immediate danger, an angel was sent to tell Joseph to take his family back to his hometown of Nazareth from where they had been hiding in Egypt."

But that wasn't what Marshall was seeing. Instead, he was witnessing a gathering of the forces of darkness at the headquarters Satan had set up. Once again, the prince of darkness was addressing his troops.

Supred, Candeg, and Zulef stood at attention in front of the throng of demons in faithful service of the prince of darkness.

"The war has changed, my friends," Satan began. "The Most High has undertaken a campaign drastically different from anything we have encountered thus far. The rules of engagement, therefore, must also be drastically altered. What has been effective for us in the past is no longer going to be functional in leading us to ultimate victory."

Although hovering several yards above the ground, Satan paced back and forth in front of the assembly like an army general addressing his troops before sending them out into battle. "Victory has, however, been ours many times over the duration of our exile," he thundered, now sounding rather more like that same army general on the campaign trail running for congress. "Four thousand earth years ago, when the Most High first created those wretched humans and placed them here on our world, we undertook a great campaign, not to simply destroy them, but to strike a heavy blow to the heart of the Most High by turning them against him. In this, we were completely successful!" He raised his arms and spread his wings wide, nodding in acceptance of the praise of his minions. "Our campaign of corruption and betrayal was so successful that, a mere 1, 500 earth years later, the Most High himself became so disgusted with them that he sent that wonderful flood, wiping all but eight of them off the face of the earth, thereby purging our world of his beloved pestilence and saving us the trouble!"

Another thunderous round of shouts and applause from the company.

"Unfortunately, those eight that he saved from the flood again filled the earth with their offspring. But once again, our efforts at turning them against the Most High were completely successful. Therefore, a mere four hundred or so earth years after he saved that one family of faithful followers from the flood, we had succeeded in corrupting the whole earth again.

"And so the Most High was again forced to change his approach. Rather than attempting to maintain an entire earth full of faithful followers, he chose one family, one specific man, through whom he would build for himself a nation of faithful followers and let the rest remain ours. And yet again, we were completely successful in leading that man's offspring away from the Most High. Each time the Most High would choose a man through whom to propagate his promise of being their God and them being his people, we also would choose one to oppose him. He had the one they called Isaac, we had Ishmael. He had Jacob, we had Esau. He had Joseph, we had all his brothers! And so it went, generation after generation. We successfully corrupted and destroyed his beloved chosen people and prevented him from having his special family!

"But now, the Most High is changing it again. Thus far, it has always been a corporate promise to a group of humans, which could be categorically besmirched and ultimately led into betrayal of the Most High. However, with the advent of this Messiah, the Most High is making it personal. No longer can an entire group of people be influenced and led astray and subsequently spiritually destroyed. No, the Most High is making it into an individual endeavor for each human separately. No longer will the fate of the whole rest on the shoulders of the whole. Instead, the fate of each individual will rest solely upon the shoulders of that individual. Therefore, our strategy must change, beginning with this Messiah. He must not be allowed to succeed in his mission. We must be vigilant, clever, prepared. One of you will be specifically assigned to every single human on planet earth. We will not pick and choose who we think merits monitoring on a grand scale with respect to his or her contribution to the race or the nation as a whole. Instead, every human will be monitored every second of every day and every night. Just like the Most High has assigned what they call a guardian angel of the heavenly host to each human, so we will assign at least one of you to deal with each human individually. You will watch them continuously. You will ascertain their weaknesses, their strengths, their dreams, their desires. You will engage in intensive and continuous reconnaissance, beginning before their birth while they are still in their mothers' wombs, using every tactic at your disposal to keep every individual human from developing or maintaining a relationship with the Most High. You have been trained. You have all witnessed the fall of the first two humans. Use that knowledge, adapt it to fit your charge, and destroy them from the inside out by deceiving them into destroying themselves. Impress upon them day and night, night and day that nothing is more important than their own will and their own desires. Convince them to place their own will above that of anyone and everyone else. In subtle ways. In small ways. In ways that seem insignificant. Start small. Create a habit of looking out for the will of self, and soon you will own them. Begin when they are tiny children. Teach them selfishness and self-centeredness until it becomes a way of life for them.

"A special detail will be assigned to the Messiah, but each of you will carry out the same instructions on a smaller scale throughout the entire earth. Your generals will have your assignments presently. Dismissed."

Satan descended to the ground in front of his generals. "Candeg," he commanded, "choose one to lead the reconnaissance and assault against the Messiah, a team of ten to assist him. And report to my chambers at once."

Marshall watched as the scene before him became a small house in the small town of Nazareth. In accordance with their master's instructions, the team of demons was intensely monitoring every word and action of the young Messiah. Some were specifically watching his facial expressions. Some were specifically listening to his words and voice inflections. Some were monitoring his reactions and attitudes toward others. Some were simply hovering and watching from above, getting the bird's eye view of every situation. Each night, as he slept, they would gather nearby and share information. Detailed records were kept of absolutely everything they saw and heard. There was nothing about him that they did not observe, record, discuss, and share with all the others.

As Marshall was carefully observing and scrutinizing the demonic activity surrounding the Son of God, he saw something else emerge into his field of vision. Out of the corner of his eye, there was another complete scene opening up to his view. It was like picture in picture television or like a separate window opening up on his computer screen. He could still see the scene of Jesus as a boy on the one side, but as the other window finished enlarging and placed itself next to the original, he was able to see a small boy of about the same age in that window as well. He looked at Gudan, who nodded that he should pay attention and gestured toward the new scene.

The two scenes began to fast forward simultaneously, years passing like seconds, while Marshall looked on. His mind was given the ability to see and completely take in both scenes at the same time as though each were playing at normal speed and without the distraction of the other. He heard the audio of each, saw the action of each, and comprehended each without error.

The boys were both monitored continuously by the forces of darkness, the only difference being that the other boy had only one demon watching him, while Jesus always had at least ten and often twelve or fifteen or as many as twenty. Regardless of the number of demons, however, their activities remained the same. They watched. They listened. They talked. They were like evil little soldiers, scampering through their subjects' minds, setting mental land mines, trip wires, and all manner of booby traps to cause their enemy to stumble, doubt, make a wrong choice, make a foolish decision, assume the worst, see the bad, miss the good, lose heart, lose faith, want to give up, feel self-conscious, feel the need to protect himself. They offered suggestions into the boys' ears. They changed circumstances to present obstacles. They even worked in conjunction with the demons assigned to other people to cause the boys' pain in ways ranging from rejection to abuse to abandonment to feelings of worthlessness and depression.

Marshall lifted his head abruptly. His eyes flashed to Gudan then back to the scenes. His eyes became wide as his breathing shortened. He had been so intently observing the demonic activity in both scenes before him that he had failed to recognize the players in the second scene. His heart rate increased as he recognized his mother and father. The little boy in the other scene was Marshall himself!

Many of the same scenes of his life that he had witnessed earlier in his journey were played again, this time with the spiritual battle around him in full view. He saw the demons hovering above him. At various points in his life, there was only one demon. Other times, there were many. Marshall noticed that during those times in his life when he had a significant life decision to make, the demons were present in force. When he was going through a difficult time, they were present in force. During the quiet, comfortable times, they tended to slacken the force. But they were always there, every day, every night. Sometimes actively engaging, often merely observing. But they were always there.

Even after hearing Satan himself order the demons to monitor every human at all times, it had never really registered that even in Marshall's time, there would still be demons assigned to monitor and destroy every human being, including himself! Again, he looked up at Gudan.

"Yes, Marshall," he said. "The command of Satan is still in force today. What many humans fail to realize is that the forces of darkness are busy at work every second of every day and every night. They still monitor every human being all the time. And they are still constantly at work to trip up every human being and keep them from being anything that the Most High wants them to be."

"I guess I never really realized the scope of Satan's plan and his activities on earth. I always knew that he was real and that he was busy trying to deceive people and to cause them to fail to live in obedience to God, but I never dreamed that his operation was so intricate and on such a grand scale! If you think about it, it would have to be, but I just never thought about it like that before. People often talk about 'the devil made me do it,' and such silly phrases, but I doubt that very many really grasp the full range and scope of the work Satan does. I mean, to have so many demons and so well organized! I just never thought of it that way."

"Yes, he truly is a formidable opponent," Gudan agreed. "The adversary of the Most High is also the greatest adversary of the human race. Remember, Marshall, Lucifer was the wisest being ever created. Becoming Satan did not diminish his intelligence or his abilities. It merely changed his allegiance."

Marshall thought for a moment. "So that is why he is so good at tricking us and how he seems to know just what to do and just how to do it, right? The intensive observation, I mean?"

"Precisely, Marshall. That is an accurate assessment. Satan has dispatched his followers across the globe, targeting every single human being on the planet. He knows the weaknesses and the strengths of every single human being alive. He knows which human beings would most likely have negative interaction with which other human beings. He knows whose paths to cross with whom to cause the most damage to both parties. He knows the bent and the potential of each one, and he knows how to deflate and discourage each one from achieving that potential or succeeding according to that bent. He is a master at deception and coercion. His troops have been well trained and are constantly and assiduously on the job.

"Most humans completely fail to realize both the reality and the implications of the constant presence of Satan and his followers in their world and in their lives specifically. And it is constant, Marshall. They never sleep. They never take a break. They know everything about everyone because they never stop gathering intelligence and sharing it amongst themselves. They know exactly how each one will react to any given situation as they act and react according to their human nature, which has been so meticulously observed and analyzed over the course of each human's life." Gudan paused for a moment, allowing Marshall time to process his explanation. "Let's move on," he said, ending the conversation for the moment.

Their forward movement ceased. Gudan nodded in the direction of a new scene unfolding on the other side of the barrier.

"When the Messiah was preparing to begin the next phase in the redemption of mankind, his personal earthly ministry, Satan was all the more eager to get to him and to stop him. Look, for example, how he attempted to get to Jesus right before he began his public ministry."

Marshall looked back into the human realm where Jesus, now a fully-grown man, strolled alone in the wilderness. The second hand on the clock of Marshall's mind ticked off days instead of seconds as time rushed by on the other side of the barrier. Jesus spent hour after hour out there in the desert wilderness with the Father, praying to him, enjoying fellowship with him, gaining wisdom, and receiving instruction.

"His body was weak from lack of food," Gudan explained. "He fasted for many days alone in the desert while he prepared himself to begin his earthly ministry in accordance with the will of the Most High. And it was there that Satan tried once again to take the ruling power from the Most High by perverting the will of his creation. He tried to offer Jesus something that the Most High could not, or would not, all the while positioning himself above both the Most High and his created beings and claiming lordship over them. As we have previously witnessed," Gudan reviewed, "that which impassioned Lucifer to rebel against the Most High in the first place and that which caused him to become Satan, the adversary of the Most High, and that which in turn prompted his all-out assault on the heart and soul of mankind remains the same as it has always been: his desire to be the highest, to be in charge, to be worshiped. Lucifer has an insatiable need to have his own false ideas of self-importance confirmed by elevating himself above those who are presently above him. In his case, there was only one: the Most High. As you saw, it began back before your world even existed, when we all still resided in the glory of heaven, when Lucifer became puffed up with pride in his own magnificence. He had foolishly convinced himself that his very existence was something of his own doing and that he himself should deserve praise for it rather than acknowledging the fact that he was nothing more than a product of the creative mind of the Most High. The grandest and most magnificent product, to be sure, but a created being nonetheless. Eventually, this warped sense of self-importance caused him to covet the worship, which rightfully belongs exclusively to the Most High. It is no surprise, then, that the most effective tool he uses against mankind is that of cultivating the very same feeling of self-importance that caused his own fall from fellowship with the Most High. To get mankind to focus on himself and his own passions and desires, to let his emotions rule his mind, to drive him to please himself without concern for others, asserting his independence from the Most High and living according to the rules of the sinful, depraved world of which he is temporarily a part are Satan's crowning achievements. Rather than allowing mankind to develop character traits in keeping with the attributes of the Most High—love, joy, peace, patience, kindness, goodness, faithfulness, gentleness, and self-control—Satan has deceived mankind into becoming more like himself by developing the rebellious attitudes of self-reliance, self-centeredness, self-righteousness, self-will, self-indulgence, self-preservation, and self-pity. He has fit mankind into the mold he has chosen for him, making him more like Satan day after day, rather than allowing him to become more like the Most High day after day as he was created to do.

"And that is precisely what he will now attempt to do to the Messiah. He will attempt to get him to fall into the trap of self-preservation and refuse to do the will of the Most High, thereby rendering himself useless to the plan of the Most High for the eternal redemption of mankind.

Marshall shuddered as the reality of what Gudan had just said slammed into his mind like a freight train. He felt as though a professional boxer had delivered a knockout jab to his chest, taking his breath and weakening his knees. He caught his breath as his eyes again began to fill with tears. He soon became overwhelmed with emotion, and the tears began to stream down his face. As he stood frozen in place, unable to move or to speak, the wisdom of God filled his mind. He felt as though his heart would explode within his chest. Marshall had heard the voice of the Lord many times while preparing a sermon or praying for his congregation, but he had never experienced anything like this before. He wanted to scream, he wanted to fall to his face on the ground, he wanted to dance, he wanted to sing, he wanted to cry—but he found himself completely unable to do anything except stand frozen like a stone statue, alone in the presence of Almighty God.

While his physical body and all its collective functions were benumbed and rendered inoperable by the incomprehensible presence of the Most High God, his mind was processing the new information at a level he had never before experienced. His spiritual eyes were opening wide to accommodate the full understanding of a fundamental truth that he had previously only grasped to the slightest degree although he had studied it and even taught and preached about it many times during the years of his ministry. Marshall looked up, and the words of God penned by the apostle Paul appeared to be written across the blankness that served this realm as a sky. They seemed to be alive, looking at him, calling to him, beckoning him to open his heart to a deeper level of understanding. It was not the letters that seemed alive, like the personified letters found in kindergarten classrooms across the country—Mrs. A., Mr. H., Mr. W.—but rather it was the words themselves that exuded life. *Hebrews 4:12*, Marshall thought to himself. *For the word of God is living and active.*

Just as a child's hand placed over a spinning top causes it to stop its motion and remain still, so Marshall's human reaction to the living Word of God was interrupted and stilled by the revealed spiritual interpretation of the same. For the first time in his life, he truly understood the words that the apostle had written to the church in Rome, and for the first time in his life, he truly understood the spiritual reality behind those words. He understood why God gave those words to Paul to be included in his letter in the first place. He understood how they applied to the Roman Christians at the time of their original writing, how they applied to the world of his own day, and how they applied to him personally—to Marshall J. Pennington—nearly two thousand years after they were written.

The impotence of the mere words written in Romans served to mask the depth of the spiritual truth behind them. Again, the blackboard of the sky became alive as the mind of God took the form of words splashing across the expanse of emptiness. Marshall read aloud the words from Romans 12:1-2, "Therefore, I urge you, brothers, in view of God's mercy, to offer your bodies as living sacrifices, holy and pleasing to God—this is your spiritual act of worship. Do not conform any longer to the pattern of this world, but be transformed by the renewing of your mind. Then you will be able to test and approve what God's will is—his good, pleasing and perfect will."

He shook his head as he realized the insufficiency of his understanding. It had been so easy to breeze over this passage, taking only the whipped cream and not the pumpkin pie beneath because the whipped cream satisfied the immediate desire for sweetness and curbed the desire to see what might lie beneath the surface. The underlying goal of curiosity was overshadowed by the immediate satisfaction of the desire—not that there was anything wrong with the whipped cream of course. It was very good whipped cream—serving both as evidence of applied effort in acquiring it and as temporary satisfaction to the sweet tooth that had desired it. Marshall had indeed gleaned truth from the passage as he preached about offering oneself to God and about not conforming to the patterns of the world. He had admonished his flock to be set apart from the world in which they lived, not living as the heathen do, not frequenting places that the heathen frequent, not participating in the activities that make the heathens heathen. But he had so missed the spiritual point of this passage that he stood before the very God about whom he had been teaching, ashamed at his own ineptitude. How many times had Marshall stood in front of his congregation as an authority on the Scriptures and preached about that very passage? How many times had he used it as a supportive reference for other sermons and Bible study classes? Oh, he understood it logically, with his mind, but his heart had failed to grasp the underlying spiritual truth. He had found the single gold nugget lying in the creek bed and had been satisfied with that alone, not realizing that had he kept digging, he would have found the mother lode of solid gold lying right beneath the surface.

But now, as he stood alone up here in this holy place, the words of Gudan and the words of Paul connected to form a revolutionary train of thought in his mind. Now that he saw the truth revealed, it seemed so simple to him, so easy, so obvious! It was almost as if he himself had chipped the small gold nugget from the larger vein of gold, but he had been spiritually blinded to a point that he hadn't even noticed that it was indeed a larger chunk of gold from which he had separated the smaller piece. Consequently, as he had merely achieved a surface understanding of the Scripture itself, so he had merely gleaned a surface instruction from it.

His mind placed the words of Gudan next to the words of the apostle Paul in the sky:

> He has fit mankind into the mold he has chosen for him, making him more like Satan day after day, rather than allowing him to become more like the Most High day after day, as he was created to do.
>
> Do not conform any longer to the pattern of this world, but be transformed by the renewing of your mind.

The "pattern of this world" is not at all the wild living and sinful activities that Marshall had believed and taught for so many years. He had admonished his flock to avoid certain sinful places and activities, to "flee from sexual immorality, idolatry, and the evil desires of youth" as Paul had commanded in several of his other biblical writings. Marshall had encouraged love, joy, peace, patience, kindness, goodness, faithfulness, gentleness and self-control—the fruit of the Spirit listed by Paul in his letter to the Galatians 5:22–23. However, like a doctor who prescribes pain relievers, which mask the true symptoms of an ailment, thereby making assessment of and subsequent curing of the root cause of the ailment impossible, Marshall had prescribed to his flock a pain-reliever level of admonition from the Bible, rather than digging deep enough to ascertain the root cause of their ailing souls and take the action necessary for their complete regeneration and restoration. Unfortunately, what he was coming to understand now was merely the fact that his previous knowledge had been insufficient; he had yet to grasp the correct answer.

So then what was the pattern of this world? What did Paul mean by not conforming to it? What was he trying to keep us from doing? To answer that question, Marshall reflected on what he had learned since this journey had begun. Using logic as a companion to both personal revelation and the truth of the Holy Scriptures, he would start at the beginning. The first step would be to determine who had initially established the pattern of this world. The obvious answer would be God the Father. He who created the universe would certainly be the one who would establish the pattern for its operation. Why, then, would he not want humanity to conform to a pattern established by himself? Something must have altered the plan from its initial status somewhere along the line. The plan must have become corrupted. The most obvious answer would be the sin of Adam and Eve—the entrance of sin into world through the fall of man. But again, this would be only a surface answer to a root-level problem. What, then, was at the bottom? A verse from the revelation of Jesus to the apostle John came to Marshall's mind. He quietly quoted Revelation 12:9 to himself, "The great dragon was hurled down—that ancient serpent called the devil, or Satan, *who leads the whole world astray*. He was hurled to the earth, and his angels with him."

"Satan has been given control of the world!" Marshall nearly shouted. "This is supported by Jesus's words in John 12:31, 'Now is the time for judgment on this world; now the prince of this world will be driven out,' and by Paul's words in Ephesians 6:12, 'For our struggle is not against flesh and blood, but against the rulers, against the authorities, against the powers of this dark world and against the spiritual forces of evil in the heavenly realms.'"

But that didn't make any sense! Why would God banish Lucifer and his angels to the earth and then give him control over it? Wouldn't that be more of a reward than a punishment? Sure, he wouldn't rule over heaven and take the place of the Most High, but he would be the supreme dictator over an entire world, which had been created just for him! No, that couldn't be how it happened, that couldn't have been God's plan! That was not justice!

Gudan, sensing Marshall's frustration, interrupted his mental wrestling.

"Lordship over the earth was not given to Lucifer by the Most High, Marshall. It was given to him by mankind."

Marshall was jerked back to reality with a start. He had been so deep in thought, he had not realized that he was pacing back and forth and talking out loud. Too focused on his mental quest to feel embarrassed about being caught, he turned to Gudan and continued his argument with himself.

"But why would he just—what did you say?" he asked, belatedly hearing what Gudan had said.

"I said Lucifer was not given control of the earth by the Most High. He was given control by Adam."

"How did Adam give him control? I mean, I know he was deceived by Lucifer and fell into sin, but—"

"Marshall, it is much, much bigger than that," Gudan stated patiently. "Don't you see? This is not like one of your baseball games where an outfielder might make an error, which allows the opposing team to score a run but which can be overcome by that same player hitting a home run on his next chance at bat and scoring a run for his own team. It is not a matter of which team can tally up the most points by the end of the game to be declared the winner. It is a war, Marshall. Mistakes cause death—permanent, eternal death—and there is no making up for a bad play simply by executing a greater quantity of good plays.

"The Most High created the earth for mankind, Marshall, not for Lucifer. Why would he create it for Lucifer? Lucifer is a spirit—why would he need a physical, tangible earth to live in? No, it was created to be inhabited by mankind. What instruction did the Most High give to Adam when he created him and placed him on the earth?"

Only by the miraculous power of God was Marshall able to recall every verse Gudan asked him about. "Genesis 1:28," he said, "God blessed them and said to them, 'Be fruitful and increase in number; fill the earth and subdue it. Rule over the fish of the sea and the birds of the air and over every living creature that moves on the ground.'"

"Exactly," Gudan said. "The earth in its entirety was given to Adam to subdue and to rule. That word, *subdue*, implies complete lordship, a total control over every aspect of the earth and everything in it. That is what was given to mankind."

"But then how was Satan able to take control over it?" Marshall asked.

"He didn't take control on his own," Gudan said. "He didn't have the power to *take* it. That is why it was necessary for him to deceive Adam and Eve so that they would willingly give it to him although they didn't really realize what they were doing at the time. Adam and Eve had the power—Satan did not. He could not force them to disobey the Most High. He could not force them to do anything. Satan's power is great, and it extends to the ends of the earth. However, it includes neither mankind nor the earth upon which he lives as its subjects. Mankind is the only creature on the earth that has maintained control of its own destiny and its own existence. As long as mankind continued to live in submission to the Most High as supreme ruler, all was well, and the balance of power remained intact. The Most High protected the dwelling place of mankind from Satan's power in the same way that he protected mankind himself from Satan's power. The protection was from Satan's *power*, but not from his *influence*. It was up to mankind to make the choice either to obey the Most High or to oppose him and follow the urgings of Satan. When Satan successfully convinced mankind to disobey the Most High, evil was allowed to enter the equation. From that point on, everything changed. The Most High removed his protective power from the earth. Forget floods and famine and suffering—Marshall, there weren't even weeds before Adam's betrayal of the Most High. We were there, Marshall. You saw it. The garden of Eden was perfect in every respect, all living things existing in harmony with each other. All the bad things present in your world came after Adam's sin. They are a direct result of mankind's choice to reject the will of the Most High and to follow his own rules. When mankind rejected the word of the Most High, mankind also rejected the protection and the sustaining power of the Most High, thereby allowing Satan to usurp the rule and to categorically corrupt and/or destroy every good thing about the earth and its inhabitants.

"The power and dominion over the earth that had originally been entrusted to Adam was turned over to Satan. By his act of disobedience against the Most High, Adam allowed his own will to be influenced by and to fall under the controlling power of Satan, thereby transferring the lordship over the earth to Satan. In your world, Marshall, sin does not appear to carry consequences—or at any rate, no significant consequences—but that is not the truth. It is nothing more than another lie of Satan. In the spiritual realm, it took but one betrayal against the Most High to get Lucifer and all his followers banished from heaven. It took but one betrayal on the part of Adam to get all mankind banished from the garden of Eden, from the full presence of the Most High, and placed under the curse of sin from birth, and it took but one succumbing to the deceitful scheming of Satan for Adam to lose his authority over the earth and everything in it. Now, that curse of sin must be overcome before mankind can enjoy the presence of the Most High and live as the Most High intended him to live. The authority can be retrieved from Satan by mankind, but only through the power of the Most High and only by each human being individually. You see, Marshall, Satan's power is infinitely greater than that of mankind, but it is infinitely weaker than that of the Most High. Satan was only able to usurp the dominion over the earth because mankind cannot stand up to him on his own. Only through the authority granted him by the Most High can he stand against the power of Satan victoriously."

Silence came between them. Marshall processed what Gudan had said, turning it over in his mind.

Gudan's voice grabbed Marshall's attention. "Now that we have established who has determined the pattern of this world, Marshall, let us go back to the previously posed but hitherto unanswered question: What is the pattern of this world?"

Marshall allowed the silence to continue as his mind raced to formulate a response. He recalled bits and pieces of his conversation with Gudan, added his own thoughts, and compared them both with verses of Scripture. He weighed them against what he had just witnessed and what he had just learned, eventually coming to the same conclusion that he had reached before his mental quest had even really begun.

"Strangely enough, Gudan, it is very simple. The pattern of this world is that which is fashioned by the imprint of the ruler of this world: defiance of the Most High by the placing of self on the throne above him."

Gudan let the words hang in the air for a moment without responding. "Hmm," he said, "defiance of the Most High by the placing of self on the throne above him. Well said, Marshall. Well said." Gudan nodded approvingly. "Please continue."

"Gudan, I always thought that the behavior evidenced by the inhabitants of this world was the pattern of this world. Now I can see that those behavioral patterns are merely the evidence of the underlying pattern established by Satan himself and unwittingly accepted as truth and as normalcy by the human race as a whole. I realize how bold of a statement that is, to include the entire human race, but I really think it is an accurate assessment of the state of mankind. We have, as a race, turned our backs on the pattern established by God. Even from many of our pulpits, we preach and teach a change of behavior but fail to address the true cause of the behavior lying beneath the surface, which can only be corrected by a change of heart. We treat the symptoms, not the disease.

"The problem has to be all of those self-issues that you mentioned earlier when you spoke of the anti-God attitudes that had caused Lucifer's own rebellion: self-reliance, self-righteousness, self-will, self-pity, self-centeredness, self-indulgence, self-preservation. All of these things are in direct contradiction to the attributes of love as described by Paul in his letter to the Corinthians and also to the fruit of the Spirit described in his letter to the Galatians." Marshall then recited these verses:

> "Love is patient, love is kind. It does not envy, it does not boast, it is not proud. It is not rude, it is not self-seeking, it is not easily angered, it keeps no record of wrongs. Love does not delight in evil but rejoices with the truth. It always protects, always trusts, always hopes, always perseveres. Love never fails."
>
> 1 Corinthians 13:4–8 (NIV)

> "But the fruit of the Spirit is love, joy, peace, patience, kindness, goodness, faithfulness, gentleness and self-control. Against such things there is no law."
>
> Galatians 5:22–23 (NIV)

Suddenly, another Scripture came to Marshall's mind. Hebrews 4:12–13 flashed across the sky, its glowing words tearing open Marshall's soul and laying it bare before him.

> For the word of God is living and active. Sharper than any double-edged sword, it penetrates even to dividing soul and spirit, joints and marrow; it judges the thoughts and attitudes of the heart. Nothing in all creation is hidden from God's sight. Everything is uncovered and laid bare before the eyes of him to whom we must give account.
>
> Hebrews 4:12–13 (NIV)

The words faded as they were replaced with the scene of Marshall's life. He saw the face of God sadden and a tear fall from his eye every time Marshall made a choice contrary to the will of God; then he saw God's heart break as the negative consequence of that improper choice played out according to the natural rules of a fallen world controlled by Satan. He saw the Father's heart break as he lovingly watched his precious child suffer the consequences of his own rebellion, himself on his knees with his hands in the air, asking God why this adversity had befallen him, and Satan doubled over in laughter at the sight of them both. As Marshall watched the scene play itself out in his mind, he reacted to what he saw. Sure, there was a modicum of anger directed at Satan, the deceiver and trickster, but the anger at Satan was completely overshadowed by the realization of his own blind ignorance and by the crushing revelation of God's emotional response.

Marshall had seen only the tiniest fringe of the glory of God, and even here, in his protected state under Gudan's presence, it was nearly more than he could handle in his humanity. He had seen the beauty of the creation of God on the earth and the grandeur and majesty of heaven. He had seen the awesome power of God displayed when he threw Lucifer out of heaven along with his followers. He had seen God as the most awesome being imaginable, an explanation of him so far beyond the capacity of humanity to understand that to attempt to describe him would be futile. He had seen all these wonders and countless more, yet when Marshall was distressed because of a foolish choice and found himself in some difficulty entirely of his own making, he saw that God was saddened because Marshall was distressed.

Marshall's chest tightened again. The temperature seemed to skyrocket. He could not look at Gudan, whom he knew had been right there beside him his entire life. He felt lower than the lowest form of life as his mind cruelly went to the times when he had willingly disobeyed God, times when he had known what was right but had knowingly chosen to disobey and to follow his own way anyway. If God was so affected by an innocent mistake on his part, the result of a foolish choice that ended up with negative consequences but which was not intentional disobedience, how terrible must it have been when Marshall, with full knowledge of what he was doing, turned from God and followed his own path? He dropped to his knees and cried out to God in humiliation. There was nothing he could say to make up for what he had done all those times throughout his life. How God could still love him was beyond his comprehension.

As Marshall's sobbing subsided, Gudan touched his shoulder and lifted him to his feet. "The Most High has forgiven you, Marshall. Long ago."

"I know, Gudan, but I never realized how awful I had been until now. I never realized how real my sins were. Most of the time, even when the consequences were adverse, it was not a big deal to me, and I easily recovered. I would ask God to forgive me, but only because I knew that I had done wrong, not because I really wanted his forgiveness. I wanted to be absolved from my sins for my sake, but I didn't care about experiencing true forgiveness for his sake. I didn't consider how my actions would affect him or whether or not his feelings might be hurt. Even when asking for forgiveness, I still made it all about me, not about God! I asked for forgiveness so that I could feel better, not even considering how God might be feeling about the situation.

"I have been so foolish, Gudan. I was like the little boy who apologized to his brother because his mother told him to, but not because he was really sorry for what he had done to his brother in the first place. I received forgiveness because the Bible promised me I would, but I never apologized personally to God for offending him. My sin is my own, Gudan. I can't blame it on anybody else, I can't rationalize it, and I can't justify it. The responsibility is all mine. When I sin, it hurts God, and it is my fault. He feels it, and I did it. Any adverse consequence that may come about as a result of my sin is nothing compared to the knowledge that I have personally wronged the Most High God and that his feelings are hurt as a result of my selfish actions. I mean, even in my earthly life, when I inadvertently hurt someone I love, it hurts me to see them hurt. The closer they are to me or the more I love them, the more it hurts me to know that I have caused them pain. God has commanded me to love him above all else, more than myself or my wife or my family or anything at all. In keeping with this command, he should be the one who matters to me the most, the one who I honestly do love the most, the one who is closest to me. Yet when I wrong him, I flippantly and callously toss up a quick prayer of repentance, asking for forgiveness for betraying him as though I'm asking him for nothing more significant than to pass the salt at the dinner table. I have treated it more like an impersonal business transaction with a clerk at a convenience store rather than like a deeply emotional interaction between two people who love each other."

Gudan smiled. "Though it has caused you great pain, Marshall, you have just grasped a mystery that most followers of the Most High never come within reach of. Only now will you be able to understand the answer to the question that began this journey for you in the first place."

CHAPTER TEN

Marshall looked back through the barrier to see Jesus alone in the wilderness. He had climbed up onto a large rock and was leaning up against another to rest. Satan walked through the barrier to stand beside him.

"Marshall, do you understand why Satan approached Jesus in the wilderness while he was fasting and praying?"

Marshall hesitated. "Gudan, my understanding of nearly everything I thought I knew has been proven to be, at the very best, negligible in comparison to the reality that you have shown me. Hence, I am hesitant even to attempt an answer to your question."

"A fair assessment, Marshall," Gudan replied, then said with a grin, "and a wise response."

Marshall's muted smile was one of humility and respect rather than satisfaction in giving a correct answer.

He and Gudan passed through the barrier, stopping a short distance away from where Jesus and Satan were talking.

"Jesus was about to begin his earthly ministry," Gudan continued. "Following the prompting of the Holy Spirit, he went out into the wilderness where he could focus all his attention on the Father and receive encouragement and instruction from him."

"So Satan took this opportunity for a last-ditch attempt at sabotaging his mission," Marshall added.

"Precisely," Gudan agreed. "But that is not what I want you to notice about what is happening. Yes, Satan is attempting one final time to prevent Jesus from even beginning his earthly mission, but that fact is not as important as the method he is employing. Watch closely."

Marshall leaned forward and craned his neck to hear better, wrinkling his forehead in concentration. He watched for a long while as Satan and Jesus talked. Scene after scene played out in front of him, like a ping-pong game upon which the fate of all humanity had been wagered. Satan would make a suggestion to Jesus, Jesus would denounce it with Scripture. Satan would resort to quoting Scripture, out of context and slightly misquoted, of course, and Jesus would again counter with a proper quotation of Scripture. Back and forth they would go, day after day, week after week, with Satan trying every trick he could come up with to cause Jesus to shy away from his task.

Sensing Gudan's movement, Marshall looked up at him.

"What have you noticed about Satan's efforts, Marshall?" Gudan asked.

Marshall didn't have to think. The answer came to him as quickly and easily as the secret code for his bank card. "He is trying to get Jesus to put his own will above that of the Father."

"Exactly. The very same thing that caused Lucifer to be banished from heaven and to become Satan. The very same thing that caused mankind to fall into sin in the first place. The very same thing that is responsible for the terrible state of the world as it is in your time, Marshall. Elevating the will of self above the will of the Most High. How was it that you stated it? 'Defiance of the Most High by the placing of self on the throne above him.' That is precisely his goal. If you look at all three of the temptations of Jesus that were recorded in the Bible, they all boil down to putting the will of the Son above that of the Father. The tactic has not changed since the very beginning, even before the beginning of time: create doubt about the validity of the word of the Most High, then twist the word of the Most High to mean something other than that which was intended, and finally, provide a self-serving alternative course of action, which makes much more sense than following the tainted logic of the Most High along with its stringent and unreasonable requirements."

Marshall shook his head at the simplicity of it. "And we fall for it," he observed. "Time after time, we walk right into it, eyes wide open, and utterly fall for it." Marshall paced back and forth, his mind processing again what he had been shown. So much information had been presented to him! So much knowledge had been given to him! So many misconceptions had been corrected for him!

Gudan stood silently a short distance away. He watched patiently as Marshall paced, talking to himself, talking to the Most High, working through the many things his mind was grappling with. It truly was a great amount of information for one human mind to grasp and understand all in such a minute time frame.

After a long while, Marshall walked back over and stood in front of Gudan. "Wow," he said, feeling foolish that that was all he could come up with. "Wow. It seems like I have so many questions about so many things, but I don't even know where to begin formulating a logical, rational one. I have seen so much and learned so much on this unbelievable trip, but I am having trouble knowing where to go from here. What is next? We have seen Lucifer's fall from glory, understood how it happened, discovered the motivation behind his obsession with destroying humanity, witnessed the activities of the demons in the spiritual realm as they pertain to all humanity, and even seen demonstrations of the power, craftiness, and cunning of Satan and his minions. But still, even though I have learned so much, I feel like I still really don't have useable answers. Maybe I am just not really getting it. What am I still missing, Gudan? I feel like the disciples must have felt when they were afraid their fishing boat would sink during the storm and Jesus asked them, 'Are you still so dull?' I don't mean to be so dull, but I feel like if we go back home now, I will still be just as frustrated—or even more so—because now I have a wealth of information in addition to what I had before, and I still have no idea what to do with it." Marshall dropped his hands to his sides, clearly at the end of himself. He looked up helplessly at Gudan.

"Be still, Marshall. We are far from finished. Your request was to know your enemy, and that request has been granted. You probably know him better than any human being ever has. However, the Most High knows that you asked in ignorance. You made a general request for what you believed to be your need. Your knowledge is limited, as is your perception of your need. Knowledge is power, Marshall, but knowledge alone is useless. Knowledge alone is power that cannot be tapped into and thus serves no true purpose. No, knowledge is merely the beginning. To be used effectively against the enemy, it must be coupled with strategy, action, resolve, fortitude, cunning, persistence, and so on. Your reconnaissance thus far has increased your knowledge significantly, but as I said, it is just the beginning.

"Therefore, as when King Solomon asked the Most High for wisdom to rule his people rather than for fame or wealth and the Most High rewarded his humility with a full measure of all three, so also since you humbly asked for knowledge of your enemy instead of church membership increase or prestige or recognition, the Most High will reward you with the addition of everything you need to be successful in standing up against your enemy and defeating him. Not that your reward will be something given only to you. You will not be acquiring anything that is not freely available to every human being as has already been clearly explained in the pages of your Bible. You will simply be given understanding at a level which few humans achieve, mainly because they are too steeped in their own selfish humanity to truly deny themselves as the Most High requires and follow him completely. You have demonstrated your desire to surpass mediocrity and be a force for the kingdom of God in your world." He nodded toward the scene of Jesus and Satan still before them. "Look again," he said. "Watch what the Messiah does. Listen to what he says. See how he defends, how he attacks. What are his weapons and how does he use them? Which of those weapons are available for you to use? Make no mistake, Marshall—this is a battle. This is the greatest battle ever fought on the face of the earth." Gudan paused. "You see, Marshall, your journey thus far has been essentially historical in nature. You have observed events as they happened to gain insight and understanding into the mind of your enemy to better understand how to deal with him. You will now begin to observe the battle. Up to this point in human history, mankind was lacking for true weapons of battle. There was basically the law as given through Moses, and mankind could choose whether or not to abide by it and have fellowship with the Most High. Unfortunately, mankind did not obey the law as the Most High intended. Throughout the years, it became merely a list of rules, the following of which would guarantee heaven upon death. The law was given and intended to be a manner of living, a manner of loving. The rules were given as example of how to treat one's fellow man and how to interact properly with each other and with the Most High himself to the great benefit of all. A heart of love and a desire for unity was supposed to have been the 'assumed' part of the equation, but the bent of mankind toward evil was too strong. Only a few remained faithful throughout the course of human history.

"Now, however, with the advent of the Messiah and the formation of the New Covenant between the Most High and mankind, everything will change. All mankind will now be granted access to the Most High individually. Each person will be responsible for his own life, his own conduct, and his own relationship with the Most High. It will no longer be a group effort, such as it was when the whole nation of Israel was cursed or blessed in accordance with their corporate obedience or disobedience. That is why the demonic activity became so much more prevalent when the Messiah was on the earth and why it has not decreased since. At first, Satan's motivation was to destroy the Messiah outright and thereby prevent him from completing the New Covenant at all. He was utterly unsuccessful in completing this task, of course, and consequently was forced to adopt an entirely new mission altogether. He would now have to work to deceive and destroy each and every human being individually, rather than as a group. He would still be able to deceive nations and peoples, but he would have to do it one soul at a time.

"It was at this point in time, Marshall, that the war of the ages became one-on-one mortal combat, engaged exclusively, individually, daily, every minute of every day and night, on the ultimate battlefield: the mind of each and every human being on planet earth."

Marshall stood silent. Of course, God would never have brought him here just to add to his confusion. He looked up at Gudan and nodded. *Ephesians 6*, he thought to himself. "God laid out the entire situation for us right there in Ephesians 6. He knew we would need detailed instruction, so he provided it for us, speaking through Paul as he wrote to his friends in the church at Ephesus."

"Yes," Gudan agreed. "And the Messiah knew exactly how to deal with Satan, his adversary and yours, because he had done the exact same thing, not only amidst his temptations while in the wilderness as specifically recorded in the Bible, but also throughout all his life on earth. The three specific temptations of Jesus recorded in your Bible are essentially three categories of temptations. They are also three general examples of how you are to engage the enemy and prevail in battle when he comes against you. Jesus underwent many, many temptations, Marshall.

Throughout his whole life on earth, Satan fought against him every single day. Every single night. Not one single moment went by where Satan was not either actively engaging him in battle or preparing his forces for the next attack. He is relentless, Marshall. When he wasn't directly attacking and taunting Jesus himself, he sent Pharisees, teachers of the law, Sadducees, false disciples, Roman soldiers, demon-possessed men, sultry, attractive women, powerful religious and political leaders, common men and women who simply doubted and disbelieved him, and a throng of demons to assail him at every turn. He threw absolutely everything he had at the Messiah to cause him to fall and fail in his mission, but the Messiah was victorious. Watch, Marshall. Watch how he defeated his adversary." Gudan nodded again at the scene beyond the barrier.

Marshall looked again at the scene before him on the other side of the barrier. "*Watch what the Messiah does,*" Gudan had said. "*Listen to what he says. See how he defends, how he attacks. What are his weapons and how does he use them? Which of those weapons are available for you to use? Make no mistake, Marshall—this is a battle. This is the greatest battle ever fought on the face of the earth.*"

Watching Jesus and Satan engage in their verbal exchange, Marshall's mind envisioned Jesus wielding the sword of the Spirit, which is the word of God, and exchanging blows with Satan and his dark sword of deception and self-will. It was just as intense and just as deadly as any swordfight had ever been, even though the weapons used for the battle were in reality merely words.

Although the scene flashed before him in fast motion, Marshall was able to comprehend every bit of it as though it were in slow motion. He saw Jesus throughout his entire ministry, including his private prayer times, his public teachings, his intimate gatherings with just his disciples, his debates with the Pharisees and teachers of the Law, his midnight talk with Nicodemus, his betrayal, accusation, mock trials, and crucifixion. He noticed that Satan was right there, every step of the way, taunting him, ridiculing him, attempting to coerce him to abandon his mission. He would point out how the very people he was there trying to save didn't even want him there! They didn't even believe in him! Was he really going to go to the cross and die for these insidious people who rejected him to his face on a daily basis? What kind of fool would go through with such an insane mission?

And every time, Jesus would counter Satan's scoffing with a verse of Scripture, silencing the taunts of his enemy. Not once did he waver, not once did he falter. Even up to the very night of his betrayal, he did not shrink back from his responsibilities. He prayed and prayed, asking the Father if there was another way to redeem the humans, but not once did he shy away from completing his mission. Up to the very last second, even when Jesus was hanging on the cross and near to his death, Satan still goaded him through one of the thieves crucified beside him.

But Marshall's mind wouldn't accept it. He wanted to raise his objection to Gudan, but he didn't dare. He trusted, but he doubted. It just all seemed too easy.

"Go ahead and say it, Marshall," Gudan requested.

That was all the prodding Marshall needed. He blurted it out: "But he was the Son of God! Of course it was easier for him to defeat Satan! But what about just a man? Just any old man? What about a man like me or Pete or Sam or any person on earth? How can we honestly do the things Jesus did? He had the power of God behind him! He *was* God! But I am just a man, Gudan. Just a man. No divine nature, rather, a fallen one, at enmity with God. No miraculous powers, no infinite wisdom. I am just a man."

"Come," Gudan said without answering. He placed his hand on Marshall's arm, and they once again moved forward in time.

Marshall wanted to object, wanted to plant his feet and say, "No! I don't understand! Please, no more until I understand!"

But he knew that his explanation lay in the next scene they would see. Or the one after that. He knew that Gudan would show him exactly what God wanted him to see, exactly when he wanted him to see it, and that it would be exactly what he needed to see to gain complete understanding of what God was trying to show him. He breathed deeply and closed his eyes, trying to prepare himself for whatever their next destination might hold.

CHAPTER ELEVEN

Marshall was quite surprised and even more confused to see what appeared to be a military training camp come into view on the other side of the barrier. A military training camp? Yes, that was what it was. There were thousands of what appeared to be Roman soldiers, clad in full battle dress, engaged in all sorts of combat training exercises. Foot soldiers wielding heavy broadswords chopped and hacked at their simulated enemies. Others honed their skills in close combat by practicing the "cut and thrust" technique using the characteristic short swords developed specifically by the Roman army for more effective and lethal hand-to-hand combat. Archers shot arrows into targets from varying distances, learning to use wind, angles, topography, and trajectory to their advantage. Horsemen raced back and forth, clubbing their enemies with broadswords, battle axes, and maces while attempting to avoid becoming unhorsed in the process.

Gudan stopped. Marshall looked up, blank faced, completely unable to comprehend any rationale behind a visit to the Roman army training camp. As he perused the scene, group after group of soldiers slowly faded into the background, becoming nearly invisible except for their outlines, like pencil drawings for a movie scene proposal. Eventually, only the close-combat infantrymen brandishing the specialized short swords remained clearly visible.

Marshall absently watched the men as they practiced—duck and jab, chop and slice, stick and jump. His mind was still so focused on his previous question of how a mere man could really prevail against the devil like Jesus had that he didn't grasp the significance of where they were or the relevance of what they were seeing.

Gudan's voice snapped him out of his reverie. "Do you remember when we discussed the war between Satan and the Most High?" he asked.

Marshall, still not quite back to the moment, blinked but didn't speak.

Gudan continued, prodding Marshall's memory. "How after Lucifer's banishment from heaven? That war was brought to the earth to be fought through the Most High's next creation, the humans?" Gudan asked.

Marshall nodded.

"For you to understand the answer to your question, it will require you to think from the perspective of both a war strategist and a front-line foot soldier. Your question, while seemingly simple, is in reality a very complex, very large question. It would not be unlike a war correspondent at a press conference asking the ranking general, 'Sir, how can we win this war quickly and efficiently and get our boys home?' While the question can be answered, the answer is no more quick or efficient than the resolution of the war itself.

"The Messiah was victorious against his adversary, not only because his power exceeded that of his opponent, but also because he engaged his enemy completely prepared and ready for the battle. The battle was won in his mind before he ever set foot on the physical field of battle. He entered the contest with a complete understanding of the entire situation. He fully understood his position, his responsibility, his capabilities, and his authority, as well as those of his adversary. He knew his opponent's battle strategy. His was practiced in using his weapons, both offensive and defensive. He knew no fear but placed his confidence in his readiness, in his authority, and in the access he had to the power of the Most High. That, Marshall, was how the battle was won."

Marshall looked quizzically at Gudan, mouth agape, unable to even formulate a question. He felt like the person who had responded to a tragic news story by asking to no one in particular, "What makes people do that kind of thing?" to which the psychologist seated next to him responded with a detailed explanation of the inner workings of the human psyche.

Gudan raised a hand to stop him before he could even start, then he continued. "What you must understand, Marshall, is this: it is a battle. It is not a misunderstanding. It is not a difference of opinion. It is neither an obstacle course nor a simulated training exercise. It is a real live daily battle. The conflict is live, and the opposition is both well trained and keenly aware. The reason why humanity has throughout their history been so soundly defeated by the enemy, then, is that humanity is neither well-trained nor keenly aware. And by that, I do not refer to merely a few of them. Not at all! In fact, sadly, the vast majority of humanity, including even those who consider themselves to be believers or Christians, is neither well trained nor keenly aware! Oblivious would be a more appropriate way to describe them. Most of humanity gives flippant, if any, attention to the reality of the spiritual realm, ignoring both its relevance and the eternal consequences of their ignorance.

"Their ignorance is no different than that of the child who assumes that since he can no longer see his father once he covers his eyes, he is likewise no longer visible to his father. Although such a lack of cognizance is cute and amusing when exhibited by a child, such a severely debilitating lack of understanding exhibited by one who is called of the Most High to be a soldier in his army is another thing altogether. It is the ultimate travesty of the creation of man in the image of his creator.

"Admitting, recognizing, and engaging in battle is the first step. Next, to emerge from the battle victorious, every human being needs to learn the fighting techniques of the spirit world.

"The battle is old, Marshall. The rules of engagement were established long ago between Satan and the Most High, as were the weapons of warfare. Humanity is defeated not because of inferior weaponry or faulty intelligence, but simply because of their ignorance, stubbornness, and self-reliance. Every single human being has everything he needs to completely defeat his enemy at his immediate disposal every hour of every day. What he lacks is simply the wisdom and courage to employ the assets already in place. The words spoken by the Most High through the prophet Hosea nearly three thousand earth years ago are still true today: 'My people are destroyed from lack of knowledge'." (Hosea 4:6)

Gudan again paused momentarily to let Marshall process what he had said. Again, he continued before allowing Marshall an opportunity to speak.

"Oddly enough, however, it is not a fight to the death. Humanity is already spiritually dead! Rather, it is a fight for life. The Most High offers life through the sacrifice of his Son, the Christ. It is Satan's mission, therefore, to prevent mankind from accepting that life by whatever means necessary. Because of the brilliance of Satan's mind, he appreciates the fact that the means by which he can do the most damage to humanity, while simultaneously causing the most severe grief to the Most High, is to deceive humanity into rejecting his gift of life completely of their own volition, without even engaging in battle and fighting for it. Therefore, he first engages them at their most vulnerable point—their minds. Consider it a preemptive strike by the kingdom of darkness. The power to defeat Satan comes through the Holy Spirit into the mind of him who has accepted the Christ's sacrifice and has yielded lordship of his life to him. You see, Marshall, once a human being has acknowledged his position as a sinful creature at enmity with the Most High and has subsequently confessed and been forgiven for his sins, cleansed from all unrighteousness, and put back into a right relationship with the Most High, he literally becomes a new creation. And *that* creation has *authority* over Satan. The apostle Paul said it in his letter to the Corinthians."

The sky was instantly lit with the words of 2 Corinthians 5:17.

> Therefore, if anyone is in Christ, he is a new creation; the old has gone, the new has come!
>
> 2 Corinthians 5:17 (NIV)

Gudan continued his discourse. "In his natural state, as a sinful human being separated from the Most High, mankind is virtually powerless against Satan. Satan's lies actually make sense to him and have the appearance of wisdom because they seem to coincide with the natural depraved thoughts already residing in the fallen man's mind. Thoughts of inadequacy, unimportance, insignificance, inability, and unworthiness work together to completely destroy that one part of the man that pushes him forward, and this is the difficult part, Marshall—the desire within each man's heart to know and to have a relationship with his creator. Do you understand the truth here, Marshall? While the sinful, unregenerate man has a bent toward evil and does not have the capability to please the Most High in and of himself, there still lies deep within every human the inherent and insatiable desire to know the Most High and to have a right relationship with him. No human will ever experience wholeness, peace, or true contentment and happiness without this relationship. Therefore, if Satan can convince a person that he is unworthy or unable for whatever reason to even achieve that relationship, his hope of completeness is dashed to pieces, the person is left defeated, and the enemy has completely destroyed his opponent and achieved victory without ever even having had to engage him in actual battle. The battle has been completely lost in the person's mind without a single weapon ever having been wielded against the enemy. The most effective way to defeat mankind, then, is simply to take away their hope and belief in the possibility of victory and thereby keep them out of the battle entirely.

"Conversely, however, once a person takes hold of his position in Christ and engages in battle, Satan's own defeat is certain. The reality of the situation is very simple and very complex at the same time. Listen carefully, Marshall," Gudan commanded, stepping in front of him and looking directly into his eyes. "Satan has already been utterly defeated by the work of the Christ when he was crucified by men and subsequently raised to life by the power of the Most High. In that work, Satan was completely defeated. However, each human being must choose for himself to accept the work of Christ, declare Satan defeated, and live in freedom and victory.

"Marshall, do you remember the cartoons you watched as a child?" Gudan asked, stepping away from Marshall so he could use his hands to illustrate. "Remember when Wile E. Coyote would chase the Road Runner until he unwittingly ran off the edge of a cliff, but the force of gravity would not take effect until the coyote looked down and acknowledged that he was no longer standing on solid ground but was suspended in midair? And then, poof! He would instantly plummet to the rocky surface far below? Of course that story is ridiculous, but the concept behind it is actually true in the spiritual world. Satan is completely defeated in the life of every single human being. However, that defeat does not take effect until the person looks down and realizes that the victory of Christ is his also. Then, once he recognizes the truth and the significance of the Christ's sacrifice, he instantly becomes that new creation that has authority over Satan, and thus his victory is sure."

Marshall paced again, deep in thought. "But..."

He gave a heavy sigh and continued pacing. "So..."

His brow wrinkled, he shook his head, putting his arms up, palms out, and then his arms back down by his sides. He shook his head, as if feeling a fly landing there. He raised his index finger in the air, then put it down, continuing to pace.

Gudan waited patiently as Marshall's mind wrestled within itself. Years and years of incomplete teaching and incomplete understanding had clouded his mind to the truth. The most powerful weapon known to man had been right there in front of him his whole life, but in all that time, he hadn't even grasped its most elementary instruction.

"Maybe this will help, Marshall," Gudan stated as the sky once again filled with the word of the Most High. "We have already discussed that Adam was given complete dominion over the entire earth upon his creation. Then, when he yielded to sin and betrayed the Most High, that dominion was handed over to Satan. Next, the dominion was retrieved from Satan by the Messiah when he rose from the dead after his crucifixion. Finally, then, it was returned to its rightful owner, mankind, individually, upon acceptance of the sacrifice of the Messiah and the submission of one's life to his lordship. Follow the logic of these verses from your Bible," Gudan said, turning to stand beside Marshall so they could both see the display of verses.

> Consequently, just as the result of one trespass was condemnation for all men, so also the result of one act of righteousness was justification that brings life for all men. For just as through the disobedience of the one man the many were made sinners, so also through the obedience of the one man the many will be made righteous.
>
> Romans 5:18–19 (NIV)

> Then Jesus came to them and said, "All authority in heaven and on earth has been given to me.
>
> Matthew 28:18 (NIV)

> The people were all so amazed that they asked each other, "What is this? A new teaching—and with authority! He even gives orders to evil spirits and they obey him."
>
> Mark 1:27 (NIV)

> So he said to me, "This is the word of the LORD to Zerubbabel: 'Not by might nor by power, but by my Spirit,' says the LORD Almighty.
>
> Zechariah 4:6 (NIV)

> But you will receive power when the Holy Spirit comes on you; and you will be my witnesses in Jerusalem, and in all Judea and Samaria, and to the ends of the earth."
>
> Acts 1:8 (NIV)

> Now to him who is able to do immeasurably more than all we ask or imagine, according to his power that is at work within us,
>
> Ephesians 3:20 (NIV)

> Finally, be strong in the Lord and in his mighty power.
>
> Ephesians 6:10 (NIV)

Marshall stood silent. Understanding was beginning to pierce the darkness of his mind like pinpricks in a black curtain, allowing the barest of rays of sunlight to penetrate into a dark room.

"It all comes down to the authority, Marshall," Gudan said. "The key to victory lies wholly in the proper exercise of authority. Victory over Satan does not come from being able to overpower him, because you will never be able to overpower him, or from being able to outwit him because you will never be able to win even the simplest argument with him, much less actually outwit him. Rather, victory comes simply from understanding one's authority over Satan and cultivating the ability to exercise it effectively."

Marshall was still confused. "Then why are we at a military training camp?" he asked. "I mean, I understand the concept of authority. Issuing of orders, following of orders, things like that. Officers have authority over foot soldiers, higher-ranking officers over lower ranking officers, and so on. But—"

Gudan raised a hand to stop him. "You will learn several things during this part of your journey, Marshall," he explained. "But first, do you understand from these verses that it is not you doing the work but the Holy Spirit of the Most High doing the work through you?" Gudan motioned with an outstretched hand to the verses that still illuminated the sky all around them.

"Yes," Marshall said.

"And do you understand that the enemy has already been defeated by the Messiah when he was raised from the dead following his crucifixion?"

Again, Marshall answered in the affirmative.

"Good," Gudan said. "And do you understand that in a war, the soldiers fight in the king's stead under his authority and exercising his authority over those against whom he is fighting?"

An uncertain, "Yes."

"Then listen carefully, Marshall. Your battle is very similar to that of the foot soldier in one way, but completely different from it in another.

"It is different from it in that while the king's soldier fights to enforce the king's authority, the soldier of the Most High fights to remind the enemy of his own authority. The soldier of the king fights to put the enemy in his place. The soldier of the Most High fights to *remind* the enemy of his place. The king's soldier must fight to achieve victory. The soldier of the Most High must fight only to remind the enemy that victory has already been achieved. It is a show of authority more than anything else. Look at the word of the Most High recorded in Ephesians 6."

Marshall instinctively looked beyond Gudan and up at the sky, which he knew would be illuminated with the word of God at Gudan's suggestion. The verses previously displayed faded from view as they were replaced by the words of Ephesians 6:10–13.

> Finally, be strong in the Lord and in his mighty power. Put on the full armor of God so that you can take your stand against the devil's schemes. For our struggle is not against flesh and blood, but against the rulers, against the authorities, against the powers of this dark world and against the spiritual forces of evil in the heavenly realms. Therefore put on the full armor of God, so that when the day of evil comes, you may be able to stand your ground, and after you have done everything, to stand.
>
> Ephesians 6:10–13 (NIV)

"What has the Most High instructed you to do in those verses, Marshall?" Gudan asked.

Marshall took a minute to read, reread, and think, all the while praying for God to give him the proper understanding of the verses.

"Forget what you think you know about this passage and allow the Most High to tell you what it means," Gudan encouraged.

Marshall began to think out loud as his mind was filled with truth.

"Well, in keeping with what you just told me, Gudan, I am to be strong in the Lord, and in *his* mighty power, not in my own. That is significant."

Gudan nodded approvingly, knowing that there was much more to come but allowing the enlightenment to come to Marshall directly from the Holy Spirit.

"Stand," Marshall said. "Three times in that passage, I am instructed to stand my ground. Take my stand, stand my ground, stand. And further, the first phrase of the next verse, verse 14, again says to stand firm then."

Gudan again nodded his approval. "Then what is your task, Marshall? What is it that the Most High has instructed you to do in light of these verses? What is your objective?"

Understanding wafted over Marshall like the blast of hot air from the opening of a bakery oven. He looked at Gudan and pointed to the words splashed across the sky.

"I have to stand firm in the truth of God's word!" he shouted. "My enemy is not one that can be defeated. I am a soldier in a battle that does not exist! It is the ultimate oxymoron."

Marshall paced back and forth excitedly, gesturing, nodding, looking at Gudan, looking at the sky, looking inside himself.

"The only way to win the battle is to utterly reject the battle because it has already been won! It is already over! I cannot defeat the enemy because he has already been defeated. Yet I must engage in the battle every day because to not fight the battle is to lose the battle. No, that's not entirely correct. To ignore the battle is to lose the battle. Yes, that's it—to passively ignore the battle is to lose the battle because that would allow the enemy free reign to cause destruction and mayhem at his whim. On the other hand, to actively reject the battle renders the enemy impotent because the ultimate truth of his previous defeat comes to the forefront. Actively fighting the enemy is futile because he cannot be defeated. The enemy cannot be advanced upon. The enemy cannot be defeated. Ground cannot be taken from him. Territory cannot be taken from him. The earth is his domain, given to him unwittingly by mankind himself. Therefore, it cannot be retrieved through battle. The enemy cannot be brought into submission through battle. That is what you meant by the rules of engagement having been established long ago by God and Satan. The battle is unlike any earthly battle. In an earthly battle, land is taken, enemy soldiers are killed or imprisoned, and when enough damage has been done to the enemy, he surrenders, allowing the victor to impose his rule upon him and all that used to belong to him. Territory can be taken. The enemy can be forced to change his allegiance and become subject to the victor. Actual, physical changes occur at the end of the battle."

Marshall wrinkled his brow and squinted into the nothingness, pointing into the air with his forefinger and beginning to pace. "In this case, however, the battle never ends. The earth belongs to the enemy, and that cannot be changed by battle. Satan and the forces of evil will never surrender and will never be forced to be subject to mankind as the victors. In the spiritual realm, they have already been defeated. Their ultimate demise is certain. That battle is finished. The Messiah won that battle where mankind never could. However, due to God's timing, the fullness of their punishment has not yet been brought upon them. And during the interim between their defeat and their ultimate punishment, mankind is allowed a second chance at life with God.

"Mankind brought destruction on himself by betraying God in the garden of Eden when they first brought sin into the world. The battle involving humanity began then. Mankind deserved to die then as punishment for his betrayal, but God would not allow it. Rather, he provided a means of redeeming them to himself with the sacrificial death of the Messiah, Jesus. The penalty of their sin was paid in full by the shedding of the innocent blood of the Christ. In that, the battle in the spiritual realm was finished. It was also at that point that the cosmic battle between God and Satan became an individual battle between each human being and Satan.

"Satan is defeated, but each human being must claim that victory individually. God tests the loyalty of each human being by allowing Satan to retain his power and his dominion over the earth as a whole while allowing each human being individually the authority to claim the Messiah's victory for his own, thereby defeating Satan's power in his own life individually and allowing him to live in complete victory over the forces of evil. It is the authority over Satan that gives mankind the victory over Satan. Satan's power is still real and strong, but he is only allowed to exercise it under the authority of the Messiah. God allows Satan to wield his sword of deceit and torment throughout the earth and against all its inhabitants, but he gives each inhabitant the authority to stop Satan cold with the mere spoken word, empowered by the authority of Jesus.

"Every human being is given complete victory over Satan and free access to the gift of life provided by the sacrifice of the Messiah, but he must choose to accept that gift by renouncing his life of sin and his succumbing to the power of his own will and the deceit of Satan. He must choose to obey the word of God and stand firm. That is the answer, Gudan. We are to stand. We do not have to defeat the enemy. We do not have to take over his territory. We do not have to advance against the enemy. We do not have to obliterate him or destroy him or make him subject to our will as an earthly army would have to do. We are required simply to take a stand against him. Our authority over him in the power of Christ gives us complete victory over him. We don't need to defeat him. We just need to live in the victory already provided. We need only to stand firm as long as we live upon this earth, his domain, and remain faithful to the will of God."

Marshall fell to his knees, weakened by his dissertation like he had been intensely preaching a two-hour Sunday sermon. His breath came in deep gasps, his mind still reeling with the enlightenment of God to his soul.

After a few moments, Gudan placed his hand upon Marshall's shoulder, infusing him with strength from the Most High. Marshall stood and looked at Gudan.

"Did I really just say all that?" he asked. "That's really how it is, isn't it, Gudan?"

"Yes, Marshall," Gudan replied. "That is exactly how it is."

Nothing else needed to be said. Gudan nodded in the direction of the training camp. "So tell me, Marshall, what then is the significance of the training camp? If there is actually no battle to be fought, why would the Most High bring you to a training camp for soldiers?"

"The only thing I can think of is that fourteenth verse in Ephesians 6. Having established the fact that my mission and objective is simply to stand firm and considering the fact that the verse begins with the phrase, 'Stand firm, then, with…' I can only assume that the remainder of the passage will tell me how to stand firm."

"Precisely, Marshall. Understanding how a Roman soldier used the weapons Paul talked about in his letter will help you explain to your parishioners exactly how to stand firm against their enemy and fulfill their mission."

Gudan noticed the gleam in Marshall's eye as he said with a grin, "Then let us proceed."

"First," Gudan advised, "let us talk about strategy."

"Ours or his?" Marshall asked.

"Let us begin with that of the enemy," Gudan suggested. "What is his objective, Marshall?"

Marshall thought for a moment. "Well, if my objective is to stand firm, then I suppose his objective is to keep me from standing firm."

"True enough, Marshall, but what does that mean?"

Marshall grinned and nodded. "Yes, I thought that would be too easy," he admitted. "Okay. God wants me to claim and receive the life he provided for me with the sacrifice of the Messiah. He wants me to live for him in accordance with the requirements of the Bible. I guess the best way to answer that would be through a series of Bible verses." Marshall cited several passages of Scripture, each of which immediately became illuminated in the sky above them.

But just as he who called you is holy, so be holy in all you do; for it is written: "Be holy, because I am holy."

1 Peter 1:15–16 (NIV)

Therefore, I urge you, brothers, in view of God's mercy, to offer your bodies as living sacrifices, holy and pleasing to God—this is your spiritual act of worship. Do not conform any longer to the pattern of this world, but be transformed by the renewing of your mind. Then you will be able to test and approve what God's will is—his good, pleasing and perfect will.

Romans 12:1–2 (NIV)

"Teacher, which is the greatest commandment in the Law?" Jesus replied: "'Love the Lord your God with all your heart and with all your soul and with all your mind.' This is the first and greatest commandment. And the second is like it: 'Love your neighbor as yourself.' All the Law and the Prophets hang on these two commandments."

Matthew 22:36–40 (NIV)

Then Jesus came to them and said, "All authority in heaven and on earth has been given to me. Therefore go and make disciples of all nations, baptizing them in the name of the Father and of the Son and of the Holy Spirit, and teaching them to obey everything I have commanded you. And surely I am with you always, to the very end of the age."

Matthew 28:18–20 (NIV)

"Very good, Marshall. Be holy. Offer your bodies, be not conformed, but be transformed. Love God, love people. Go and make disciples. A very good selection of verses. And you could easily add a hundred more to those. But let's narrow it down a little more. That is too broad. What specifically is your mission? Look at it in light of what we have just discussed. Where is the battle fought? How is the soldier defeated? Where does the defeat begin?"

Marshall thought for a moment. "You said the battle is in the mind. Then defeat must happen first in the mind, as well as victory."

"Very good, Marshall. Very good. That is exactly right. Defeat and victory both happen first in the mind of the soldier. Consider this. A random thought enters the mind. Suppose that thought is contrary to the will of the Most High. What, at that very point, is the soldier supposed to do?"

"Follow the command in 2 Corinthians 10:5," Marshall replied. The passage flashed onto the screen of the sky.

> We demolish arguments and every pretension that sets itself up against the knowledge of God, and we take captive every thought to make it obedient to Christ.
>
> 2 Corinthians 10:5 (NIV)

"Very good. And if that action is taken immediately, the random thought is found to be contrary to the will of the Most High. It is summarily rejected and dismissed, and the soldier has maintained his victory over the enemy. He has stood firm.

"However, suppose the soldier failed to follow that procedure. Suppose that thought was permitted to remain in his mind. As time progresses, that thought will likely become less offensive. It will likely become more appealing. It will likely become a desire.

"And at that point, the soldier again has a choice to make. The desire basically acts as a new thought, which must then be subject to the scrutiny of the law and will of the Most High. If it is set up against the law and will of the Most High and found wanting, then it is to be immediately taken captive and made obedient to Christ, which in this case would mean eradication.

"However, suppose the soldier again failed to execute his orders properly and the desire was again permitted to remain in the mind. As time progresses, the desire will likely become an action. The thought was not sin. The desire was not sin. But when the progression was allowed to continue to the point at which that desire became action, it became sin. Consider the words of the apostle James. How did it become sin, Marshall? 'but each person is tempted when they are dragged away by their own evil desire and enticed. Then, after desire has conceived, it gives birth to sin; and sin, when it is full-grown, gives birth to death' (James 1:14–15)."

"It was not eradicated immediately upon detection," Marshall replied.

"Correct," Gudan agreed. "The random thought was permitted to fulfill its life cycle of evil, which eventually led to death. So then how could that life cycle have been stopped so that the random thought did not lead to an act of sin?"

Marshall smiled and nodded. "It must be stopped while it is still in the mind," he answered.

"Yes, Marshall. Every thought, every day. But why? Why is it so important to keep the mind pure? Because the only weapon in Satan's arsenal that has any ability to defeat mankind is deceit. He is completely powerless against mankind, Marshall. He is very powerful, to be sure, but his power is useless against mankind. He cannot make someone sin. He cannot make someone betray the Most High. But he can deceive someone into doing it. He is a master of deception.

"Remember how we witnessed Satan talking to his troops and issuing orders to reconnoiter mankind? Remember how thorough he commanded his demons to be? That was for the sole purpose of gathering intelligence against every single human being alive so that they would then know the most effective means by which they might deceive each one into disobeying the law and will of the Most High.

"Satan knows he cannot defeat mankind outright. He knows that there are very few human beings to whom he can simply appear and suggest that they join him in rebellion against the Most High. Even though all humans are born with a sinful nature that is in opposition to the Most High, they are still born with a desire to know him and to have that relationship repaired. But because of that sinful nature, it is much easier for Satan to deceive them into disobedience. He doesn't need to attack them outright. He merely needs to encourage them to do the very things their sinful minds want to do anyway.

"Which brings us to the reason for our visit to the military training camp," Gudan concluded, closing the subject for the moment. He waved his arm in a large arc, which acted like an enormous blackboard eraser, clearing the sky for the next series of verses that materialized in their place. "First of all, let us go directly to the word of the Most High, in which you will find all answers to all questions."

> Finally, be strong in the Lord and in his mighty power. Put on the full armor of God so that you can take your stand against the devil's schemes. For our struggle is not against flesh and blood, but against the rulers, against the authorities, against the powers of this dark world and against the spiritual forces of evil in the heavenly realms. Therefore put on the full armor of God, so that when the day of evil comes, you may be able to stand your ground, and after you have done everything, to stand. Stand firm then, with the belt of truth buckled around your waist, with the breastplate of righteousness in place, and with your feet fitted with the readiness that comes from the gospel of peace. In addition to all this, take up the shield of faith, with which you can extinguish all the flaming arrows of the evil one. Take the helmet of salvation and the sword of the Spirit, which is the word of God. And pray in the Spirit on all occasions with all kinds of prayers and requests. With this in mind, be alert and always keep on praying for all the saints.
>
> Ephesians 6:10–18 (NIV)

As the sky filled with words, Marshall looked again at the training camp and at the soldiers engaged in simulated battle. He studied the scene, knowing that Gudan would soon ask him many questions about the soldiers and their equipment. He watched them move. He observed their various pieces of armor and their weapons. He watched them move toward each other, jump back, thrust, kick, swing, chop, block, slice, jab. He carefully observed how each piece of armor and weaponry assisted the soldier in defending against or besting his sparring partner.

The pair over to his left caught his eye. They were on a slight incline—well, one of them was. Crispus One—so named by Marshall as it was the only Roman-sounding name he could think of at the moment—was standing on a relatively flat piece of earth while Crispus Two, having been forced backward in response to Crispus One's advances, found himself standing on a gentle slope just past the edge of the plateau. It was obvious that the soldiers were friends. Between the clenched-jaw scowls of exertion, their faces betrayed their admiration of each other's techniques and abilities.

They had fought together in battle. They had learned together, trained together, taught together. These men were elite soldiers. They had progressed beyond merely learning and practicing the basics of close-combat infantry fighting techniques and were now learning to adjust for and adapt to such variations in the dynamics of close-combat as topography and terrain, elevation, and weather conditions. This particular session was focused on adjusting the technique to correct for the unpredictability of ground irregularities. The angle of the sword's arc, the direction of the applied and resulting forces, even the feel of the blow received differ significantly with the change of only a few inches in elevation between contenders. Such differences must be accounted for and corrected for to ensure victory over the enemy.

Marshall watched as the soldier he had named Crispus One hammered relentlessly against the shield of his friend below him. As Marshall studied the man on the slope, he could actually see him straining at the awkwardness of his swing, making a correction by changing his grip on his sword slightly, then swinging again with noticeably less difficulty. Crispus One raised his sword high above his head to deliver what was sure to be the final knockout blow to Crispus Two beneath him. Having suffered the effects of his friend's signature blow in previous spars, Crispus Two braced himself for it as he tried, within the course of a split second, to find some means of defending himself against it.

Suddenly, Crispus One disappeared. Marshall heard a thud followed by a clank of metal, then heard a man laughing hysterically. Crispus Two looked down to see his friend lying flat on his back at his feet, sword on the ground on one side of him, shield on the ground on the other. The man's legs were up in the air, arms across his belly in a fit of laughter. Dropping to his knees to join his friend, Crispus Two's mind caught up to what his eyes had seen.

The upward momentum created by the swift raising of Crispus One's sword hand, coupled with the slight reduction in friction between his feet and the ground due to that same upward momentum, had caused his feet to slip on the grass and shoot right out from under him. At that point, the uncompromising force of gravity took over and returned his body quickly and decidedly to the ground, albeit back first rather than feet first.

Gudan's voice startled Marshall. "Did you see how that happened, Marshall?" he asked.

"Yes," he chuckled. "He raised his arm with such force that it basically lifted him off the ground, and his feet slipped out from under him! That was really funny!"

"Yes," Gudan agreed. "But watch what happens next."

Marshall looked back at the scene to see Crispus Two pointing at the sole of his sandals, tapping them with pride.

"Spikes," he said with a satisfied grin. "I told you about my idea of putting spikes in the soles of my shoes! You should have listened. Then it would probably be me lying on the ground right now instead of you!"

"Spikes, huh?" Crispus One said, admiring his friend's handiwork. "Tell me how you made those…"

"You see, Marshall, it doesn't matter how skilled the soldier might be—no one can fight effectively lying on the ground on his back!"

Marshall smiled. "Gudan, did you just make a joke?"

"Simply pointing out the necessity of sure footing," Gudan replied, feigning innocence of any such endeavor. "The Most High is the creator of humor after all," he added as an afterthought. Each permitted himself a private grin.

Marshall quoted Ephesians 6:15, "'And with your feet fitted with the readiness that comes from the gospel of peace.' The one who fell was obviously the superior soldier," he observed. "But the less skilled soldier defeated him because of his sure footing. Even though he appeared to be fighting from a disadvantage, he prevailed because of his preparation. His feet were stable. He was able to fight with greater confidence and success because he knew his footing was sure. He could be at peace during the battle knowing that he would not slip even on the grassy slope.

"And before you ask," Marshall continued, "I will try to relate that to Paul's admonition in Ephesians. The Christian soldier's peace and confidence comes from knowing that he is secure, that his footing is sure, that he is on the side of right, and that his power base, the Spirit of God, is unfaltering. He will never slip and fall, regardless of the battle or the situation, as long as he has his feet readied and his mind at peace, resting secure on the gospel of Jesus the Christ."

"Well said," Gudan agreed. "How, then, does a mere man defeat and prevail against the enemy like the Messiah did? You must begin with placing your confidence and security in the gospel provided by the Messiah. The Christian soldier is definitely on the side of truth and righteousness, and the power of the Most High will always prevail no matter what comes against it. You are exactly correct, Marshall. Begin with the sure footing and peace provided by the gospel of Christ."

Marshall knew without words being shared that it was time for the next lesson, which would again come from watching the soldiers spar. He turned his attention back to the Crispi on the other side of the barrier.

Crispus Two jumped to his feet and extended a hand to Crispus One, who took it and also returned to his feet.

"Round two?" Crispus Two asked with a slight bow and a mocking grin.

Crispus One retrieved his shield. "Round two," he agreed, returning both the bow and the grin, and positioning himself for battle. "And this time, I will not let you win so easily!" he countered.

"If you are so confident," Crispus Two taunted, "then you take the low ground this time."

"Gladly," Crispus One agreed.

The soldiers, their swords and shields at the ready, hunched slightly and circled each other until One was on the slope and Two was on the plateau. They exchanged blows, swords glancing off shields. They stabbed and sliced, blocking and parrying each other's advances. Crispus One launched an intense offensive, striking blow after blow in rapid succession, forcing Crispus Two back until One climbed the slope and joined his friend on the plateau. Crispus Two lunged backward with arms spread wide to dodge Crispus One's signature death blow. In one quick motion, Crispus Two then lunged forward with dizzying speed, slapped Crispus One's sword to the side with the blade his own, and kicked hard against Crispus One's shield. The sheer force of the impact knocked the unsuspecting man off balance. Crispus Two kicked hard again. His friend was driven over the side of the plateau and onto the slope. As he frantically tried to regain his balance and his footing, Crispus Two came straight down from above with a great sweeping arc that would have been his own version of the death blow. He changed his assault at the last minute and instead used the side of his sword blade to deliver a harmless thump to the top of Crispus One's head.

Crispus One regained his footing, then bowed to his friend, conceding his defeat.

"What if he had not halted his offensive, Marshall? What if that final blow had been delivered full force?"

"Well, without his helmet, it would have pretty much removed his head, or at least part of it. With the helmet, it probably would have knocked him unconscious or at least made him really dizzy for a while."

"True," Gudan agreed. "Without the helmet, death and defeat would have been certain. However, with the helmet in place, the soldier may have been wounded but would not have been killed or defeated. Paul called it the helmet of salvation. Without the assurance of salvation protecting his mind, the soldier is easily defeated. Remember how I said that causing the soldier to doubt his salvation, his worth, his value, his ability, etc., is the most effective way to debilitate him and render him useless to the battle? Satan knows this as well, and he knows that he doesn't have to defeat the soldier in a battle of wits or even best him blow for blow. If he can get the soldier to doubt himself, his worth, and the truth of his salvation, the battle is lost to him before it even begins. Human beings thrive on hope. On belief. If they believe their cause is right, they will die for it. If they believe they can achieve something, they can achieve beyond their actual abilities. Conversely, if they do not believe, they will be defeated before even approaching the end of their abilities.

"How, then, can a mere man defeat Satan like the Messiah did? The battle is in the mind, Marshall. Belief and hope are extremely strong weapons. The helmet of salvation protects the sanctity of the mind, keeping the assurance of salvation and the hope for victory foremost in the mind of the soldier. With the battlefield clear of the obstruction of Satan's lies, the soldier will have strength far beyond himself and will be able to come from the battle victorious."

The Crispi on the other side of the barrier squared off again, this time both on the plateau. They circled each other, striking and blocking, kicking and punching. Once again, Crispus Two's rapid succession of sword chops, fist punches, and kicks unbalanced his opponent, allowing him to stab his sword straight into the open chest of Crispus One. While Crispus One's body armor prevented the sword from actually piercing his chest and killing him, it did partially force the air out of his lungs. He stepped back from Crispus Two and dropped his arms to his sides. With an approving grin, he bowed his head and again conceded his friend's victory.

"The breastplate of righteousness," Marshall stated. "In this case, the breastplate protected Crispus One's major life support organs from being wounded. His heart, his lungs. Damage or wounding to the extremities might not have rendered the soldier defenseless or unable to attack, but damage to the upper torso would have debilitated or likely killed him. The breastplate must be in place to protect the soldier and allow him to remain engaged in the battle."

"Correct," Gudan simply stated. "The breastplate armor protects the life force of the soldier. The same is true for the soldier in the army of the Most High. The breastplate of righteousness is actually a multifaceted piece of armor. In one respect, the breastplate is like the pin awarded to the soldier to signify his membership in a specialized unit or having achieved a particular level of competency. For example, the army rangers or the navy SEALS in your time, Marshall. The pins they wear on their uniforms signify that they have completed the training and have demonstrated sufficient competency to be known as members of the most elite fighting forces in your world. Similarly, the breastplate of righteousness signifies that the soldier belongs to the army of the Most High. It is where he wears his colors. It is external evidence of his membership in the most elite fighting force in any world.

"Secondly, the breastplate of righteousness provides an internal witness to the standing of the soldier as being in a right relationship with the Most High. The enemy will attack the soldier's character, trying to convince him that he is not good enough or that he is failing at being a soldier or that he as no value to the Most High or to his cause. This contradicts 2 Corinthians 5:21, where the Most High says that, 'God made him who had no sin to be sin for us, so that in him we might become the righteousness of God.' Where the helmet of salvation protects against the enemy trying to convince the soldier that he is not even a member of the army of the Most High, the breastplate of righteousness protects the soldier against the enemy's attempts to convince him that he is incapable or not good enough to be a soldier. Satan will tell the soldier that unless he is perfect and has always been perfect, he is not fit to serve. The word of the Most High says that if the soldier is forgiven, he is fit to serve. Satan will try to tell the soldier that his past can never be forgiven, so therefore he will never amount to anything as he pretends to be a godly person and a soldier for the Most High. The word of the Most High says, 'So if the Son sets you free, you will be free indeed' (John 8:36). 'If we confess our sins, he is faithful and just and will forgive us our sins and purify us from all unrighteousness' (1 John 1:9). The breastplate of righteousness protects the most vital tenets of the Christian's existence from the lies of the devil. With the breastplate securely in place, doubts as to the soldier's position or value or worth or usefulness are dispelled the instant they are suggested by the enemy.

"How, then, can a mere man defeat the enemy like the Messiah did? Wear the badge of righteousness with pride. Know your position in Christ. Accept the complete forgiveness from all sin and the purification from all unrighteousness freely offered by the Most High, and claim your status as forgiven and free. Do not allow the lies of the enemy to debilitate you or to render you weak and useless in the battle. As the Most High himself said to one of the greatest soldiers recorded in your Bible, "Have I not commanded you? Be strong and courageous. Do not be terrified; do not be discouraged, for the LORD your God will be with you wherever you go. (Joshua 1:9)"

"Archers!" the centurion yelled, his right hand raised high above his head. The Crispi glanced at each other, then looked back across the field at the line of archers standing at the ready, with their blunt-tipped, paint-dipped practice arrows loaded into their bows, poised and waiting in firing position. The centurion dropped his hand, and instantly one hundred arrows shot through the sky toward the other end of the field where the line of infantry soldiers stood two feet away from each other and hiding behind their shields. Men screamed as some of the arrows got past their shields and thumped into legs, feet, arms, heads, chests, and shoulders. Much more prominent, however, were the dozens and dozens of clanks of arrows being stopped by the shields of the warriors who knew how to properly use them. The Crispi again looked at each other. Crispus One had thirteen paint splotches on his shield, while Crispus Two had only nine on his. Neither had allowed any to pass his shield and strike his person.

"In addition to all this, take up the shield of faith, with which you can extinguish all the flaming arrows of the evil one," Marshall quoted.

"Precisely, Marshall. One important thing to note, however, is the ultimate power of the shield. In your time, a shield really doesn't mean much, but understand that at the time when the apostle Paul wrote this letter, there was no weapon in existence that could penetrate the soldier's properly maintained and properly utilized shield. Arrows, flaming arrows, battle axes, maces, swords, spears—none of them could penetrate the shield. Every single attack of the enemy could be thwarted by properly utilizing the shield. It didn't merely reduce the severity of the attack. It didn't stop some of the arrows. It stopped all of them. A good, strong shield in the arm of a well-trained soldier could make that soldier basically impervious to the onslaught of the enemy—even multiple enemies attacking at the same time.

"In the same way, Marshall, a good, strong faith in the heart of the well-trained soldier can basically make him impervious to the attacks of Satan. No weapon of the enemy can strike down the soldier with an unshakable faith in the Most High. That is not to say that the soldier will not suffer any battle damage. On the contrary, there will probably be more battle damage due to the increased severity and frequency of the attacks! The soldier will be beaten up for sure, but he will not be beaten." Gudan paused for a moment. It just wasn't enough. "Marshall, this one is too important to leave so quickly," he said. "It is very simple, so further explanation may not necessarily be prudent, but fully grasping the significance and scope of the shield of faith may require more discussion about it.

Gudan again paused for a moment, then continued. "Faith addresses the overall mind-set of the believer. It gives the soldier the ability to know without a doubt that the words of the enemy are false even when they appear to be true. Even when the believer doesn't understand something, he believes fully in the word of the Most High. Even when the words or actions of the Most High do not make sense to him, still he believes. Regardless of anything he may see or hear, he stands firm in the knowledge of the truth of the Most High.

"Many people claim to have faith, claim they believe, claim lots of things, but when difficult times come or when the attacks of the enemy get personal, they buckle under the lies, begin to doubt the truth of the Bible and the reality of God's unfailing love for them, and they fall victim to the attack of the enemy. They are defeated by their doubt, by their lack of faith.

"The shield of faith, so properly designated by the apostle Paul, truly does keep the wise soldier safe from every attack of the enemy. No lie, no distortion of the truth, no exaggeration, no hint or suggestion of evil, no feigned misunderstanding of the truth will even begin to take root in the mind of the soldier who effectively employs the shield of faith. His total faith in the ultimate, undeniable, all-powerful, undefeatable word of the Most High gives him the ability to see every single thought, word, or action of the enemy for exactly what it is before it even gets close enough to him to begin to do any harm. He will not succumb to the lies of the enemy because he will not even entertain them for the briefest period of time. They will hit his shield and will fall harmlessly to the ground at his feet, rendered completely useless and ineffective by his rock-solid adherence to and confidence in the inerrant word of the Most High.

"Another aspect of the shield of faith is the firm belief that even if things don't work out as the soldier would have them work out or even if terrible things happen to him or even if he seems to be getting beat up again and again and again at the hands of those who do not believe, the Most High is still in control, still has a plan for his life, and will take care of him in any and every situation, regardless of how bleak or impossible that situation may appear to be. It is easy to agree with that sentiment when things are going well. Strong, true faith will remember and still believe without being discouraged when things are not going well.

"How, then, can a mere man defeat the enemy like the Messiah did?" Gudan again asked. "By looking beyond himself and putting his faith absolutely, completely, and solely in the word and character of the Most High. By categorically refusing and rejecting any and every thought, inkling, or idea that does not definitively line up one hundred percent with the word of the Most High. By not giving the enemy the slightest foothold in his life by even considering for a moment any suggestion that in any way violates the truth of the word of the Most High. By properly utilizing the shield of faith, Marshall."

The centurion gave the command to cease the archer exercise and resume normal scheduled training drills. The Crispi walked across the field, chatting with their fellow soldiers, teasing those with multiple hits on their bodies, bragging in jest of the relative cleanliness of their own armor. As they walked, a particularly devious man came up close behind Crispus Two. As he leaned in close to him and mock-whispered something in his ear to the amusement of his fellows, he deftly removed his dagger from his belt and sliced partway through the leather belt that held Crispus Two's armor in place. The slice was not enough to completely sever the belt, but it was enough to weaken it such that it would not last the remainder of the training session without failing. He and his team proceeded to their stations to resume their drills, casting side-glances at the Crispi every few moments to watch for the sabotaged belt's failure.

Once again, the Crispi faced off on the plateau. As one might expect of elite soldiers, the intensity of their sparring increased as the day went on, rather than waning due to fatigue or lack of motivation. They adjusted their armor, checked their weapons. Crouching, they again began circling one another, swords and shields at the ready. The practiced dance of battle went on, footwork complementing swordplay, reaction complementing action. They shouted as they attacked, grunted with exertion. Metal clanged. The swiping whoosh of swinging swords could be heard as blows were anticipated and avoided. The dull thud of fist or foot making contact with body armor could be heard as blows were delivered and received by each.

Crispus One launched an intense offensive against Crispus Two. He lunged forward, swinging his sword with practiced efficiency, quickly delivering three blows aimed at his opponent's upper body. He jumped back and to his right, then lunged forward again, swiping his sword at Crispus Two's legs. Capitalizing on that momentum to propel him, he spun to his right and leapt into the air, delivering a roundhouse kick to Crispus Two's chest. Crispus Two blocked the three sword swipes with his shield, jumped above the fourth swipe to his legs, and turned his body quickly to his left to avoid the kick coming at his chest. His defense was nearly successful. The foot of Crispus One failed to make contact with his chest, catching him instead mid-rotation and landing squarely on his right hip. The force of the kick spun Crispus Two the rest of the way around, also knocking him backward. Crispus Two flung his arms like a bird to regain his balance, righted himself, and positioned himself for his own offensive attack. He lunged at Crispus One, swinging hard with his sword. Crispus One jumped backward to deflect the blow. Crispus Two raised his sword to deliver another. As he did, the stress on his belt finished the tear, which his fellow soldier had begun on the archery range. His belt fell to his feet, taking with it the sheath for his sword and his dagger in its sheath.

Raucous laughter filled the air as the soldiers who had seen the belt's sabotage pointed, shouted, and fell to the ground in hysterics. Other soldiers stopped sparring and looked to see what the commotion was all about. They joined in the laughter.

Crispus Two, however, did not let the loss of his belt take him out of the battle. He continued his offensive against Crispus One, then defended himself against the next attack from his opponent.

"Watch, Marshall, the significant effect of the loss of the belt on the soldier's ability to fight," Gudan instructed.

Crispus Two, who was very nearly the equal to Crispus One on even fighting ground, was quickly and soundly defeated by Crispus One.

"What happened, Marshall?" Gudan asked. "Why did he lose so quickly after his belt failed him?"

Marshall didn't even have to think about it. "His belt was holding everything else in place!" he answered. "When his belt fell off, his breastplate began to flop around, exposing his chest to his opponent. He lost his dagger and would have lost his sword as well, had he not been holding it. His shield, which protects him from most of his opponent's attacks, was too heavy for him to hold without being able to rest the bottom of it in that little holder on his belt, which had been designed for just that purpose. His own armor and weaponry actually worked against him when he lost his belt, and he was soundly defeated."

"Excellent, Marshall. Very well done. Although I presume that your last statement contains a depth of truth, which I doubt you even realize yourself, my friend," Gudan said. He waved to the sky, upon which Marshall's last statement appeared.

> His own armor and weaponry actually worked against him when he lost his belt, and he was soundly defeated.

"Marshall, that is exactly how the enemy, Satan, defeats followers of the Most High. The apostle called it the belt of truth. It is the belt that holds the soldier's armor in place, keeps his weapons at the ready, and holds his shield in place. The belt is the crux of everything for the soldier. Even so, the truth is the crux of everything for the soldier in the army of the Most High. The truth holds his armor in place. The truth keeps his weapons at the ready. The truth holds his shield in place. Without the solid foundation of truth, the soldier's armor and weaponry are rendered useless and can actually be manipulated by the enemy to be used against the soldier. What was meant by the Most High to be used for the soldier's benefit and the defeat of the enemy can instead be used to the soldier's detriment and often leads to his ultimate defeat.

"What is Satan's only real weapon? Deceit. Therefore, truth is paramount in the soldier's ability to stand against him. Deceit is all he has. If he can get a foothold in the life of the soldier, he is a master at using that to his advantage and bringing about the destruction of the soldier. Truth is vital. Truth is deadly. Truth is the crux of everything for the soldier of the Most High.

"How, then, can the mere man defeat the enemy like the Messiah did? Hold fast to the truth. Never ever let the enemy have even the slightest foothold in your mind. Never ever doubt the word of the Most High. Any of it. If Satan can convince you that maybe some tiny part of the word of the Most High is suspect, he can get you to doubt the whole thing. And once he does that, your defeat is virtually guaranteed. Truth is the crux of everything. Consider the words of the Messiah as he was praying for his disciples shortly before his crucifixion: 'My prayer is not that you take them out of the world but that you protect them from the evil one. They are not of the world, even as I am not of it. Sanctify them by the truth; your word is truth. As you sent me into the world, I have sent them into the world' (John 17:15–18). "Truth, Marshall. Guard the truth. Guard your heart and your mind against deceit. Again, consider the words of the Messiah: 'To the Jews who had believed him, Jesus said, "If you hold to my teaching, you are really my disciples. Then you will know the truth, and the truth will set you free' (John 8:31–32).

"Freedom comes with knowledge of the truth. Victory comes with keeping the truth in your heart and mind. That, Marshall, is how you, a mere man, can defeat the enemy like the Messiah did." He paused. "And now, one last look at the soldiers."

Marshall looked back through the barrier. The Crispi, Two having replaced his defective belt, once again faced off on the plateau. This time, the focus was on their swords. Marshall noticed that not only were they the only offensive weapons, they were also the only weapons that could be both offensive and defensive. They could deflect a blow from the enemy, deliver a blow to the enemy, or if held properly and with enough ferocity, ward off an enemy attack altogether.

"With the shield in one hand and the sword in the other," he remarked to Gudan, "nearly every attempted blow from the enemy can be blocked. The shield provides a strong wall of protection between the soldier and his enemy while the sword not only allows him to deflect any renegade blows that might have gotten around the shield but also allows him to strike back against the enemy in answer to the attack."

"That is correct, Marshall," Gudan agreed. "But look closer. What else can you notice about their use of the sword? Look deeper."

Marshall watched the soldiers carefully for a long while. Eventually, he began to notice something. These soldiers had been fighting each other for a long time, and they were learning as they fought. Crispus One poised himself for an attack. Crispus Two recognized his stance and how he was holding his sword, so he reacted to it in such a way that would allow him to successfully answer the attack and render it futile. He explained as much to Gudan, who smiled approvingly.

"That's right, Marshall. And this is very significant indeed. The adept soldier can anticipate the coming attack of his enemy and, by positioning his sword in a fashion that would be sure to successfully answer the attack and possibly inflict retaliatory damage of its own, can cause his enemy to abort the attack altogether. Something of a preemptive strike, as it were. It works with soldiers in battle, and it can work with Satan's attacks and those of his warriors. If the soldier can begin to recognize the methods of his enemy and anticipate his attack, he can be defeated, and some of his attacks prevented before they can even begin.

"This is very important to the soldier of the Most High, Marshall. Knowing an enemy's attack strategy will show the soldier how to position his sword effectively to defend against the attack. In the same way, knowing Satan's attack strategy will show the soldier of the Most High how to position his sword, the word of God, to successfully defend against or possibly even prevent his attack. Through prayer, the Most High will bring verses to his mind to stop Satan's attack before it can even begin. Do you understand all this, Marshall? The weapons? The armor? The battle strategy?"

"Yes, Gudan. I believe so," Marshall answered.

"Do you understand the tactics of the enemy, Satan, as we have witnessed them on our journey thus far?"

"I believe so," Marshall again stated.

Gudan nodded. "Then let's recap," he said. "Let's briefly review what you have learned thus far, just to make sure you have gained sufficient understanding."

"Okay," Marshall agreed, reluctant at the likelihood of appearing dull if he couldn't recall or explain his recollection sufficiently and eager at the opportunity to solidify his own understanding of the many things he had witnessed thus far. He was also a bit apprehensive about the necessity of a review, deducing that what was coming next must be very significant to deem confirmation of complete understanding of what had already been. Considering the depth of what had already been seen and experienced, Marshall refused to even let his mind wander to the possibilities of the next lesson. Instead, he steeled himself for the questioning.

"Let's go back, Marshall. Let's discuss the initial status of Lucifer. At his creation, he was perfect. His focus was on the Most High, where it belonged. His only desire was to please the Most High and to bring him glory. Unfortunately, sin crept in. Lucifer allowed sin to enter his mind and pervert his desires. Eventually, Lucifer's focus turned inward, and he began to be completely focused on himself. His only desire became self-gratification rather than glorifying the Most High. The end result of this infiltration of his mind was full-scale betrayal of and eventually opposition to the Most High. He became completely focused on self. He created and became the epitome of self-reliance, self-centeredness, self-righteousness, self-will, self-indulgence, self-preservation, and self-pity.

"Lucifer allowed sin to enter his mind and pervert his desires. He gave in to selfishness, and in the end, Lucifer, the anointed cherub, guardian of the throne of the Most High, became Satan, the adversary of the Most High."

Gudan's gaze fell to Marshall, who sensed that it was his turn to take over the discussion.

"And mankind did the very same thing," Marshall said, the conclusion resonating through his mind. "Mankind was also created perfect, in perfect submission to God and in a perfect relationship with him. His focus was also wholly on God, and his only desire was to please God and to bring glory to him. And just like Lucifer, he allowed sin to enter his mind and pervert his desires."

Marshall's understanding became complete even as he spoke the words to Gudan.

"For mankind, it happened much more quickly, but the result was the same. Through Satan's deception, mankind's focus also turned inward. He believed that he could take care of himself better than God could. His desire for self-gratification also overcame his desire to please and bring glory to God, so he succumbed to sin, yielded to its call, and betrayed God. Again, as with Lucifer, this infiltration of his mind led from what appeared to be a minor elevation of self and a slight pushing aside of God to a full-scale betrayal of God and a total focus on self. Mankind became the perfect imitation of the original, but not the original that the Most High had intended. Rather than becoming the imitation of God, with all the character and attributes of the supreme holy being, mankind fell into depravity and became the imitation of the original *adversary* of God—the exact duplicate of self-reliance, self-centeredness, self-righteousness, self-will, self-indulgence, self-preservation, and self-pity. Mankind became the exact imitation of Satan."

"Very good, Marshall," Gudan responded. "That is an excellent explanation. And that is exactly what happened."

Marshall looked at Gudan expectantly, knowing that this particular discussion, while summarizing in nature, was not a conclusion at all, but rather a transition.

In keeping with Marshall's expectation and true to his form insomuch as Marshall had come to know him throughout this journey, Gudan posed a question.

"Marshall, what do you know about espionage?"

Marshall looked at him with a blank look on his face as though he could not possibly have heard him correctly, and said, "Uh…"

"Yes, Marshall, espionage. What do you know about espionage?"

"Well, just what I have seen in movies or read in books. Not a lot, really, I suppose."

"Let's go back to those two soldiers you labeled as the Crispi at the Roman military training camp," Gudan said with a grin as they were instantly transported to the place they had left only moments earlier. Again, Marshall could see thousands of soldiers going about their training regimen.

"Marshall, suppose the Crispi were dispatched to lead a team on a top secret mission to assassinate an enemy king. What would be their most effective means of gaining access to the king to accomplish their mission?"

Marshall thought for a while before offering an uncertain reply. "I suppose the best way would be to send in a man on a reconnaissance mission to infiltrate the king's castle, determine the time, place, and method that would offer the greatest chance of success, then plan and execute the mission."

"Okay," Gudan agreed. "And what would be the best way to accomplish that reconnaissance and subsequent infiltration?"

"Probably to recruit an inside man and either bribe him or threaten him to divulge whatever information might be necessary to ensure the success of the mission," Marshall suggested.

"Yes, yes, very good, Marshall," Gudan agreed. "An infiltrator and an inside man. Very good. And which of those—the reconnaissance team, the infiltrator, or the inside man—do you think poses the greatest threat to the king? Which one is the most important, the most significant player? The most detrimental to the king? Which one holds the greatest amount of power over the situation? Which one has the capacity to inflict the most devastating amount of damage? Which one is the key to the success of the whole operation?"

Marshall thought for a moment. "Well," he responded at last, "I suppose it would be the inside man. I mean, he is the one with access to the king and the castle. If he can keep the king and his guards distracted while the infiltrators gain access, the mission can be accomplished successfully and efficiently. However, if the inside man makes a mistake or for some reason fails to execute his part of the plan, the whole mission could be an utter failure. So, really, regardless of how good the intelligence acquired by the reconnaissance team and regardless of how proficient and flawless the infiltrator's execution, it all comes down to the effectiveness of the inside man."

"Crude, but reasonable," Gudan agreed again. "And therefore, since it is definitely the top—albeit not at all a secret—mission of Satan every minute of every day to assassinate the soul of every human being on the face of the earth, what do you suppose might be the most effective way for him to gain access to those souls and to accomplish his own mission?" Gudan asked.

Although uncertain of why it was the correct answer, Marshall faithfully followed Gudan down the path along which he was being led and answered what he knew Gudan was expecting to hear. "An infiltrator and an inside man," he offered.

Gudan sensed Marshall's hesitation. "You seem unconvinced, Marshall," he said. "Were you under the impression that Satan worked alone to accomplish his mission?"

"Well, yes. Er—well, no. I mean, not really alone, no. He has all those legions of demons to assist him," Marshall responded. "But yes, I always thought he worked alone. I mean, Satan is our enemy. He is the one who is prowling around like a roaring lion seeking to devour us. He is the one Paul talked about when he told us about the armor and resisting the devil and his schemes. He is the one Jesus even warned us about as he taught the multitudes during his three years of ministry. Right?"

"Yes, but that is not exactly what I mean," Gudan said. He pointed through the barrier to the Roman soldiers still training and sparring on the other side. "Look at those soldiers training, Marshall. When they go into battle and when they defeat their enemy and capture their city, who is going to get the credit for the victory? Each man? Each squadron? Each battalion? Of course not. The credit for the victory will go to the senior commander of the Roman army. Further, the credit for the success of the entire campaign will not even go to the generals commanding the armies but rather to the supreme ruler of the nation—in this case, the caesar.

"When the Israelites were about to enter the promised land under the leadership of Joshua, whom did the nations of Canaan fear? Joshua. And later, under the rule of King David, whom did the Philistines fear? David. Not the Israelites, not the clan of Ephraim or the house of Rueben, but David, the commander in chief of the army. 'Saul has killed his thousands, but David has killed his tens of thousands,' as the women sang. The credit goes to the commander.

"Likewise, when your Bible refers to the works of the devil, or Satan, it is referring not only to that one specific being, but also to all the minions under his charge, the entirety of the kingdom of darkness. The verse you referred to in 1 Peter could just as well read, 'Be self controlled and alert. Your enemy, the devil, *along with the legions of demons at his command,* prowls around like a roaring lion, seeking whom he may devour.'"

Marshall nodded his understanding. Gudan continued. "With that in mind, then, look at Satan's mission and potential battle strategy in the context of reconnaissance, infiltration, and the inside man. We have already seen the reconnaissance mission—Satan sent his followers on the moment mankind was placed upon the Earth," Gudan began.

Marshall instantly recalled Satan's address to his minions shortly after the humans had been created when he had sent them all out on a reconnaissance mission throughout the entire globe, demanding absolute knowledge of the humans and their every activity.

"Now let's take it a step further. Let's look at it in comparison to your suggested method of accomplishing the assassination of an enemy king. Read this verse, Marshall," Gudan said as he waved his arm in an arc, causing the words of the apostle Paul to fill the sky. "And tell me how Satan accomplishes his mission. Does he work alone? Does he have help? Is there an infiltrator? Is there an inside man?"

> So I find this law at work: When I want to do good, evil is right there with me. For in my inner being I delight in God's law; but I see another law at work in the members of my body, waging war against the law of my mind and making me a prisoner of the law of sin at work within my members.
>
> Romans 7:21–23 (NIV)

Marshall thought for a long moment, turning the question over in his mind. *Who was the real enemy? Did 'the devil make me do it,' as the old adage goes? Or is there more to it than that? Is the father of lies the real enemy? Is he the only enemy? Does he work alone? Is there an infiltrator? And if so, who is it? Is there an inside man? And if so, who is that?*

Even as Marshall read the words aloud again, his mind went back over years of study. Never once had he found a verse in his Bible that told him that the devil had caused someone to sin. Yet there are so many verses that warn us about him. *True, he did command the forces of darkness, but Gudan was talking about the method being reconnaissance, infiltration, and the inside man. Clearly, Satan and the forces of darkness were the ones doing the reconnaissance. And since they are an outside force attacking the person, Satan and his followers must also be the infiltrators. That leaves the inside man. Who, then, is the inside man?*

While Marshall was wrestling with the question, Gudan again waved his arm in a sweeping arc. The word of God filled the sky.

But each one is tempted when, by his own evil desire, he is dragged away and enticed. Then, after desire has conceived, it gives birth to sin; and sin, when it is full-grown, gives birth to death.

James 1:14–15 (NIV)

Those who live according to the sinful nature have their minds set on what that nature desires; but those who live in accordance with the Spirit have their minds set on what the Spirit desires. The mind of sinful man is death, but the mind controlled by the Spirit is life and peace; the sinful mind is hostile to God. It does not submit to God's law, nor can it do so. Those controlled by the sinful nature cannot please God.

Romans 8:5–8 (NIV)

Rather, clothe yourselves with the Lord Jesus Christ, and do not think about how to gratify the desires of the sinful nature.

Romans 13:14 (NIV)

For the sinful nature desires what is contrary to the Spirit, and the Spirit what is contrary to the sinful nature. They are in conflict with each other, so that you do not do what you want.

Galatians 5:17 (NIV)

Do not be deceived: God cannot be mocked. A man reaps what he sows. The one who sows to please his sinful nature, from that nature will reap destruction; the one who sows to please the Spirit, from the Spirit will reap eternal life.

Galatians 6:7–8 (NIV)

> As for you, you were dead in your transgressions and sins, in which you used to live when you followed the ways of this world and of the ruler of the kingdom of the air, the spirit who is now at work in those who are disobedient. All of us also lived among them at one time, gratifying the cravings of our sinful nature and following its desires and thoughts. Like the rest, we were by nature objects of wrath.
>
> Ephesians 2:1–3 (NIV)

> Dear friends, I urge you, as aliens and strangers in the world, to abstain from sinful desires, which war against your soul.
>
> 1 Peter 2:11 (NIV)

Marshall slowly began to understand what Gudan was showing him. He again perused the selection of verses Gudan had placed in the sky, noticing that nowhere in that whole selection of verses did God warn us against the works of the devil. *Not once did God caution us against the devil's activities or his schemes. No, in this selection of verses, we are cautioned against the sinful nature and against the sinful mind.*

"The sinful nature within the mind of a man actually conspires to work against him!" Marshall concluded aloud. "The inside man is, quite literally, the inside man! The inner man!"

Again, the revelation of the Holy Spirit into Marshall's mind caused the teacher in him to verbally conclude the concept his mind had been wrestling with.

"So then Satan is only a catalyst to sin, not the actual cause of it. Satan does not cause us to sin. He only encourages and empowers us to go through with what we want to do anyway. All that armor and weaponry is to be used to defeat ourselves, not the devil. *We* are the enemy. He is only a coconspirator with us in our betrayal against God. If we resist *us*, we can defeat *him* as well and stay true to God. One does not sin by yielding to Satan. One sins by yielding to his own sinful desires at the suggestion, encouragement, possibly even the coercion, and definitely the deception of Satan. The sin may be that of doing something forbidden, or it could be that of refusal to do something required, action or inaction. It could be the desire to do something, or it could be the desire to be complacent and simply do nothing. It could even be in thought only, never having manifested itself in the form of a deed. Sin can take a variety of forms with varying degrees of severity. Nevertheless, whatever its form, at the end of the day, the cause of the sin was the choice of succumbing to the desires of the mind. The true enemy, then, is the desire. The sinful nature, and the desires it produces."

"Exactly right, Marshall," Gudan again confirmed.

"But—" Marshall began, then stopped, searching for the right words to explain his uncertainty.

"Go ahead," Gudan encouraged. "It is critical that you fully understand this. There must be no confusion at all. Talk me through your confusion."

"I have always taught my people that when they are saved, when they experience salvation, their heart is made pure again, like it would have been had there never been original sin in the garden of Eden. The sinful nature is eradicated."

Gudan nodded.

"But clearly that is incorrect because Paul even struggled with a sinful nature, and he was definitely saved and following Christ!"

"Marshall, your frustration is apparent and understandable," Gudan comforted. "Satan has twisted mankind's understanding of the word of the Most High to such a degree that it is often extremely difficult for the average human being to understand the most basic of its truths. Put aside what you think you know, Marshall. Wipe your mind clean from tradition and from man's wisdom, and fill it with the truth of the Most High.

"You see, Marshall, when Adam was created, he was perfect in every way. He was created in the image of the Most High—perfect, holy, sinless. His heart, having never known evil, was one with the

Holy Spirit, in perfect unity. His mind, having never made the choice to sin against the Most High, was also one with the Holy Spirit, in perfect unity. However, when Adam chose to disobey the word of the Most High and enter into sin, his heart was changed. In fact, his very nature was changed. At that point, his once pure heart became sinful. His nature became sinful. His mind, having made the choice to sin, ceased to be basically good with the option to choose sin and became basically evil with the option to choose righteousness. That was the point at which these words"—Gudan extended his arm to indicate the verses of Scripture illuminated across the sky—"became accurate and applicable. That is also why the psalmist accurately requested, 'Create in me a pure heart, O God, and renew a steadfast spirit within me' (Psalm 51:10).

"It took an act of the will from both parties—Adam and the Most High—for the restoration of that relationship to take place. The work of the Most High is in the area of the heart, whereas the work of the creature, Adam, is in the area of the mind. Adam had not exercised positive control of his mind when he allowed himself to be coerced into betraying the Most High and falling into sin. Therefore, the first step in making things right was for Adam to regain positive control of his mind and to make the choice to obey the Most High and to once again yield to his lordship. Once he did that, the Most High was pleased to forgive his betrayal and his sin and create once again a pure heart within him so that their fellowship could be restored to some degree. The Most High purifies the heart and sets things right, but the man must control his mind and refuse to yield to the influence of the sinful nature. The heart must be renewed only once for all time, but the mind must be continually renewed day by day, moment by moment as the man makes the conscious effort to call upon the name of the Most High and daily yield to his lordship. No longer was 'every inclination of the thoughts of his heart only evil all the time,' as it was in the days of Noah. His heart was restored to perfect unity with the Most High. His mind, however, would continue to struggle day after day to remain faithful to the Most High and to resist the influence of the sinful nature and the coercion of Satan."

Gudan paused, allowing Marshall the opportunity to clarify his understanding.

Marshall attempted to recap. "So the heart and mind were both created pure and holy, and both were basically destroyed when Adam sinned. And although the heart can be made new again when a man repents of his sin and confesses to God and asks forgiveness, the mind remains sinful."

"In its barest form, yes," Gudan agreed. "All mankind was born into sin because of the sin of Adam. Their hearts and minds were born sinful. When one accepts the sacrifice of the Messiah to pay for his sin and yields to the lordship of the Christ over his life, his heart is made new, and his mind is purified. His status as a forgiven, holy being is established by his acceptance of the Messiah's sacrifice. This is what you call becoming a Christian or experiencing salvation. The mind, however, is purified, but is not made new. It is still susceptible to the influence of evil, both from the outside sources, the kingdom of darkness, and from the inside source, the sinful nature. It can only be temporarily purified. Hence, its purification must be an ongoing process. It must be the result of the joint effort of the man training and disciplining his mind and the Holy Spirit enabling him to overcome the combined powers of Satan, the host of demons under his control, and the man's own sinful nature. The heart is made new by the Most High. The mind must be controlled by the will of the man through the power of the Holy Spirit."

Marshall contemplated for a long while. *So then it really was just that simple. The only thing keeping men and women from living a sinless life like Jesus did is their failure to control their own minds. They do not lack the power or the ability to do it; rather, they lack the discipline and the desire to do it. Their heart might desire to please God and make right choices, but they fall short of overcoming the desire of their mind to fulfill its own selfish desires, which are nearly always contrary to the choice of obedience to God.*

Yes, that was it, Marshall thought. *No matter how you slice it or what color you paint it or how you look at it or how many metaphors you use to attempt to describe it, the bottom line is that it really is just that simple. You either choose to obey or you don't. No matter how many things get in the way or how strong the influences are one way or the other or what kind of anticipated repercussions or consequences might result from either decision, it all comes down to that one thing: controlling one's own mind and choosing above all else to walk in obedience to the word of God.*

Gudan's look interrupted Marshall's thoughts. He repeated his conclusion aloud. Gudan nodded with satisfaction at Marshall's understanding. "Yes, Marshall," he agreed. "It is very simple indeed. In fact, nothing could be simpler. Yet," he added dolefully, "for mankind, it appears at the same time as though nothing could be more difficult."

They stood in contemplative silence for a long moment, neither feeling the need to speak. Eventually, however, Gudan's voice broke the silence.

"So then," he asked, not facing Marshall, but rather looking out over the training camp still in view on the other side of the barrier, "how does one defend against it? How does one defeat the true enemy—the enemy of selfish desire? How does one win the battle for the mind? You see, Marshall, even though the human mind is an unbelievably strong force, there is a force that is much stronger working right alongside the human mind—Satan and all the powers of the kingdom of darkness at his command. Not only must the selfish desires of the human mind be overcome and defeated, but the external influence of the powers of darkness on that human mind must also be overcome and defeated."

In keeping with the spirit of the journey, Marshall offered the only reasonable answer.

"Just like Jesus did," he concluded.

"Just like the Messiah did," Gudan agreed with a nod. "And just like the Messiah said," he added. "Recall these words of the Messiah from your Bible," Gudan said, nodding toward the expanse where the words would appear.

> When an evil spirit comes out of a man, it goes through arid places seeking rest and does not find it. Then it says, 'I will return to the house I left.' When it arrives, it finds the house swept clean and put in order. Then it goes and takes seven other spirits more wicked than itself, and they go in and live there. And the final condition of that man is worse than the first.
>
> Luke 11:24–26 (NIV)

Marshall nodded his head in understanding. "It is not enough merely to eradicate the negative influence in one's mind. The empty space must then be filled with something. In this story, Jesus indicated that if the man rids himself of the influence of the evil spirits alone and does not then take the next necessary step and fill the space with the positive influence of the Holy Spirit and the Holy Scriptures, the evil spirits will just come back in force and make the man much worse off than he had ever been."

"That is correct, Marshall. And that is why the Messiah was able to subsequently defeat Satan during his temptation. Evil was never given a place in his mind for one thing, but just as important to mankind is the fact that his mind was filled with the knowledge of the Most High and of the Holy Scriptures. This knowledge was the weapon he used to completely and utterly defeat Satan during his temptation. The Messiah never said, 'We don't do that' or 'That is not a good idea' or 'People wouldn't understand' or even 'It's against my religion' or any such weak, ineffective argument. No, in each case of his temptation—which, allow me to remind you, was much more extensive than what is recorded in your Bible—the Messiah defended himself and overcame the temptation by quoting straight from the word of the

Most High. His mind was filled with the wisdom and knowledge of the Most High. His arsenal was completely full, and thus he soundly defeated the enemy at every turn. He didn't rely on his own standards or his own reasoning—which, as the Son of God, would have been sufficient at the very least—but rather, he relied completely on the wisdom and knowledge of his father, the Most High. He filled his mind with the wisdom and knowledge of the Most High, and he let that wisdom and knowledge manifest itself as power to completely defeat the enemy."

"But Jesus didn't have a sinful mind!" Marshall objected. "It isn't the same!"

Gudan smiled. "Good, Marshall. Very good. But this is the difference that makes it the same." Gudan pointed a finger as he spoke, resembling a professor about to reveal the secrets of a chemical chain reaction that had mystified his students for weeks. "The Messiah wasn't the only one who had a perfect, sinless mind. Lucifer did too at his creation. Mankind is the only one born with a sinful nature. In fact, the Messiah could have given up his perfection just like Satan, and later mankind, had done. He could have succumbed to Satan's influence and betrayed the Most High in the same manner and for the same reasons. But he didn't. He chose rather to be faithful to the Most High and to keep his mind always filled with the wisdom and knowledge of the Most High. Living in the fallen world, the Messiah was subject to the desire to give up and give in just like the rest of humanity. He overcame it, however, by keeping his mind focused on the Most High. He did not lose sight of the goal but kept it always before him. He did not entertain thoughts contrary to what he knew to be the will of the Most High. His house was swept clean, just like in the story he told, but instead of merely keeping it free of the influence of the devil, he went a step further and kept it filled with the power of the Holy Spirit. Therefore, he did not have to feel the full force of every blow of the enemy. His own mind acted as a shield against the attacks of the enemy. The truth he filled his mind with made the taunts of the enemy ridiculous and impotent. The righteousness of his mind made the suggestions of inadequacy and insufficiency from the enemy laughable and easily defended against. His inherent standing of holiness—which in the case of humanity would be an acquired, rather than inherent, standing of holiness and would thus be referred to as salvation—before the Most High as a result of keeping his mind filled with the fullness of the wisdom and knowledge of the Most High made Satan's attacks against his worth, value, and ability meaningless and ineffective. Inasmuch as the truth of the word of the Most High is foolishness to those who do not know him, so also the attacks of Satan are just as mush foolishness to those who do know him. Consider the words of the apostle Paul in his letter to the Corinthians: 'For the message of the cross is foolishness to those who are perishing, but to us who are being saved it is the power of God' (1 Corinthians 1:18).

"Marshall, the attacks of Satan should sound so ridiculous to people that they are immediately rejected and utterly disregarded. But they are not because of the sinfulness of the human mind. The attacks of Satan merely stoke to flame the smoldering coals of sinful desire always present in the mind of sinful man."

Gudan paused. "Marshall, are you hearing anything familiar in my words? What is it that I am getting at?"

Marshall nodded with a wry smile. "The armor," he answered.

"The armor," Gudan confirmed with a satisfied smile. "You have seen how to use it as a soldier in battle, and you have seen why you use it with respect to the powers at work in the spiritual realm."

Gudan placed his hand on Marshall's arm. "Next, the two will be brought together. You will see how you, in the human realm, can use your weapons of warfare in the spiritual realm to defeat your enemy and remain victorious."

Together, they ascended into the vast nothingness, leaving the training camp far behind them.

Chapter Twelve

What Marshall saw next was the closest thing he had ever been able to imagine for how God himself must see the earth and those who live upon it even though he knew its presence was for his benefit alone. To the best of his mind's ability to comprehend and describe it, he thought it was like a video comic book; there was a bank of thousands upon thousands of television screens, arranged top to bottom, left to right, each carrying live feed of some time, place, person, or event occurring on the other side of the barrier. The arrangement of the screens was chronological with respect to the events taking place within them.

As Marshall looked from screen to screen, he slowly began to understand what they were and how they worked. The ones he was being permitted to see were all the life of one person. Although they were happening live and in real time to the people in the scenes, Marshall could see them all at the same time. He could look up and to his left to see the baby being rocked and fed as an infant; in the middle of the bank, he could see who the boy's friends were at school and how they played on the playground; down and to his right, many, many screens later, he could see who he chose to marry, how many kids he had, and eventually how he died and where he was buried. The man's entire life, from birth to death and every single moment in between, was displayed simultaneously on that bank of screens. Marshall watched in amazement as he was allowed to, by the simple touch of his finger, bring to the forefront any specific scene he wished to see in close-up detail while the others remained in the background in a sort of picture-in-picture arrangement. With another touch to the screen, that scene was returned to its original position, and the full bank was restored. It was like a three-dimensional, touch-screen menu selector, allowing the viewer access to a video log of the entire life of every human being on the face of the earth.

Marshall's incredulous eyes were riveted to the huge bank of screens. Gudan reached up and began working his fingers across the menu screen, bringing up scene after scene for Marshall to view. Scene after scene, life after life, battle after battle, Marshall observed the varying degrees to which the subjects used, ignored, or were completely oblivious of their spiritual armor and weapons.

→ ✣ ←

Steve shouted into the air, "No! I have been forgiven for that! First John 1:9 tells me that if I confess my sin, he is faithful and just and will forgive me my sin and cleanse me from all unrighteousness!" As Marshall watched the scene unfolding before him, Gudan touched the screen, allowing Marshall to see not only the events as they happened in the natural realm but also those occurring simultaneously in the spiritual realm. In the natural realm, he saw Steve standing alone in a kitchen, talking to the empty room as though arguing with someone who wasn't there. In the spiritual realm, however, he saw Steve in full battle dress, having put on the full armor of God, standing, sword in hand, poised and ready for battle.

And in the spiritual realm, Steve was not alone. He faced off with a demon, also armed and ready for battle.

As Steve quoted the truth of God's word, his belt—the belt of truth—began to glow. Then his sword—the sword of the Spirit, which is the word of God—began to glow.

The demon growled in fury as he leapt at Steve, swinging his sword of lies and guilt from above his own head to deliver a crushing blow on the top of Steve's. "No!" he shouted. "You are wicked! You are sinful! You are a bad person! You could never be forgiven for something that terrible! You made her kill her own baby! You killed your own baby!"

In the kitchen, Steve, sensing intense feelings of guilt building up in his heart, making his chest tighten turned sharply to his left as if expecting to see someone there. He pointed his finger in the air and again shouted, "No. You lie! I have been forgiven. Romans 8:1 tells me that there is now no condemnation for those who are in Christ Jesus! I reject these feelings of guilt and condemnation by the authority of Jesus! I have been set free from sin, and according to John 8:36, I am free indeed!"

Instantly, Steve's helmet—the helmet of salvation—began to glow with an intensity that not only stopped the demon cold but knocked him backward and sent him rolling head over heels until he finally came to rest at the other end of the room. He jumped to his feet, seething with rage, shouting curses at Steve. Then he sheathed his sword and vanished in a puff of yellow smoke.

→ ✣ ←

Janet didn't bother wiping the tears from her face. Her makeup would have been virtually gone, the washing with tears so thorough, had she even bothered applying it in the first place. "I don't deserve to live," she muttered, so deep in the depths of despair that her voice failed even to register emotion at all.
Behind her, the demon chanted: "Murderer! Murderer! You killed your own daughter! Baby killer. You don't deserve to live. Baby killer! You don't deserve to live!"

The demon grinned an evil grin as he listened to Janet say, "I don't deserve to live. I killed her. I killed my own baby. I am a murderer." A new deluge of tears followed.

The single tear that Marshall wiped from his own eye upon hearing and empathizing with Janet's pain also became a deluge when his view of the scene was altered to include the spiritual realm. His heart broke for Janet as he saw her stagger and fall to her knees. She was wearing the short robe of the Roman soldier, but she had no armor. She had no weapon, no shield. She did not even have the helmet of salvation or the sure-footed stability of the gospel of peace. She was weak, pathetic, defenseless. The demon attacking her thrust and slashed and stabbed, beating her down with the flat of his blade, crushing her, destroying her. It was all Marshall could do not to scream at her—run to her—make her understand that she has the authority to defeat her attacker! She does not need to be crushed under the weight of her own sin! There is forgiveness! There is freedom!

But without the helmet of salvation,
Without the sure-footedness of the gospel of peace,
Without the shield of faith,
Without the breastplate of righteousness,
Without the belt of truth,
Without the sword of the spirit,
There is no hope.

There is nothing but despair, nothing but grief, guilt, condemnation. There is no defense against the attacks of the enemy.

⇾ ✣ ⇽

Rachel sat alone in the hallway between what used to be their master bedroom and what used to be their family room. She had just been lying on her son's bed quietly crying to herself.

Marshall jolted as the spiritual realm came into focus, and he saw the complement of demons posted in and around her house.

Rachel stood and walked into Sarah's room. She knelt beside her bed and tried to pray, but the words seemed to bounce back at her from the ceiling of Sarah's room, unheard by anyone but herself. She asked God to protect them both while they were with their father and to let them know the truth even while spending time in the deception that had become their father's life. Rachel tried to have faith. She tried to believe. She tried to trust. But she felt so alone. Where was God? Why didn't he hear her anymore?

Marshall felt his throat constrict as though he had attempted to swallow too big of a bite of food and could not get it to go down the rest of the way. He tried swallowing again out of instinct. While the physical reaction may have produced a slight excretion from his tear ducts, and the subsequent emotional response may have further triggered a flow of tears, it was the spiritually discerned comprehension of the whole situation that caused the large tears to begin flowing from his eyes and rolling down his cheeks.

With slightly blurred vision, Marshall looked past Rachel to the far side of the room. There, propped up against the wall in the corner, stood a magnificently bejeweled shield. Draped across one corner of it was a worn leather belt, its sheath containing an equally magnificent double-edged short sword. The armor and weaponry were rusted and dusty from a combination of age and lack of use.

As Marshall looked again at Rachel, he noticed her tattered tunic. Her shoes were on but unfastened, the long leather laces lying loosely on the ground. Her breastplate hung limply off to one side; her helmet dented, cracked, and pushed haphazard to the back of her head, seemingly forgotten. The demons surrounded her in a tight circle, chanting and jabbing their swords at her like a group of young boys tormenting a wounded bird. Their chanting was so loud that Rachel could hardly hear anything else; it came across to her as deep, intense silence. She tried to pray and to listen for God's voice, but there was only the deep, intense silence.

"God, I know you are there, but where are you? Why can't I hear you anymore? Why have you left me?"

"God can't hear you, Rachel!" the demons jeered. "He can't hear you because of what you have done! You are no longer fit for service. He can't use you now! You are worthless! Useless! God could never use someone like you—someone who would do what you have done! All those prophecies people said about you? You have ruined them! You have slapped God in the face by your actions, and he does not want you anymore! He could never want you! You are a failure, and you will never be able to do anything for God! You are not good enough! You are not good enough!"

Rachel's body shook with the force of her weeping. "But all I have ever wanted was to serve God!" she screamed to the empty room, beating her fists into the mattress. "I have tried so hard to live my life for him! Yes, I messed up, but there has to be something left for me! This can't be the end. It can't all be over." She buried her face into the mattress as the sobs again overtook her.

"No!" the demons yelled in unison. "It *is* over! You have ruined it! You will never be good enough to serve God again! God could never forgive you or trust you to serve him again! You will never be good enough to serve him again!" The demons positively convulsed with laughter as they watched the woman drowning in the bottomless pool of her own grief and emptiness, accepting their lies as truth more and more, and slowly, helplessly, giving up hope.

Marshall was crawling out of his skin. Their taunting was more than he could stand. He had not even noticed, but his body had gone rigid. His hands were sweating. As he watched Rachel sink deeper into the depths of despair where even the mere idea of hope is an unattainable puff of smoke, he began to groan in empathy. His heart literally broke for this poor, wounded child of God who was falling so hopelessly for the lies of the enemy. Finally, he could take no more. With his voice raspy and his words choked by the emotion overcoming him, he rushed at her with all his strength, screaming at the demons, pleading with her not to listen to them and not to give up.

Although the scene before them was being watched on what appeared to be a normal-sized TV screen in the middle of a bank of similar screens, as Gudan stepped aside, that particular screen resized and became part of the barrier itself. As Marshall lunged forward with his arms outstretched, pleading with Rachel to stand firm and cling to her faith, he felt himself drop through the barrier. He fell headlong on the floor at Rachel's feet.

Righting himself quickly, he knelt beside Rachel and attempted to comfort her and pray for her. He began quoting Bible verses to her, but when he reached his hand up to place it on her shoulder, it passed right through her body as though she were a hologram. It was then that he realized that she had not seemed to even notice him at all. She had not responded in any way to his arrival. He yanked his hand back as if it had landed on a hot pan just taken out of the oven. He leapt to his feet a couple of steps behind Rachel, looking quizzically at Gudan.

"You can't help her, Marshall." Gudan stated. "Remember? You will not be able to influence or participate in what you see during this journey in any way. No being in either dimension can see you, hear you, or even sense that you are here."

Marshall sighed heavily, coming back to himself. "Yes, I remember. I am sorry, Gudan. I just became overwhelmed with sorrow for that girl, and I forgot myself."

"Let us return, Marshall," Gudan suggested.

Gudan led Marshall back through the barrier, stopping in front of the bank of screens.

Ava walked to her locker at the end of the crowded hallway. She felt alone. In a sea of people, she felt alone. Between classes, the hallway was so full that she couldn't even walk along it without bumping into other kids. And still, she felt alone. Lonely.

"Nobody here cares about you, Ava. Nobody loves you. You don't even matter. If you died tonight and never came back here, you wouldn't even be missed. There is really no point. Your life is insignificant."

Even as the wave of loneliness came over her, Ava's eyes squinted in defiance. *Why am I feeling this way?* she asked herself. *I feel so alone, but I am not alone—I have lots of friends! But still, I feel alone. It doesn't even make sense! It just—*And then it hit her. It didn't make sense because it was a lie! It was an attack of the enemy against what her spirit knew to be true.

"That is not true!" she whispered to herself. "Jesus loves me. I am significant to *him*! I may not be the most popular girl in this school, but that does not determine my identity or my value! I am a child of God, and that is what really matters."

As she spoke, her shield and belt began to glow. The demon fired back at her.

"That's just a cop-out. A cliché. A bumper sticker. 'Smile, God loves you!' But so what? What is that doing for you? Is that getting you invited to parties? Asked out on dates? Is that getting you friends? You are a nobody. You don't contribute. You are not important."

"You are a liar!" Ava said aloud as she pulled open her locker door. Then she smiled as she looked at the paper she had taped to the inside of her locker door. It was a list of Bible verses under the caption "Who I Am in Christ." As the smile covered her face, the sword in her hand began to glow with an intensity that caused the demon to shudder. Her helmet of salvation glowed brightly, matching the brilliance of her shield and belt. As she began to speak, a fiery bolt of lightening shot out of the tip of her sword toward the demon, knocking him backward. As he staggered back toward her in pain, barely able to clutch his sword, he stopped cold when he saw Ava's face.

Ava began to grin. She stepped closer to the demon, her shoes and helmet now glowing with a brilliance rivaled only by her sword and shield.

"You know, you are right," she smiled, nodding her head up and down as she stepped still closer to the demon. "I am insignificant. In fact, I am dead. According to Galatians 2:20, I don't even live, but Christ lives in me!"

"Shut up! Shut up!" The terrified demon shrieked. He was losing this battle. The truth was overtaking him. He clapped his hands to his ears to shut out the sound of Ava's voice. "No! You are nothing! God doesn't love you! It's just a fantasy—something made up by weak people who can't face their lives on their own! You are just too weak to stand on your own! You are nothing!"

"Enough!" Ava commanded. "I don't have to be strong. In fact, Christ's strength is made perfect in my weakness—2 Corinthians 12:9. I stand with Paul, who said that he will boast all the more gladly about his weaknesses so that the power of Christ may rest upon him. In fact, he goes on to say that for Christ's sake, he will delight in weaknesses, insults, hardships, persecutions, and difficulties because when he is weak, then he is strong through Christ!"

The demon shuddered and staggered backward as Ava slashed with her sword, crushing him blow after blow and forcing him backward even farther.

She pointed to the words printed on the paper as she read aloud, "I have been crucified with Christ and I no longer live, but Christ lives in me. The life I live in the body, I live by faith in the Son of God, who loved me and gave himself for me. Galatians 2:20. And even if that were not the case, Ephesians 2:10 says that I am God's workmanship, created in Christ Jesus to do good works which God prepared in advance for me to do! And in Colossians 3:12, it says that I am chosen by God, holy and dearly loved! That is the truth, and I do not accept your lies! Depart from me by the authority of the blood of Jesus, the Christ!"

With a final deadly swipe of her sword, Ava set the demon to flight. As the peace and security of having a personal relationship with her father God washed over her, she quietly bowed her head and thanked him for loving her and for giving her strength to stand up against the enemy.

Gudan turned to face Marshall, allowing the bank of screens to fade into the background. "Observations?" he prompted.

Marshall paused, knowing that this particular question held more substance than a mere inquiry into his impression of the scenes he had just witnessed. Gudan was looking for an analysis, a deeper understanding than what a quick glance or brief viewing would produce.

Marshall replayed each scene in his mind, attempting to look beyond the surface to grasp the big picture of what was happening. Knowing that Gudan would ask him to repeat his thoughts aloud anyway, he simply opted to work through his answer aloud while Gudan listened on. He began with Steve.

"Steve appears to be a veteran Christian soldier. His armor and weaponry is in good repair and in good working order. He wears it properly and uses it effectively as though seasoned through frequent use. He knows his position and his authority. He understands his role. He does not doubt the word of God, and he uses it authoritatively. He is very effective in battle.

"Janet is a kitten released into the wild. Defenseless and weak, she has no way of standing up against or warding off an attack from an enemy.

"Rachel is a fallen soldier. She is severely wounded. She could recover and live to fight again, but she is fading fast. She knows the truth in her heart, but she is alone, and the enemy's ruthless attack is destroying her faith and blinding her to the truth.

"Ava is young, but strong and effective. She quickly recognizes the attack of the enemy and quickly employs her weapons to defend against it. She stands firm on the truth of God's Word and resists the devil's lies."

Marshall paused, thinking. "But th—" he began, then hesitated. Considering how to formulate his question, he reluctantly continued. "I...I guess it just seems too easy. Or like something is missing—like we're watching the stripped-down-for-TV version of a full-feature movie or reading the abridged version of a full-length novel instead of the entirety of the text. I'm sorry, but there just isn't enough there. Am I missing some critical part of those scenes? Unless I am just missing something, it seems incomplete. What is it that makes the difference between them? One person fights valiantly and effectively while another is swiftly defeated. Both hear the same taunts from the enemy, and while one rises above it and sends the enemy fleeing, another buckles under its weight and is crushed. What is the difference? There has to be something more going on that I am not seeing."

Gudan smiled with satisfaction.

"Well done, Marshall. Very well done," he said. "So if, as you surmise, some part was missing, then which parts were you able to see? We will get to what was missing in a moment. First, let us discuss what was present."

Marshall again thought for a moment, trying to determine exactly what answer Gudan might be looking for. He forced himself to look at it from the standpoint of a military strategist, thinking back to Gudan's example of assassinating an enemy king.

"Well, Steve and Ava and the others would be the king upon whom the assassination attempt is being made, and the demons attacking them would be the infiltrators," Marshall concluded.

Gudan raised an eyebrow. "Go deeper," he suggested. "Don't look at it from a human point of view. Think bigger."

Marshall thought for a moment but still could not follow the path Gudan was pointing toward.

"Merely saying 'Steve' is too broad. Remember, Steve is a triune being," Gudan prompted.

"Ah," Marshall exhaled, nodding his head up and down. "Right—body, soul, and spirit."

"Or," Gudan offered, "in reference to our recent conversation about the true enemy—body, heart, and mind."

Marshall, still unsure, again nodded his head and attempted to take his thoughts down the course Gudan had indicated.

"Okay, we have a body, a heart, and a mind. But which is which? Because we also have an infiltrator, a king, and an inside man."

Marshall began to pace, working out his thoughts in his mind and speaking them aloud. "Okay, we have already determined that the mind is the inside man, and obviously the demons are the infiltrators. That leaves heart and body. So if the heart is the king, then—but wait—then who is fighting the demons? It can't be the body because the body is in the physical realm and therefore can't be a player in the spiritual realm. So then if the heart is the king, then who is fighting the demons? Well, since it can't be the body, but there is fighting going on, then it has to be the...no, I am missing one. There aren't enough players. Okay, start over. Mind and infiltrators are set. No possibility for change there. So who is the soldier fighting the demons? If it isn't the body or the mind, then it has to be the heart. Yes, that makes sense. The unsaved heart, like Janet's, has no armor or weaponry with which to put up any fight at all against the attacks of the demons. The saved heart, like Steve's, is fitted with and can use the Ephesians 6 armor and weaponry. Yes, and it is the heart that is created anew at the point of salvation. Then who is the king?"

"The man as a whole, Marshall. That is the king," Gudan prompted.

"Yes! Of course!" Marshall shouted, the concept coming together in his head. "The entire being is the king who the enemy is trying to assassinate. The physical body itself is irrelevant to this discussion because the man is a spiritual being and the physical aspect of his existence is merely temporary and therefore not pertinent to the battle. The infiltrator is the member or members of the kingdom of darkness assigned to that particular man. The soldier defending the king is the heart, which is empowered and imbued with authority by the death and resurrection of Jesus. King, infiltrator, defensive soldier. And the last one, the inside man, is the man's own mind."

"Exactly, Marshall," Gudan confirmed. "So then which one was missing from the scenes we viewed?"

Marshall only thought for a moment before answering. "The inside man. We didn't see the part the people's mind played."

Gudan nodded. "That is correct, Marshall. You're feeling that something was missing as we viewed the scenes the first time was accurate. We only saw the demon/infiltrator attacking and the heart/soldier defending. This time, as we view them again, we will also be able to see the contribution of the person's mind, the inside man.

Gudan turned to stand beside Marshall as the bank of screens again displayed the scene of Steve standing alone in his kitchen.

Steve (king) stood alone in his kitchen. The demon (infiltrator) appeared and began hurling lies at him, thrusting and jabbing at him with his sword. Steve's heart (defensive soldier), in full battle dress, assumed a fighting posture and began deflecting the blows of his attacker. The demon was stronger than Steve's heart and was easily overpowering him. The lies he threw at Steve's heart caused him to take pause, to doubt himself, to consider the words of the demon as potentially valid.

Suddenly, Steve's mind (inside man) recognized the attack of the demon and engaged in the battle. He acted as a power source for Steve's heart, infusing him with strength and bringing his weapons to life. As Steve's mind shouted out the truth of God's word, his heart's belt began to glow. Then his sword began to glow as well.

The demon chopped and jabbed and swiped at Steve's heart, spewing forth lies meant to confuse and disarm him. But Steve's mind was quick and sharp and well trained. Every time the demon uttered a word, Steve's mind recognized it as being in violation of God's word and refuted it with the truth of the Scriptures. This infusing of Steve's heart with the power of God's word gave the heart unlimited power, allowing him to easily defeat the demon and claim victory in the battle.

Janet fell to her knees. The demon hurled lies at her, attacking her worth and value and denying the power of God's forgiveness. Janet's heart fell to her knees, defenseless. She tried to block the swipes of the enemy's sword, but it cut deep into her arms and hands. Occasionally she tried to swing at him, but she had no strength, and her fists passed through the air in front of him, serving only to make him laugh and fueling the fire of his ruthless attack against her. Janet's mind, slow, dull, and completely untrained for battle, accepted the lies of the enemy. Janet succumbed to capture and destruction at the hands of a powerless, weak enemy because her heart did not know the forgiveness of God, and her mind did not know the power of God. She was completely unfit for battle and was soundly defeated at the hands of a weak enemy whose only weapon was deceit.

Rachel's heart was broken. The demons attacked her relentlessly, feeding her lies about herself, about God, about his lack of willingness to forgive and restore. She tried to defend herself against them, but she had very little strength. She was knocked down repeatedly. Still having enough will to at least get up, she refused to completely yield and give up the fight.

Rachel's mind heard the taunts of the demons. She was confused. She knew that God loved her and would forgive, but she was uncertain. "But God said he would always be there!" her mind shouted. "God forgives people who make mistakes!"

One jewel on the dusty shield flickered. Quickly, several demons dashed in front of it to block it from her sight. They countered her confession of truth with more lies. "God can't hear you, Rachel! You are no longer fit for service. God could never forgive you or trust you to serve him again!"

Rachel's untrained mind did not argue. She fell to the floor in front of the bed and cried, knowing somewhere deep in her spirit that there must be more, must be a way out, but she was too weak and defeated to find it.

Ava walked to her locker at the end of the crowded hallway. She felt alone. The demon drew his sword and slashed at her. "Nobody here cares about you, Ava. You don't even matter. Your life is insignificant."

Instantly, Ava's mind, quick and strong, sensed that something was wrong. There was a renegade thought about that just didn't seem right. She sounded the alarm, rousting her heart into position, poised and ready for battle.

Why am I feeling this way? Ava asked herself. *I feel so alone, but I am not alone. It doesn't even make sense!*

Her mind latched onto the attack of the enemy. "That is not true!" Her mind shouted at the demon. "Jesus loves me! I am significant to him!"

"That's just a cop-out. A cliché. You are a nobody. You don't contribute. You are not important."

"You are a liar!" Ava's mind shouted. As the word of God came to her mind, Ava began to grin. Ava's heart stepped closer to the demon, her shoes and helmet now glowing with a brilliance rivaled only by her sword and shield.

As her mind poured verses from the word of God into her consciousness, Ava's heart smiled, slowly nodding her head up and down as she stepped still closer to the demon. "You know, you are right. I am insignificant. In fact, I am dead. According to Galatians 2:20, I don't even live, but Christ lives in me!" Ava's heart wielded her sword, slashing, clanging, cutting deep into the demon's flesh.

"Shut up! Shut up!" The terrified demon shrieked. "No! you are nothing! God doesn't love you! It's just a fantasy—something made up by weak people who can't face their lives on their own! You are just too weak to stand on your own!"

Ava's mind quoted 2 Corinthians 12:9. "But he said to me, 'My grace is sufficient for you, for my power is made perfect in weakness.' Therefore, I will boast all the more about my weaknesses, so that Christ's power may rest upon me."

"Enough!" Ava's heart commanded, further strengthened by the word of God. "I don't have to be strong. In fact, Christ's strength is made perfect in my weakness. 2 Corinthians 12:9."

Ava's heart continued walking toward the demon, slashing and chopping with her sword, relentlessly driving the demon further back, weakening him with every blow.

"Stop it! That is not true!" The terrified demon shouted in desperation, trying to lift his sword to strike.

Ava's mind quoted 2 Corinthians 12:10, "That is why for Christ's sake, I delight in weaknesses, in insults, in hardships, in persecutions, in difficulties. For when I am weak, then I am strong."

Ava's heart continued, still purposefully marching toward the demon. "I stand with Paul, who said that he will boast all the more gladly about his weaknesses so that the power of Christ may rest upon him. In fact, he goes on to say that for Christ's sake, he will delight in weaknesses, insults, hardships, persecutions, and difficulties because when he is weak, then he is strong through Christ. When I am weak, then I am also strong through Christ!"

The demon shuddered and staggered backward as Ava's heart slashed with her sword, crushing him blow after blow and forcing him backward even farther.

Ava's mind pointed to the words printed on the paper as she read the next three verses aloud.

"That is the truth, and I do not accept your lies!" she stated with stern finality. "Depart from me by the authority of the blood of Jesus, the Christ!"

With a final deadly swipe of her sword, Ava's heart set the demon to flight.

Marshall stood still, silently processing the scenes again after the role of the mind had been added.

"What role did the mind play, Marshall?" Gudan asked.

"The pivotal role," Marshall answered. He recalled their discussion about the heart being re-created new and pure and sinless while the mind is only cleansed.

"The heart draws its power from the mind. The mind, being the inside man, can either work for or against the heart. If the mind is controlled by the Spirit, it will entertain only those thoughts or ideas or influences that come from and fall in line with the truth of the word of God. On the other hand, if the mind is not controlled by the Spirit—the mind of a sinful man—anything and everything that is contrary to the word of God will be freely given access and will be allowed to take up residence in the heart. The heart can be created anew, but the mind can still choke out the influence of the word of God and render the heart, therefore the person, ungodly and ineffective for the kingdom."

"You have learned well, Marshall," Gudan complemented. "But the two variations of the scenes you have observed so far dealt with only one aspect of the battle—that of a direct attack from an external enemy. Next, you will see something completely different. You were correct in stating that the mind plays the pivotal role. Remember when we concluded that the inside man was the most powerful and vital of them all because of his proximity to the king? He could choose at any time either to betray his king at the behest of the enemy and bring about the king's downfall or remain faithful to the king and assist in the destruction of the enemy. The victor, then, is essentially determined by which side is successful at winning the allegiance of the inside man, at winning the allegiance of the mind.

"Bearing that in mind, then, consider this," Gudan continued. "What if the attack is more subtle than a full frontal assault? Remember, Marshall, Satan is shrewd, cunning, and extremely wise. He is a master strategist with virtually limitless intelligence and reconnaissance. Often he does not even have to launch an offensive against someone to cause them to fall. He can merely lie in wait until the sinful mind of the man himself opens the door to his influence. And to take it the final step, many times Satan doesn't even need to intervene at all to get the man to fall into sin. It is as the apostle Paul said in his letter to the Romans: 'The sinful mind is hostile to God. It does not submit to God's law, nor can it do so. Those controlled by the sinful nature cannot please God' (Romans 8:7–8).

"Make no mistake, Marshall. The influence of Satan is crippling and deadly to the heart of a man, but even more crippling and deadly to any man is the influence of his own sinful mind."

Gudan turned back toward the bank of screens as a new scene came into view.

"That's awesome, bro!" Jerald said into the phone as he pushed himself away from his desk, stood up stiffly, and walked toward the break room. He plugged one end of his headset into the jack on his phone, hooked the other end over his ear, and dropped his cell phone into his jacket pocket. The coffee was old and stale, with that sheen of oil or something covering the surface that Jerald could never really identify and never really trusted. And how in the world could coffee—even fresh coffee—smell like an old barn? With a heavy sigh, he dumped the too-thick and too-dark black liquid into the sink and began the ritual of making a fresh pot while chatting with his brother on the phone. It was a typical afternoon at the law offices of Rufler, Clovis, and Kinderschwartz, of whom Jerald was merely a junior associate.

In the screen to the left of Jerald, Marshall could see Bryan, Jerald's older brother, walking around a spacious corner office with glass walls, contemporary furniture, and a view of the city in two directions. His phone lay on his desk, the blue light of his wireless headset blinking lazily on his ear.

"I know!" he nearly shouted at his younger brother on the other end of the line. "I've only been here two years, and already they are talking *partner*! It's crazy! Not that I didn't earn some kind of award or promotion for all the work I put into that *Bladwell v. Johanssen* case last year, but I never expected this!"

"I'm really happy for you, Bryan," Jerald said sincerely. "You've earned it. When do you hear the details?"

"First of the week. The partners are having their annual cookout at the senior partner's estate this weekend—business meeting on Friday night, mixed with a whole lot of pleasure for the rest of the weekend. They usually have an all-firm meeting on Monday morning where they make all the prudent announcements of promotions and policy changes and that sort of thing."

"That is so great, bro," Jerald said. "I can't wait to hear all the details! You'd better call me right away!"

"You know I will, Jer. Gotta go. Talk to you soon."

After returning the salutation, Jerald pulled the headset off his ear, dropping it and his phone onto his desk.

He completely forgot about the coffee.

After a few moments, he realized that he was pacing. He was in the office alone at the moment, so he continued his pacing and began muttering to himself.

"That is so unfair. I mean, I am really happy for Bryan, but what is the deal? Everything he touches turns to gold in his hand. Great for him, but what about me? When is it my turn? I am as smart as he is! I work as hard as he does! But things just have a way of not working out for me. We got about the same grades in high school, both graduated from the University of Alabama with a law degree, and had basically the identical resume for our job search. But I am still stuck here in this second-rate firm after five years, not even being considered for senior associate! And here Bryan is, three years in a firm like this one, then snatched up by Colburn, Snayhousen, Binkley, Pottersham, Borschyme, and Sneyd, one of the most prestigious firms in the greater San Francisco area! And if that's not enough, now *partner*!"

Suddenly, Jerald stopped walking, frozen in place as if someone had zapped him with some kind of futuristic ray gun. He shook his head from side to side, hearing his own words but uncertain whether he had heard them correctly.

"What am I doing?" he gasped. "What am I saying? He is my *brother*! I can't believe I am actually feeling *envious* of my own brother! That is unacceptable!"

Jerald planted his feet and took an aggressive posture as though defending himself against a physical attacker.

Aloud, he shouted to the empty room. "Feelings of envy, I reject you. I am a child of the Most High God, ransomed from sin by the blood of Jesus on the cross, and I do not accept the influence of such terrible thoughts."

Marshall watched as Jerald's heart, now poised and in full battle dress, chopped and sliced with his sword. All his armor was glowing brightly, his movements polished and smooth.

"He is my brother, and I love him, and I am very happy for his success. My life is my own, and I will live it as God wills. I refuse to entertain thoughts of envy or jealousy or anything else that implies that God is incapable of running my life properly. By the authority of the blood of Jesus and in accordance with 2 Corinthians 10:5, I take that evil thought captive, and I make it obedient to Christ, which in this case means complete eradication from my mind. Such thoughts are contrary to the character of God and are therefore contrary to my character, and I refuse to entertain them!"

Jerald stood still, his hands falling to his sides, allowing peace to wash over him.

"Thank you, Father," he said peacefully. "Thank you for giving me the wisdom to recognize those evil thoughts for what they were, and thank you for the authority to banish them from my mind. And God, may you bless Bryan a hundred times over. Thank you for his promotion, and I pray that he will be able to use his new position to bring glory and honor to your name.

Praise you for your presence and for your work in his life and in mine. Amen."

His heart sheathed his sword, also bowing and praising God for another victory.

Scott looked out the driver's window of his dad's Buick at the clear, star-filled sky. The moon was so big and so bright, he could have sworn it had been put there just for him, just for Amber, just for tonight. It was as if somebody had planned the entire evening, and everything was falling into place like a well-rehearsed acting troupe following a familiar script. For her part, Amber had never looked better. It had been a fantastic night, and it looked like it was about to get a whole lot better.

Look at her, man! Holy moly, look at her! She is so hot! And tonight, she is all about you! Tonight is your night, dude. It is your night! All that—he looked over and feasted his eyes again on her beauty—*is going to be all yours!*

Somewhere deep in his heart, he felt the slightest twinge of guilt. They had just come from a youth function at the church, and here he was, about to leap headlong into sin with Amber. *But look at her*, his mind screamed. *She is so amazing, and she actually wants to be with me! How many times have we done this in my mind? And now, here it is, ripe for the picking, right in front of my face! Amber. Holey moly, Amber Stinson!*

The twinge of guilt in his heart didn't have a chance; it was so overshadowed by the desire for Amber in his mind. All around the Buick, the demons laughed and whooped, pointing and shaking their heads. They knew they had him, and they hadn't had to do a thing! Scott's own teenage hormones and his weak—allegedly "Christian"—mind had done it all for them! Still, in the spirit of leaving nothing to chance, a couple of them perched on the dashboard and taunted Scott's mind.

"Come on, Scott! She's ready, man! And you know you want her too! Make your move before she changes her mind! Go for it, man! Can you even imagine the thrill? Go for it!"

That's it, I'm going for it, Scott's mind said. *She is amazing, and tonight, she is finally all mine!*

As Scott leaned over and kissed her, his heart fell to his knees in defeat, gasping and choking in the stranglehold of the sinful desire of Scott's mind.

Gudan turned to Marshall. "What significant difference did you notice about these two encounters?" he asked.

Marshall thought for a minute before answering. Finally, he realized that there had not been an attacker throughout the whole scene.

"There was no outside attacker! The enemy was the man's own mind—Jerald's own mind and Scott's own mind! Neither was influenced by the devil or even by one of his demons. It was nothing more than the thoughts of their own minds acting on their own."

"That's exactly right," Gudan agreed. "It was a day like any other day in the life of Jerald and in the life of Scott. There was no barrage of attacks from Satan and the forces of darkness, no cataclysmic event signifying an opportunity to choose good or evil. It was just another telephone call on just another day in the life of Jerald, just another drive home in the life of Scott. However, on this day, each was presented with an opportunity.

"The natural human tendency of the sinful human mind in Jared's situation would have been toward envy and jealousy as it was in the first few moments of the scene. And what would likely have happened had Jerald simply allowed that envy and jealousy to fester in his mind and heart? It would have gotten stronger. It would have grown into anger and self-pity. It may have had a negative effect on his attitude toward his employer and his coworkers. When he arrived home from work, he probably would have been grouchy and unpleasant to his wife and children. He would have had a negative demeanor. It could have even affected his relationship with his brother. The natural consequences of failing to 'take that thought captive and make it obedient to Christ' could have been disastrous to Jerald and his entire family. And in this case, it would not have been the result of a coordinated and well-planned assault by the enemy. It would have been the result of merely entertaining the sinful thoughts of the sinful human mind.

"The natural human tendency of the sinful human mind in Scott's situation would have been toward gratifying his sensual desires with total disregard to the cost and the ramifications of his actions. Becoming a sexually active teenager does extreme damage to the heart of both participants. Were we to view the future for both Scott and Amber, we would see that Scott, having conquered his prize, would lose all interest in Amber as anything other than an object to be used for his pleasure, which he did on several occasions. Amber gave up her innocence in a futile attempt to gain acceptance and self-worth, only to learn that she had sacrificed both in the process and gained only emptiness, rejection, and self-loathing. In this case, the natural consequences of failing to 'take that thought captive and make it obedient to Christ' was indeed disastrous to Amber and Scott. In this case as well, it was not the result of a coordinated and well-planned assault by the enemy. It was merely the result of entertaining the sinful thoughts of the sinful human mind.

"You see, Marshall, a person must be careful to give each enemy the attention he deserves. When the attack comes from a demonic source, the person must be prepared to either rebuke the demon or cast him out, but when the attack comes from the person's own mind, that person must then be prepared to disregard other potential sources, resist blame-shifting altogether, and have the courage to rebuke his own mind.

"Knowledge is power also in that once one is able to recognize and distinguish between different attackers, he will have the spiritual and mental acuity to ascertain how to most effectively combat and overcome the assailant, regardless of the source of the attack. Satan is a formidable adversary, but he often gets much more credit than he deserves. The pride of the average human being prevents his mind from considering that he, the human being himself, is his own worst enemy. He is quick to blame the devil for every bad thought he might have or for every bad thing he might do when often it is merely that person's own mind acting out its own sinful thoughts and desires all by itself without any external provocation at all."

Unwittingly, Marshall's immediate reaction and nearly verbalized response to Gudan's words provided not only a perfect proof of Gudan's explanation but also grounds for a sharp self-rebuke for Marshall. His very first thought had been to disregard that information with respect to himself but to quickly stipulate his acquiescence of that theory for the rest of humanity. Knowing that he didn't even need to say anything, he simply looked up at Gudan and nodded acknowledgement of what he sensed Gudan had already surmised.

"So what you are saying is that through the devil's accomplished use of deception and trickery, he allows the conclusion of man's search for a culprit in any given situation to pinpoint himself and his minions with their overt attempts to influence men in ways contrary to God, thereby allowing the true enemy—the man's own sinful mind—to remain in place as the covert driving force of rebellion against God," Marshall concluded.

"That is correct, Marshall," Gudan agreed. "And this shift of attention from the tacit influence of the human mind to the more explicit works of Satan and the kingdom of darkness allows that tacit influence to persist largely unchecked, thereby causing the human first to doubt his own ability and authority to resist Satan since his influence or presence never seems to be eradicated and second to doubt either the power of the Most High to overcome Satan or his willingness to do so."

"The result being a defeated, weak, ineffective Christian who doesn't even understand why he is defeated, weak, and ineffective," Marshall again concluded, "further solidifying his doubts about

God's willingness or ability to defeat Satan and rescue the man from his mediocrity, and this would naturally lead to the man losing faith in God's love for him and his supposed desire to give the man everlasting and abundant life and peace that passes understanding and to make him more than a conqueror, and so on."

Gudan's somber silence and slight nod both punctuated Marshall's conclusion and confirmed its validity.

"It is different than it was in the beginning," Gudan continued. In the garden of Eden, Adam and Eve had sinless minds. They wanted to please the Most High, and they were perfectly capable of doing so. That is why Satan had to first deceive and confuse them and then tempt them to disobey the Most High. As a consequence of their failure, the fall of man, as it is commonly called, every human child is born with original sin as his inheritance, complete with a mind that does not even want to please the Most High. In fact, as we learned earlier, it is not even capable of doing so without first being renewed by the Holy Spirit. And even then, although the heart can be regenerated and made holy, the mind can only be renewed by the Most High and subsequently controlled by the human. It cannot be made perfect this side of death."

Gudan nodded back to the screens. "Jerald has a heart that has been regenerated and a mind that is led by the Spirit of the Most High. That does not mean that any of the selfish thoughts will not attempt to creep in from time to time. It simply means that his mind will recognize them for what they are and will give his heart the power to take appropriate action against them."

"Think of it this way, Marshall. This morning when you arose, part of your morning ritual was to shave your facial hair, leaving a smooth, clean-shaven face. Not to proliferate a groundless stereotype, but for the sake of this illustration, let us say that the facial hair represents your sinful nature, and the face itself represents your mind. Every morning, you wake up to find that your face, left unattended for the night, has experienced a natural growth of facial hair upon it. In like manner, the mind left unattended will experience a natural infiltration of the sinful nature upon it. If left unattended, both the facial hair and the sinful nature will be allowed to follow their natural course of increasing both their presence and their influence. There is nothing wrong with you—the man—when your facial hair grows. It is simply the natural course of the follicles on your face. So also, there is nothing wrong with you when the sinful nature attempts to grow into your mind. It is simply the natural course of the mind of fallen man. The key is what you do about it.

"If, for example, you take a sharp razor and apply it to your face every morning, shaving the hair away, you will be left with a clean, smooth face for the better part of the rest of the day. And supposing you had a formal event to attend in the evening and desired a clean-shaven appearance, you might once again take the sharp razor and apply it to your face, once again removing the facial hair and leaving the clean, smooth appearance you desire.

"The same is true for the mind. If you take the razor-sharp word of the Most High and apply it to your mind every morning, you will be left with a clean, God-centered mind for the better part of the day. Further, as in the case of the facial hair that never ceases to grow, if you want to retain your clean, God-centered mind throughout the day and into the evening, you must continue to apply the razor-sharp word of the Most High as the day progresses.

"Take note that in both cases, the growth continues as long as you live. That is normal. But as a follower of the Most High, you have the power to overcome. That is why both King David in Psalm 51:10 and the apostle Paul in Romans 12:2 used the present progressive tense of the verb *renew* to imply the continued, repetitive action of renewing the mind. Every day you must shave your face to maintain a smooth, hairless appearance. Every day you must invite and allow the Holy Spirit to renew your mind to maintain a clean, God-centered mind. That is what it all comes down to, Marshall. It is just that simple."

Gudan waited for a moment, then looked up at the bank of screens. Marshall did likewise.

"One more thing I want you to understand from these scenes, Marshall," Gudan stated. "Look at all six again, and take note of how the battle was won, lost, or fought in each case, giving consideration to the different attackers present."

As the same six scenes again played across the screens, Marshall watched them intently. He took special note of each of the players, their actions, their words, their behavior, their demeanor. Steve, Janet, Rachel, Ava, Jared, Scott—just like before. Three overcame and were victorious; three failed and were virtually destroyed. Same words, same actions, same inaction. Same everything. Marshall shook his head as he realized that for all his intense study of the scenes, he did not notice anything different! How could he have missed it so completely? He was reviewing them again in his mind when he felt Gudan's penetrating stare. Marshall lifted his head and turned it hesitantly in Gudan's direction.

Gudan looked at him expectantly, not saying a word.

"I missed it, Gudan. I am sorry, but I completely missed it. I have been going over them in my mind, but I still can't see anything different in how the battle was fought—or not fought—regardless if the attacker was the devil and his minions or the person's own mind. There was attack and defense in some cases, attack and defeat in others. I—"

Gudan stopped him with an upraised hand and paused, allowing the silence to clear Marshall's thoughts.

"And what do you think that means, Marshall?" he asked.

Marshall allowed the answer to be the obvious. "That there really is no difference," he concluded. He quietly thought through the ramifications of his conclusion, then continued. "So if there is no difference in the actual spiritual battle regardless of whether the infiltrator is the influence of the forces of darkness or the influence of the person's own sinful mind, then they must be treated alike to be defeated alike."

Gudan opened his mouth and began to lift a finger to sort of agree and sort of correct at the same time when Marshall stopped him with an upraised hand of his own.

"Wait. I know. Close, but not really. Sorry, I like the rhymes, but they are no substitute for accuracy. Let me see if I can clear it up and state it better myself."

Gudan stifled a grin and nodded with outstretched hand to yield the floor.

"Thank you," Marshall said graciously. "What I mean is, if the enemy acts the same and uses the same tactics, regardless of whether it is the influence of the forces of darkness or the influence of the person's own mind, then the defense against the enemy can also be the same. The truth of God's word effectively defends against both the lies of the enemy and the ungodly desires of the sinful human mind. The difference being that the forces of darkness can only be driven off. They cannot be trained or educated. They cannot be controlled. Their power and influence cannot be diminished. The sinful human mind, however, *can* be trained and educated. It *can* be controlled. Its power and influence *can* be diminished—or rather, *transformed* into a positive influence instead of a negative one."

The sky became illuminated with the word of God as Marshall continued. "It is as the apostle Paul stated in his letter to the Romans, 'Do not conform any longer to the pattern of this world, but be transformed by the renewing of your mind. Then you will be able to test and approve what God's will is—his good, pleasing and perfect will,' Romans 12:2. The mind can be renewed by the power of the Holy Spirit!"

Marshall continued to expound as the Spirit continued to give him understanding. "The battle is unfair!" he stated with a cross between incredulity and surprise. "No matter what the state of the man, the battle will always be unfair! It will either be the man's new heart and renewed mind against the forces of darkness, two good against one bad, or the man's new heart against his own unrenewed sinful mind and the forces of darkness, one good against two bad. For the man who is trying to live in accordance with God's plan of redemption and in concert with the Spirit of God, the battle will always be unfair."

"And that is the key," Gudan agreed. "The infiltrator—the sinful mind—is the key to the battle. Unfortunately, Satan also knows this. And it is in the sinful mind of men where he exerts the most force and puts forth the most effort.

"Mankind has already been redeemed, Marshall. The penalty for sin has already been paid. There is no longer any reason for any man to remain estranged from his creator, who loves him so much that he himself paid the penalty for mankind to provide that very redemption. *That* battle has already been won! Satan has already been defeated, and his ultimate goal, completely denied. The only battle that remains, then, is the battle for the allegiance of the sinful human mind. The allegiance of the inside man."

"That makes sense, Gudan," Marshall said, "But how do you actually make that happen? I mean, if the mind cannot be transformed like the heart can and if it always has a sinful bent, then how am I able to control it and win its allegiance? It sounds impossible! That would be like telling the alcoholic, 'Just stop drinking!' when he asks you for help in overcoming his addiction."

Gudan raised an eyebrow. "True, Marshall, that does sound like an insurmountable task. 'Just stop drinking.' Again, you have chosen wisely the comparison utilized to illustrate your point. Wisely because it is quite an accurate comparison! The alcoholic is often consumed by his need for a drink. The sinful mind is often consumed by its need for self-gratification. It is not natural for the sinful mind to focus on the things of the Most High any more than it is natural for the alcoholic to focus on sobriety. Therefore, even as the alcoholic must overcome his craving for a drink one drink at a time, one craving at a time, so the man desiring to honor the Most High must overcome his craving for sin—rebellion, self-gratification, whatever you wish to call it—one thought at a time. In fact, this very subject was addressed in the word of the Most High by the Apostle Paul in his letter to the Corinthian believers."

Marshall instinctively looked toward the sky where he knew he would find the illuminated word of God displayed, even though he knew the words well enough to quote them as he read them.

> For though we live in the world, we do not wage war as the world does. The weapons we fight with are not the weapons of the world. On the contrary, they have divine power to demolish strongholds. We demolish arguments and every pretension that sets itself up against the knowledge of God, and we take captive every thought to make it obedient to Christ.
>
> 2 Corinthians 10:3–5 (NIV)

"I see that you are quite familiar with that passage, Marshall. But do you do what it says? Do you put it into practice? Do you take captive every thought and make it obedient to Christ? It's easy to know the words and to say that you do, but do you *really* do it? That is how you overcome the sinful mind, Marshall. One thought at a time.

"Yes, the human mind has a bent toward evil, and yes, there is an ever-present and extremely lethal force working night and day to push that mind as far away from the design of the Most High and as deep into a state of depravity as it can. However, knowledge is power, Marshall. As the screen on the computer in your office said, knowledge is power. The power to overcome and subdue the sinful human mind comes in direct proportion to the depth of knowledge the person has of that sinful human mind. Put another way, a thorough knowledge of your own sinful human mind—its bent and true state, its tendencies and limitations—is what in the end gives you the power to overcome and subdue that same sinful human mind. As we discussed previously, the *authority* to overcome and subdue it was well established by the sacrifice of the Messiah, but the *power* to do it comes only from wisdom and understanding, the direct result of knowledge.

"Of course, it takes extreme discipline and intentional focus, but that does not make it impossible. The sinful human mind can be controlled and overcome one thought at a time by following the instruction given by the Most High to Paul, which we just looked at."

Chapter Thirteen

Marshall felt foolish. He thought that after all he had seen he should have a better or deeper understanding than he did. But he was still confused. He still felt as if he had been shown one page at the beginning of a ten thousand-paged instruction manual on how to build a working spaceship, and although he had a deep understanding of that particular page, it served only to make him aware of how much he still did not know. He looked up at Gudan.

"Forgive me, Gudan," he stammered. "This seems like a very silly question, but still I must ask it. If our weapons make us invincible and our power source is infinite and our shield is impenetrable and the battle is already won in one sense and not even ours but God's in another, then why do we inevitably fail so completely? Why are those who call themselves Christians most often characterized by the same attributes and vices as the unbelieving world around them? It can't be just that simple, and due to the overwhelming failure of humanity as a whole, obviously it isn't just that simple. So then what are we still missing? What am I still missing? What causes that infinite power not to be enough? What causes that impenetrable shield to allow sin through? What causes the sword, the belt, the shoes, the helmet, the breastplate to be ineffective? Why doesn't it work? Why do so many refuse to believe and become Christians at all? Why do so many who do become Christians have to be such rotten people? Why do so many who claim the name of Jesus still fail so miserably in their attempt to live for him? Why do people refuse to actually believe the Bible? And those who claim to believe it or even those who honestly do believe it, why do they refuse to live in accordance with what it says? Why, when confronted with the truth of the Scriptures, do they attempt to argue away the fact that it does in fact apply to *them* and not just to everybody else? Why, when admonished to change their lives, do they resist and fight? If it really is just that simple, then why do so few understand and obey? Why do so few succeed? Why do so few submit to the lordship of Jesus and live completely for him? I mean *really* live for him?"

Marshall clearly wasn't finished, but he stopped talking and threw up his hands in exasperation, having so much yet in his mind and on his heart but unable to continue putting it into words.

Gudan smiled an understanding smile at Marshall's flood of frustrated emotion. It was a sad smile. "Why, indeed," he simply said, nodding his head, interlacing his fingers and beginning to slowly stroll. "Why, indeed."

Without being told, Marshall knew to look at the illumined sky above him.

"It is as the Messiah himself said, as recorded in your Bible by Matthew." Gudan quoted the text:

> "Enter through the narrow gate. For wide is the gate and broad is the road that leads to destruction, and many enter through it. But small is the gate and narrow the road that leads to life, and only a few find it."
>
> Matthew 7:13–14 (NIV)

Marshall began to walk, quickly catching up to Gudan and matching his stride.

"Forgive me, Gudan. I don't mean to be disrespectful, but… that is not an answer! That is merely a crib note restating the problem. That doesn't help me. I mean, I have learned so much on this journey—things so far beyond imagination that I know I couldn't even comprehend them if you were not here with me—but still, the same questions I had back in my office remain! Why? Why do so few find the narrow way if it is so simple?"

Marshall took a breath to continue, but Gudan stopped him with an upraised hand.

"Do not confuse simplicity with ease, Marshall," Gudan warned. "Defeating Satan and living in the Spirit or 'with the mind set on what the Spirit desires,' as Paul said, is very simple. You read and obey the words, precepts, and commands of the Most High as recorded in his word. That is really all there is to it. Extremely simple. You read it, and then you just do it. You do not weigh the options, you do not count the cost, you do not consider the pros and cons. You just do it. You just obey. It is neither intricately complex nor difficult to comprehend or understand. It is very simple.

"The difficulty arises when you genuinely attempt to overcome the innate human tendency to put self above all else and earnestly follow the will of the Most High. And that, Marshall, is the most difficult thing a human being will ever have to do. Lucifer was the wisest and most powerful being ever created, and he couldn't do it. It is simple, yes. But it is also extremely difficult."

Gudan motioned to the sky, illuminating it once again with the word of God.

"Consider the words of the Messiah to anyone who would follow him," he said.

Marshall looked up at the sky.

> Then he said to them all: "If anyone would come after me, he must deny himself and take up his cross daily and follow me. For whoever wants to save his life will lose it, but whoever loses his life for me will save it.
>
> Luke 9:23–24 (NIV)

"And the words of Paul describing the actions of the Messiah," Gudan said, again motioning to the sky.

> Do nothing out of selfish ambition or vain conceit, but in humility consider others better than yourselves. Each of you should look not only to your own interests, but also to the interests of others. Your attitude should be the same as that of Christ Jesus: Who, being in very nature God, did not consider equality with God something to be grasped, but made himself nothing, taking the very nature of a servant, being made in human likeness. And being found in appearance as a man, he humbled himself and became obedient to death—even death on a cross!
>
> Philippians 2:3–8 (NIV)

"One could find verse after verse after verse in the word of the Most High that speaks of putting others above self. In fact, do you recall the series of self attitudes that we talked about earlier?"

Marshall looked blankly at Gudan. "Self attitudes?" Then, realizing what Gudan meant, he finally said, "Oh, you mean like self-centeredness? Self-reliance?"

"Yes, those."

"Well, I may not be able to quote the list verbatim, but yes, I do remember discussing them," Marshall answered.

"Allow me to refresh your memory," Gudan said. "Self-reliance, self-centeredness, self-righteousness, self-will, self-indulgence, self-preservation, and self-pity."

Marshall nodded.

"And do you remember what we said about those when we first discussed them?" At Marshall's blank look, Gudan continued, "We referred to them as the rebellious attitudes of Satan, in contrast to the fruit of the Spirit of the Most High. Those attitudes that Satan works feverishly day and night to instill into all humanity to keep them from professing allegiance to the Most High—those are all negative concepts, all things to be avoided. However, there is a single corresponding positive to every one of them."

Marshall remained silent for a long moment, knowing that the statement was also a question and knowing also that he did not know how to answer it.

"Trust," Gudan provided. "It is trust, Marshall. The opposing positive to every single one of those negative concepts is trust. Complete, utter, unreserved, unlimited, unadulterated, supreme, and selfless trust in the Most High. Trust in his will, his methods, his purposes, his faithfulness, his rewards. Absolute trust that the Most High is so superior to any human being that his will *will* be better, his plans *will* be better, his methods *will* be more effective, his rewards *will* be greater. Anything and everything that the Most High might do in the life of any given human would be so much greater and better than anything that human could possibly come up with or accomplish on his own. It would be utter foolishness to rely on oneself rather than trusting completely in the Most High."

"Yet that is exactly what most people do on a daily basis and most for their whole lives," Marshall admitted. "Reject the leading of the Holy Spirit, reject the law of God, and then complain that their life isn't going as they wanted it to or hoped that it would."

"Exactly," Gudan agreed. "And that is the short answer to every one of the questions you asked, Marshall. Valid, reasonable questions, all—and the answer to each at its barest reality is simply refusal to trust.

"What causes that infinite power not to be enough? Refusing to trust that the power really is greater than the enemy.

"What causes that impenetrable shield to allow sin through? Lack of faith, or trust, that the Most High will protect.

"What causes the sword, the belt, the shoes, the helmet, the breastplate to be ineffective? Why doesn't it work? Refusal to trust that the word, truth, peace, salvation, and righteousness provided by the Most High is powerful enough to defeat Satan.

"Why do so many refuse to believe and become Christians at all? Lack of trust that the Most High will take care of their needs, wants, desires if they turn their lives over to his control.

"Why do so many who do become Christians have to be such rotten people? Refusal to trust that if they truly deny themselves and put others first, the Most High will take care of them, their needs, wants, desires, etc.

"Why do so many who claim the name of Jesus still fail so miserably in their attempt to live for him? Failure to trust in the strength, wisdom, and power of the Most High and failure to believe that that strength, wisdom, and power has been given to them to use against their enemy, Satan, and therefore, failure to attempt to use it against him.

"So on and so forth, Marshall. Take the rest of your questions, apply the same answer. People refuse to trust that the Most High will do right by them and take care of them to their standards. They either foolishly believe that they can do it better or their fear of the unknown is so great that they refuse to trust in the Most High at all. Instead, they cling to the seven rebellious attitudes of Satan, foolishly believing they can do better on their own. After only minimal scrutiny, you will find that one or more of the seven attitudes on that list is the root cause behind each of the human failures you asked about, and every one of them is the direct result of a simple, yet debilitating lack of faith in the Most High, resulting in a failure to completely and wholeheartedly trust him and yield to him in every aspect of life.

"I will say that again, Marshall. One or more of the seven attitudes on that list is the root cause behind each of the human failures you asked about, and every one of them is the direct result of a simple, yet debilitating lack of faith in the Most High, resulting in a failure to completely and wholeheartedly trust him and yield to him in every aspect of life.

"In that, we have the perfect example of the passive resistance to the prompting of the Holy Spirit leading to or resulting in active resistance to the lordship of the Most High. The passive resistance is simply failing to trust in the Most High and take action against those thoughts that are contrary to his will. The active resistance is where one or more of the self attitudes is allowed to take over the mind and lead it to outright disobedience. How did you put it? 'Defiance of the Most High by the placing of self on the throne above him.'

"You see, Marshall, human beings were designed and created to exist in a state of oneness with and absolute submission to the Most High. In that state, man is invincible. He cannot be defeated. The enemy is powerless, the infiltrator is routed, and the inside man is rigidly controlled, being made subject to the will of the Most High. Victory is guaranteed. However, refusal to completely surrender to the Most High makes the man easy prey. He can be quickly and profoundly defeated. The enemy becomes extremely powerful, the infiltrator is given free reign, the inside man is free to manipulate and betray, and defeat becomes guaranteed rather than victory. It is as we discussed during our visit to the military training camp—Satan doesn't need to attack men outright. He merely needs to encourage them to do the very things their sinful minds want to do anyway.

"You have acquired much knowledge on our journey thus far, Marshall," Gudan said. "But the acquisition of knowledge is useless without the ability, will, and desire to apply that knowledge. We have seen how Lucifer became Satan, the adversary of the Most High. We have learned much about the workings of the human mind and Satan's plan and strategy to infiltrate, destroy, and ultimately control that mind. The seven things we are about to discuss comprise the crux of Satan's offensive against mankind. Everything you have learned thus far serves to assist you in understanding this offensive and developing a means of defending against it. You have been given tools and weapons, and you have seen demonstrations of how to use them. But now, our journey will turn to focus on defeating the most formidable adversary of all: yourself.

"Why do humans fail, you ask? Why, with all the power and wisdom and strength and ability and authority of the Most High behind them, do humans continue to struggle and fight and succumb to sin and depravity? Why, with all the glorious promises given to them by the Most High, with all the examples of blessings and wonder lavished on mankind by the Most High in return for love and obedience, with the peace and joy and contentment poured out upon mankind simply because the Most High loves them so much and wants the best for them, does mankind still struggle to obey him even in the least of things, let alone the greater things? It is very simple, Marshall, and you said it yourself—defiance of the Most High by the placing of self on the throne above him. The reason for that defiance? Simple lack of trust."

Gudan looked up, clearing the sky, then back to Marshall. "Let us now examine the seven self issues, defined individually by one of your dictionaries. After each, the perspective of the Most High will be expressed via a series of verses taken directly from his word. Then we will discuss how a simple lack of trust is at the heart of every one."

As Marshall looked up, words materialized in the sky above him. On the left, the word *self-reliance* appeared with the definition beneath it.

Self-Reliance

Reliance on one's own powers and resources rather than those of others; reliance on one's own efforts and abilities.

To his right, a series of verses also appeared, which Marshall read aloud.

> Trust in the Lord with all your heart and lean not on your own understanding; in all your ways acknowledge him, and he will make your paths straight.
>
> Proverbs 3:5–6 (NIV)

> "For my thoughts are not your thoughts, neither are your ways my ways," declares the Lord. "As the heavens are higher than the earth, so are my ways higher than your ways and my thoughts than your thoughts.
>
> Isaiah 55:8–9 (NIV)

> He who trusts in himself is a fool, but he who walks in wisdom is kept safe.
>
> Proverbs 28:26 (NIV)

> And I'll say to myself, "You have plenty of good things laid up for many years. Take life easy; eat, drink and be merry." "But God said to him, 'You fool! This very night your life will be demanded from you. Then who will get what you have prepared for yourself?'
>
> Luke 12:19–20 (NIV)

> "I am the vine; you are the branches. If a man remains in me and I in him, he will bear much fruit; apart from me you can do nothing.
>
> John 15:5 (NIV)

"As you can see, Marshall, the definition of *self-reliance* is in sharp contrast to the precepts of the word of the Most High," Gudan observed.

The sky slowly scrolled text like movie credits as Marshall read aloud each of the next six self words, followed by its definition, and a handful of Bible verses contradicting each one.

Self-Centeredness

Concerned solely with one's own desires, needs, or interests.

Do nothing out of selfish ambition or vain conceit, but in humility consider others better than yourselves. Each of you should look not only to your own interests, but also to the interests of others.

Philippians 2:3–4 (NIV)

Nobody should seek his own good, but the good of others.

1 Corinthians 10:24 (NIV)

"If anyone comes to me and does not hate his father and mother, his wife and children, his brothers and sisters—yes, even his own life—he cannot be my disciple.

Luke 14:26 (NIV)

But whatever was to my profit I now consider loss for the sake of Christ. What is more, I consider everything a loss compared to the surpassing greatness of knowing Christ Jesus my Lord, for whose sake I have lost all things. I consider them rubbish, that I may gain Christ.

Philippians 3:7–8 (NIV)

Self-Righteousness

Convinced of one's own righteousness, especially in contrast with the actions and beliefs of others.

All of us have become like one who is unclean, and all our righteous acts are like filthy rags; we all shrivel up like a leaf, and like the wind our sins sweep us away.

Isaiah 64:6 (NIV)

You say, 'I am rich; I have acquired wealth and do not need a thing.' But you do not realize that you are wretched, pitiful, poor, blind and naked.

Revelation 3:17 (NIV)

Everyone has turned away, they have together become corrupt; there is no one who does good, not even one.

Psalms 53:3 (NIV)

For by the grace given me I say to every one of you: Do not think of yourself more highly than you ought, but rather think of yourself with sober judgment, in accordance with the measure of faith God has given you.

Romans 12:3 (NIV)

'For in him we live and move and have our being.' As some of your own poets have said, 'We are his offspring.'

Acts 17:28 (NIV)

Self-Will

Stubborn or willful adherence to one's own desires or ideas; obstinacy.

Then Jesus said to his disciples, "If anyone would come after me, he must deny himself and take up his cross and follow me.

Matthew 16:24 (NIV)

As a result, he does not live the rest of his earthly life for evil human desires, but rather for the will of God.

1 Peter 4:2 (NIV)

"I am the Lord's servant," Mary answered. "May it be to me as you have said." Then the angel left her.

Luke 1:38 (NIV)

Going a little farther, he fell with his face to the ground and prayed, "My Father, if it is possible, may this cup be taken from me. Yet not as I will, but as you will."

Matthew 26:39 (NIV)

Your kingdom come, your will be done on earth as it is in heaven.

Matthew 6:10 (NIV)

Self-Indulgence

Excessive or unrestrained gratification of one's own appetites, desires, or whims.

For to me, to live is Christ and to die is gain.

Philippians 1:21 (NIV)

I have been crucified with Christ and I no longer live, but Christ lives in me. The life I live in the body, I live by faith in the Son of God, who loved me and gave himself for me.

Galatians 2:20 (NIV)

Those who belong to Christ Jesus have crucified the sinful nature with its passions and desires.

Galatians 5:24 (NIV)

All of us also lived among them at one time, gratifying the cravings of our sinful nature and following its desires and thoughts. Like the rest, we were by nature objects of wrath.

Ephesians 2:3 (NIV)

So I say, live by the Spirit, and you will not gratify the desires of the sinful nature.

Galatians 5:16 (NIV)

Self-Preservation

Preservation of oneself from destruction or harm.

Then he said to them all: "If anyone would come after me, he must deny himself and take up his cross daily and follow me. For whoever wants to save his life will lose it, but whoever loses his life for me will save it.

Luke 9:23–24 (NIV)

There is a way that seems right to a man, but in the end it leads to death.

Proverbs 14:12 (NIV)

Who of you by worrying can add a single hour to his life? Luke 12:25 (NIV)

Self-Pity

Dwelling on one's own sorrows or misfortunes; excessive, self-absorbed unhappiness over one's own troubles.

> Before I formed you in the womb I knew you, before you were born I set you apart; I appointed you as a prophet to the nations.
>
> Jeremiah 1:5 (NIV)

> "For I know the plans I have for you," declares the Lord, "plans to prosper you and not to harm you, plans to give you hope and a future.
>
> Jeremiah 29:11 (NIV)

> And we know that in all things God works for the good of those who love him, who have been called according to his purpose.
>
> Romans 8:28 (NIV)

> Cast all your anxiety on him because he cares for you.
>
> 1 Peter 5:7 (NIV)

> Do not be anxious about anything, but in everything, by prayer and petition, with thanksgiving, present your requests to God. And the peace of God, which transcends all understanding, will guard your hearts and your minds in Christ Jesus.
>
> Philippians 4:6–7 (NIV)

Marshall stood silent, thinking about all the definitions and verses he had just read. Gudan continued the lesson.

"For each of the self issues, there is a simple lack of trust coupled to an underlying concern of 'But what about me?' In each case, the man is concerned that the Most High will not do as good a job in taking care of his wants, needs and desires as the man can do for himself. For example, the self-reliant man might think, 'If I don't rely on myself, God might not give me what I want.' Or the self-centered man might think, 'I have to be concerned about myself all the time. If I don't look out for Number One, who will? Nobody else is going to take care of me!' The self-righteous man might say, 'If you really knew me, you would know that I don't need God to be any better. And if I practice self-denial and humility, how will people know how great I am? No, I will continue to build myself up so nobody will ever question me.' The self-willed man might suggest that nobody could have a better plan than he, not even God. 'Why should I yield my will to anyone else's, even God's? My ideas are perfect. My way is the best. I don't want my plans messed up by allowing somebody else to have input.' The self-indulgent might say, 'I might not have all the happiness and contentment I want if I yield my will to God. I'm not going to follow rules that restrict what I can do or how I can enjoy myself.' The man concerned with self-preservation might not trust God to take care of him and keep him safe. *I'm not going to put myself out for anyone else—what if something bad happens to me? No, taking care of myself is more important than anything else.* The man wallowing in self-pity will not trust God to bring good things to pass because circumstances at the moment appear grim, and even when things are going well, he doesn't trust that they will continue. He refuses to find joy in anything and acts as though he is the only one ever to have suffered. *Too bad for them, but I have my own problems to deal with and I don't have the energy to help anybody else. Besides, nothing ever goes my way, and if it did, it wouldn't last anyway. God won't even do anything for me, why should I put myself out there for anybody else?*

"Every one of those pitfalls begins with a lack of faith perpetuated by the mental question 'But what about me?'"

Marshall nodded. "I had never really considered it that way," he said. "But it makes sense. If one really knows God, he knows that he can trust in God completely for everything. Not so the man who doesn't."

"Yes, Marshall. I know that was a lot of reading, but it was important for you to see the words of the Most High on this subject. Those seven attitudes creep into the life of every human being all the time. The assault on the mind is continuous. Knowing them well and recognizing their appearance is critical in defeating the enemy when he uses them against you. You must know with certainty what the Most High says about each of them so you can combat the enemy effectively. Do you see, then, how each of your questions was answered by one or more of these self issues?" Gudan asked.

Marshall thought back through his ranting about people failing even when there is just no reason for it, and he knew Gudan was right. For every one of his questions, he could now point to a lack of faith or trust relating to one of the seven self issues.

Gudan said, "The weapons and armor are only as good as the soldier wearing or using them. If the soldier doesn't have complete trust in his shield, he will not use it effectively to extinguish the darts of the enemy. If he doesn't trust his sword with his life, he will not wield it with confidence. Helmet, shoes, breastplate, it is all the same. Faith in the Most High is the basis of everything. One must accept and believe that the Most High is everything he says he is and that he will do everything he says he will do.

"It really comes down to love and discipline, Marshall. One has to love the Most High enough to want to serve and please him, and he has to be disciplined enough to follow through with obedience. He has to be willing to sacrifice short-term gratification—getting what he wants or what looks good right now from a human perspective—for a much better long-term gratification—getting what will absolutely be best for him from the perspective of the all-knowing Most High. In every case, it will always be better to forego immediate gratification in order to receive anything that the Most High might have planned for the future. It will always be better by comparison. A human being can never outdo the Most High. Human, worldly satisfaction will never ever compare to the inner peace and spiritual satisfaction lavished by the Most High onto those who love him and keep his commands. His way will always be better, his rewards always greater, his peace always deeper. It boils down to trusting that his way is better, regardless of what one might think or see or feel or think he knows. That is what faith is all about."

Marshall's chest tightened as he thought back to so many times when he had expressed the attitude if not the actual words Gudan had said, *But what about me? If I forgive that person and let it go, where is my revenge? What happens to the satisfaction I get from quietly holding a grudge, knowing that I am just that much better than him? If I obey God and give of myself to this or to that, what's in it for me? When do I get taken care of? If all I ever do is serve, serve, serve and give, give, give, when is it my turn? What if nobody else is obedient, so I never "get mine"? Sure, maybe I'll get an extra jewel in my crown by and by, but what about now? Wow, what a horrible attitude to have! Do I really doubt that God can reward me sufficiently? Or more to the point, do I love God enough to want to serve and obey him even if I never do "get mine" while here on this earth? Do I love God enough to respond as the three Hebrew children in Daniel's account responded to King Nebuchadnezzar when he demanded that they worship a golden idol he had set up?*

> Shadrach, Meshach and Abednego replied to the king, "O Nebuchadnezzar, we do not need to defend ourselves before you in this matter. If we are thrown into the blazing furnace, the God we serve is able to save us from it, and he will rescue us from your hand, O king. But even if he does not, we want you to know, O king, that we will not serve your gods or worship the image of gold you have set up."
>
> Daniel 3:16–18 (NIV)

Marshall was beginning to understand. Once again, like so many times before on this journey, he bowed his head and wept at his own failure. His own behavior. His own selfishness.

He repented of his evil attitude and asked God to forgive him. Feeling the peace wash over him, he opened his eyes and looked around at Gudan.

"Is there anything in your world that could ever possibly compare to the peace and love you are feeling from the Most High right this moment, Marshall?" Gudan asked.

Marshall pinched the bridge of his nose with his fingers and wiped his eyes. His face hardly seemed big enough to accommodate the smile.

Gudan reached out his hand and touched his arm like he had done in his office so long ago. Together, they began to ascend into the emptiness above them.

"You have learned well, Reverend Dr. Marshall J. Pennington of Community Gospel Church. Your heart is open and willing. Your love for the Most High is strong. Not only have you watched and learned well during this journey, but you have gone the extra step to see your own failures mirrored in the things you have seen. You have quickly repented with tears of sorrow and have thus been quickly forgiven. Your humility and servant's heart have served you well, and they will continue to do so throughout your life so long as you remain faithful to the Most High."

Marshall, detecting the finality in Gudan's voice, knew their journey was coming to an end. "We're going back now, aren't we?" he asked.

"Yes, Marshall, we are going back. This part of my mission is nearly complete."

"Nearly?"

"Nearly. There is one final subject to be discussed," he said as they ascended into the black nothingness.

"You need to be aware, Marshall, that in petitioning the Most High for such a degree of knowledge of the enemy and particularly by accepting this journey, to put it in your terms, you have picked a fight with the devil."

For some reason, the statement caught Marshall off guard. It made sense, of course, that the devil would know about it and not be amused, but he had not given it much thought. However, for it to be important enough for Gudan to bring it up—well, that got his attention.

Gudan continued, "Recall that Satan has his minions everywhere, watching everything, every minute of every day and night, and reporting back to him on what they observe. And they interfere with humans any time they believe such interference will further their cause against the Most High or any of his loyal servants. Taking a step as significant as this journey will not go unnoticed, and it will not go unanswered."

Marshall felt a cold chill go up his spine—not of hopeless fear, for this journey had done nothing if not strengthen his faith in God—but rather the physical reaction to sensing danger. Beneath them, Marshall could see his city materializing out of the inky blackness. He recognized the lighting scheme, the road layout, his lighted church steeple jutting up between the treetops. He watched two demons talking as they looked through the barrier in what seemed to be in the direction of his church—his own office! The larger demon was shouting something at the smaller one and gesturing, apparently reprimanding him for something. Gudan took them close enough so that they could see and hear everything taking place on both sides of the barrier.

The larger demon growled and shook his head, muttering angrily to himself. *The demon assigned to work on this pastor is failing miserably! It was my own rotten luck that the loser was assigned to my division in the first place.* His voice thundered as he shouted out a reprimand to the small demon, who cowered in fear of his superior. *I'll show this pastor a thing or two, not to mention schooling this incompetent underling who has botched his assignment so badly. Wanted to get to know the enemy, did he? Well, I can get right up close and personal if that's what he really wants. Maybe scare the life right out of him. Or maybe just kill him and be done with it. Or better yet, get his wife involved with that new guy at the Children's Center where she volunteers part time. Yes, a sleazy affair—that did it every time. And—bonus—it would provide a good old-fashioned scandal for the church too! Oh, but I am a clever one! Now let's occupy his attention and get his mind off that ridiculous praying.*

Marshall continued to look on in horror as the scene unfolded, the little demon's eyes glued to the larger one, the one he referred to as Manevid. The little demon watched in fascination as Manevid's form slowly transformed. His stature became much smaller, nearly the size of the little demon himself. Hair grew out of his head, long and brown, and fell straight across his shoulders until it reached the middle of his back. His clothing also changed, becoming blue jeans and a sweater, shrinking until they clung snugly and seductively to a flawless female human body. His indiscernible face became a lovely female human one, its beauty rivaled only by the body of which it was a part.

"Watch and learn!" Manevid sneered as he stepped through the barrier and into the foyer of Community Gospel Church, forcing tears to stream from the young girl's pretty blue eyes. He dabbed at his sniffling nose as he lifted his hand to knock on the office door of associate pastor Dr. Marshall J. Pennington.

Marshall jumped back against Gudan as a bright white light filled Community Gospel Church with such intensity that it knocked Manevid back through the barrier, sending him rolling head over heels. As he regained his footing, having already instantaneously reverted to his natural form, he cursed and growled and poised himself to rush at the angel of light who had had the gall to confront him. Manevid had only taken two steps toward the barrier when his head thumped into the chest of Mugray, a very large and imposing member of the heavenly host. Mugray was flanked by a pair of angels on each side, standing tall and strong and ready for battle.

Meanwhile, a sixth member of the heavenly host stood in Marshall's office, directly in front of his desk. Sensing a presence in the room, Marshall removed his hands from his face and looked up inquisitively.

The man stood perfectly still, hands clasped loosely in front of him, his eyes never leaving Marshall's.

"Uh...sorry, I didn't hear you come in," Marshall stammered.

Even with all that he had seen on his amazing journey thus far, Marshall was still shocked and stunned as he watched the scene play out before him. He had watched events take place on both sides of the barrier, observing the actions and interactions of demons, angels, and humans, been present in spirit during their planning, strategizing, and scheming, seen demons fall and conquer, humans fall and overcome, and spirits do battle. But that had all been someone else's story! Other than a few childhood clips of his own life, he had only been witness to the struggles and victories of other people he didn't know. But now—this one—was his own life, and it was happening in real time, right now! He was watching the very last thing that had happened to him right before he was taken up to experience this magnificent journey! And the presence of the demons—that caused him to shudder again. No, not their presence, the intimacy with which they dealt with him, Marshall J. Pennington, as though they had always been a part of his life and this was just one more day on the job. And he knew now that that is exactly how it was.

"You asked to know the enemy, Marshall," Gudan reminded him. "The Most High was not the only one who heard you, not the only one to witness your struggle.

"We were sent to protect you. You have found favor with the Most High. There is work for you to do, which threatens the kingdom of darkness. Satan knows that, and he wants to destroy you. Your zeal to see the kingdom of heaven manifested on earth is matched by Satan's zeal to see you destroyed to prevent it. And now, after the journey you have just taken, it will get worse. The kingdom of darkness was prevented from seeing what happened to you—where we went, what we saw, what you learned—but they are not fools. They will know that something great has happened to you, and they will be watching. I anticipate reinforcements will be sent to find out what happened and to launch some semblance of a counterattack. Be on your guard, Marshall. You have picked a fight with the devil, and he lives to fight. He is relentless. He will not back down. He will not give up. The power of the Most High is immeasurably greater than his, and you have full authority over him, but he will fight you to the death. He will lie, cheat, steal, kill, destroy—whatever it takes to discourage and defeat you. Do not waste what the Most High has given you, Marshall.

"As the apostle Paul admonished the Ephesians: 'Finally, be strong in the Lord and in his mighty power. Put on the full armor of God so that you can take your stand against the devil's schemes' Ephesians 6:10–11. So that you can say with the great apostle as he said to Timothy: 'I have fought the good fight, I have finished the race, I have kept the faith' 2 Timothy 4:7."

Gudan and Marshall stepped through the barrier and entered Marshall's office as time became the exact moment they had begun to ascend into the heavens at the beginning of Gudan's visit.

"The 'girl' will not be coming to your door, Marshall," Gudan said. "We have taken care of that for the time being."

He extended his hand toward the human—his assignment—as his shape slowly changed from the sharp-dressed business professional to the glorious creature he truly was. Marshall's jaw dropped as Gudan grew in stature until his upper body protruded through the ceiling, his brilliant wings open and spanning the whole office plus the rooms on both sides of it. Not being bound by human constraints, his form expanded right through the walls and ceiling as though they were not even there, all the while remaining completely visible to Marshall through them. His glistening white robe positively glowed, covering his humanoid form but not diminishing in the slightest the power and majesty it exuded. He wore a headpiece that appeared to have been weaved from gold and was covered with jewels—not a crown, but clearly indicating rank and status. A matching golden sash was strung from his left shoulder to his right hip, where a magnificent sword, glistening in the light, hung from his belt. The sword, with a handle that had been fashioned into the exact fit for Gudan's hand, was made from a single diamond, sharpened beyond any razor's edge.

"It has been an honor to meet you in person, Marshall Pennington," he said. "As it will continue to be my honor to serve the Most High as your guardian. All praise and glory to him forever and ever!"

Marshall's eyes teared at the beauty and magnificence of Gudan, his guardian angel, standing visible before him. "Thank you, Gudan," Marshall said, bowing. "I will treasure this privilege for the rest of my life. And one day, we shall meet again, when *my* assignment is finished."

Gudan smiled warmly as he slowly faded from view, leaving Marshall standing alone in his office. Books and study materials were still strewn across his desk, the cursor still blinked silently on the computer screen.

"Thank you, Lord Jesus!" he quietly prayed as he fell to is knees. He bowed with his face to the floor, lost in worship. He sang, he praised, he wept. Finally, when the Spirit released him, he stood up and walked behind his desk to straighten up. "Thank you for that awesome privilege—that gift of knowledge that nobody else has ever been given! I am so unworthy to have received it, Lord. I am so humbled. Oh Father, all I ask is that you help me to be faithful to the task you have given me. Grant me the courage to face whatever opposition the devil and his minions might throw at me. Help me to be faithful no matter what happens, no matter how hard it gets, no matter how much I might have to suffer for your name. Be with me, my Lord and my God, and give me strength!"

He wanted to stop right then and write down everything he had seen and heard and felt and learned from his journey, but he wanted even more to share the experience with Sandra, his wife. Concluding that it would still be very fresh in his mind tomorrow, he slipped on his jacket and locked his office door. He turned off the lights as he pulled the door shut behind him and walked out through the dark foyer, repeated the process with the external door, and started down the sidewalk that led to the back parking lot. The cool night air felt good as he inhaled deeply, still basking in the wonder of his experience. Nothing would ever look the same to him. Nothing would ever be the same to him.

Chapter Fourteen

Marshall was cruising south on Route 4 in his dark-blue Ford Crown Victoria, windows cracked open to let in the clean, crisp autumn air. He looked around, through each of the windows, taking in the beautiful evening. It would have been a wonderful evening even if Marshall hadn't just had the most amazing experience of his life, but somehow his elation just made everything that much more magical. The sky was free of clouds and filled with bright stars, and the full moon lit up the night in the most incredible way. Marshall flipped his cell phone shut and tucked it back into his pocket. He had called to tell his wife, Sandra, that he had had the most amazing, indescribable, wonderful experience while working at the church, and he couldn't wait to tell her all about it when he got home, which would be in about ten or twelve minutes if he took the country roads instead of dealing with the traffic lights through greater Stanhope, thereby shaving about three or four minutes from his trip.

Seven minutes into that trip, Marshall was singing praise songs to his Lord and worshipping his way home when his diaphragm involuntarily froze in position. No air moved in or out of his lungs. He could feel his heart beating slow and hard, his head throbbing with each beat as if the strong man from a circus were pounding both his temples with the hammer used to make the big tower bell ding for a prize. From about a quarter mile away, he noticed a car sitting beside the road ahead, its headlights pointing at an odd trajectory out into the cornfield. He absently dismissed the sight as it was likely teenagers shining for coon in the trees along the road or looking for deer along the edge of the adjacent woods. His involuntary bodily functions nearly stopped, however, when he realized that what he had seen from afar was the very same car he had bought for his daughter, Melanie, after she had gotten her driver's license that previous summer. But Melanie had not been shining for coon or looking for deer—or at least she wasn't anymore. Her car was crushed and mangled, wedged between two trees with part of a third tree jutting out from where the engine compartment should have been.

Marshall slammed the brake pedal so hard he thought it would go right through the floor of his car. Gravel and rocks sprayed in all directions as the car fishtailed and finally came to a stop a fifteen or twenty yards beyond the wreck. He slammed the shifting lever into reverse and jammed the gas pedal to the floor, the rear tires throwing road matter against the undercarriage of the car with a deafening noise as the car lurched backward toward the wreck. Locking the brakes again, he cranked the wheel hard to the left, swinging the front end of the car ninety degrees to the right, bringing it to a stop just off the road facing directly toward the wrecked vehicle in the trees. He shoved the transmission into park and leapt through the door which he had opened before the car had even stopped moving. Sprinting blindly toward the car, shouting Melanie's name, begging God to let her be okay, Marshall vaulted the tiny ditch and grabbed the door handle with both hands. In an instant, he took in the entire scene: the blood splattered onto the windshield; pieces of the shattered driver's window—thousands of them, speckled with blood and glittering in the moonlight as if adding beauty to the scene would make it less grisly and horrifying—covered the dash, the seat, the floor, and the beautiful, sweet young face of his wonderful, precious seventeen-year-old daughter.

"Melanie!" he shouted as loud as he could as though volume were the deciding factor in determining the reality of the situation. "Melanie! Oh God, no! God, please no! Oh God, no! Not my baby girl! No! No! No!"

Terrified, his limbs worked automatically without conscious thought as he reached through the empty window opening and into the mangled car. Disregarding the blood and broken glass, he angled his body and stretched to his right because the steering wheel had been pushed back into the seat where his daughter should have been. He lifted her wrist to check for a pulse. And he waited and waited, willing his fingers to feel the slight pumping of blood flowing through her veins and arteries as the beating of her heart pumped it throughout her body, proving that her life was still in her. But he knew better. He knew there was no way any human being could have survived that crash. There was no way the body inside the car could still be alive, no chance that his Melanie had survived. Marshall removed his fingers from her wrist, and gently holding her lifeless hand in his, he cried—as intensely and mournfully as any man has ever cried.

That was how Sandra found him eighteen minutes later. He was still leaning through the missing driver's window, caressing his daughter's hand, picking pieces of bloody glass off her face and talking to her. His own face was streaked with her blood, random shards of glass stuck into his skin where he had wiped tears away. Sandra rushed over to him, crying and shrieking. He backed out of the car window and stood up just as she collapsed into his arms.

"She's gone, Sandy," he said. "She's gone. Our baby girl is gone." He held her tightly as she cried, screamed, begged, wailed, trying to wrap her mind around the fact that her daughter was dead.

Two minutes later, the emergency vehicles began to arrive. At some point, Marshall must have dialed 911 on his cell phone and reported the accident although that memory never did resurface. The first deputy sheriff to arrive on the scene found his cell phone, with the line still connected to 911 emergency dispatch, lying in the muddy grass at his feet.

Marshall and Sandra sat side by side on the back of one of the ambulances, with the flashing lights surrounding them punctuating the night like a silent Fourth of July fireworks display, albeit it somberly announcing the death of a child instead of the birth of a nation. The vehicles of four county sheriff deputies, one fire truck, two ambulances, a tow truck, a state trooper, the county coroner, three volunteer firemen, and a local news van cluttered the area, parked haphazardly in the tiny ditch and along the narrow shoulder of the small county road. Marshall refused treatment beyond cleaning the blood and glass shards off his face but accepted a handful of moist towelettes with which he wiped the dried blood from his hands and arms. He watched as the firemen worked the Jaws of Life—a cruelly inappropriate moniker in Melanie's case—to cut the twisted metal away and remove the body from the crumpled vehicle. Sandra sat beside him, shivering, still wrapped in the wool blanket the paramedic had given her. Shock had fully set in for Sandra. She sat silent, staring into the darkness, unable to cope with the magnitude of the situation. Her crying had diminished to a whimper although her grip had not lessened as she clung white-knuckled to Marshall's arm. Her breathing was shallow, her dark eyes empty and lifeless.

Marshall, on the other hand, was fully aware. Aware not only of the situation as the emergency personnel took stock of it but also aware of the activities in the spiritual realm all around them. He went over his story again to the deputy sheriff, explaining that he had been on his way home from the church, had taken the back roads to save a little time, and had noticed the car sitting off in the trees. As he got closer, he noticed that it was his own daughter's car, and everything was kind of a blur from that point until his wife leapt across the ditch and fell into him.

When he was finished with the deputy, he went over the story again in his mind. Not the story he had just recounted for the deputy, but the full story as it had unfolded on both sides of the barrier.

Gudan had warned him about it. He had warned him that he was picking a fight with the devil and that it would not go unchecked. Granted, Marshall had not expected retaliation to be this severe or this immediate, but he had expected something nonetheless. And no matter how he stacked it, *they* were responsible. He didn't know how they had done it, but he knew that this was no accident. He knew that the forces of darkness had somehow caused Melanie to crash her car into those trees. Gudan was right. Marshall had indeed picked a fight with the devil, and now the devil had drawn first blood. He had killed his daughter—deliberately, mercilessly, strategically, and yes, personally—killed her.

It was a message, Marshall thought. *It was a challenge.* "And now," he growled to himself, "it's *on*..."

→ ✦ ←

Marshall sat in the office of the senior pastor of Community Gospel Church, his longtime friend and colleague Dr. Steven Morrow. His office was similar to Marshall's, but larger. Both had knotty pine paneling stained with deep brown on all four walls, with bookshelves built into three of them and an alternating pattern of matching wooden filing cabinets and tall, narrow windows covering the fourth. Steven's office was much larger but set up nearly the same way as Marshall's, except for the comfortable and disarming living room arrangement at the other end of the room from the desk. The living room area consisted of a couch on one side of a long oval coffee table and a pair of armchairs separated by a lamp and stand on the other. The room boasted two ceiling fans, one above Steven's desk and the other above the coffee table, neither of which was needed in the cool of the autumn afternoon. Steven guided Marshall to the pair of armchairs where the refreshment tray sat on the coffee table. He poured two cups of fresh, hot coffee, handing one to Marshall, who gratefully accepted it, and sat down in one of the armchairs. Steven added a little bit of cream and too much sugar to his own cup before lowering himself into the other armchair.

It was Wednesday afternoon, two days after Melanie's death and two days before her funeral. Marshall and Sandy had spent the rest of a nearly sleepless Monday night riding a roller coaster of intense emotion. Anger, rage, fear, sorrow, uncertainty, regret, loss, and everything in between fought for position while devastation and emptiness held a firm grip on first place. The tears seemed to flow endlessly from their eyes as if their hearts were ships sailing in a sea of sorrow and Mel's absence was a torpedo hole blasted into the hull below the waterline. No amount of shoring and patching could stop the flooding. They dealt with the trauma the only way they knew how—by baring their souls to Jesus and pouring their hearts out to him. They prayed, they cried, they sat in silence, they screamed at the top of their lungs. They questioned, they vowed, they wished, they cried. And eventually, when they were so exhausted they could no longer stay awake, they rested, holding each other tightly as they almost instantly fell into a fitful, shallow sleep.

Tuesday morning, the emotion had come crashing back again when Mel didn't come downstairs to the breakfast table. She never would again. Reggie had decided to go to school, reasoning that being home all day with nothing to do but think about his sister's death would be more difficult than just going about his usual daily business. After he left for school, Marshall and Sandy sat at the breakfast table, and he told her all about the vision he had experienced at the church the night before. He found himself very angry that the magnificence of his journey was being tainted by the death of his daughter as if Satan could negate the positive by causing such a devastating negative in his life. He wrapped up his story by telling her about Gudan's warning that the kingdom of darkness would likely retaliate and that he firmly believed they had killed Mel to counter his amazing experience in the spiritual realm. As he expected, even through her pain, Sandy's anger matched his own. Mel was no longer the victim of a random traffic accident; she was the victim of a calculated, well-planned assassination. She was a casualty of war. Even though Marshall and Sandy were still grieving parents who had just lost their precious daughter in a senseless, random traffic accident, they were also seasoned soldiers who had just had one of the junior soldiers in their unit assassinated by an enemy sniper right in front of their faces. Yes, they were fully engaged, fully human parents of a murdered teenager, but they were Christian soldiers first, so focused on God and on doing his will that they were able to maintain that focus even through the death of their beloved Melanie and see the spiritual reality behind the earthly events taking place around them.

"I was going to meet with you today anyway," Marshall began, "to share what happened to me while I was here Monday evening, so I guess we'll just add funeral details to the agenda."

Steven looked incredulous. "'*Add* funeral details?' What could you possibly have to talk about that is more important than Melanie's funeral arrangements?" he asked in surprise, wondering how Marshall could have anything else on his mind at all, let alone something else they would need to talk about two days after losing his daughter in a traffic accident.

"Just wait," Marshall said, holding up a hand. "You'll see. In fact, I believe it all ties in together."

"I was sitting in my office at my desk last night, trying to prepare for this weekend's services, when a feeling of hopelessness and helplessness came over me. My mind wandered over the congregation, the church, the past decade, and I became very frustrated at what I can only describe as the stagnation of our church. We preach sermon after sermon, offer program after program, launch group after group, study after study, course after course, but nothing ever seems to make any lasting difference. I don't see the growth, the change! It is like they hear but don't understand. They smile and go about their business as though we just meet on Sundays to punch a time card for God and pay our dues. Anyway, I was very frustrated about that, and I was praying, praying so hard for them, for you, for me, for us, for anything that might get through to them and knock them loose, out of their rut. I poured my heart out to God, begging him to search my own heart and see if there was anything in me that was causing the spiritual constipation of our church family.

"Well, praise his name, God heard my pathetic cries and answered my prayer. In a very unusual, unexpected and completely wonderful way. Reggie had accidentally mixed up one of his game CDs with one of my reference discs, and well, when I was trying to bring it up to do some research, a phrase flashed on my screen that said, "Know Your Enemy." Well, that got me thinking—how well did I really know Satan? How well did I know his tactics and methods? Was there something I was missing there that might help me figure out how to be more effective here in the church? So I set to studying Ephesians, Romans, Ezekiel, Isaiah, and a bunch of places to learn more about the devil. That wasn't exactly new ground for me, so even after almost three hours, my study didn't really turn up anything revolutionary. Well, I was again pretty frustrated, but then I remembered that you always said that God can't answer you when you're still talking, so I just buried my face in my hands and sat at my desk and waited quietly. Next thing I knew, it seemed like somebody was there, so I looked up, and there was somebody in my office, standing right there in front of my desk! Yeah, right there in my office! I hadn't opened the door or even heard anybody knock, so it really startled me. I didn't know how he had gotten in or who he was, but there he stood!

"Obviously I was quite shocked! I greeted the man. He was very well dressed and looked clean-cut and professional, so I wasn't really afraid he was a hoodlum or anything, and he introduced himself. Are you ready for this? He said his name was Gudan, and he was my guardian angel! I know this sounds ridiculous, and I would have trouble believing it if anybody came to me with this same story, but I'm telling you, it's true! He said that the Most High—he always referred to him as the Most High—was pleased with me and was going to answer my request. He said he had been given permission to make himself visible to me and take me on a journey into the spiritual realm so that I could see firsthand everything I needed to know about the enemy, about the devil. And that is exactly what happened! I spent what seemed like days in the spiritual realm with Gudan, and then I was brought right back here to my office at the exact moment I had left it."

Steven carefully placed his coffee cup on the table, not disbelieving but very tentative. He knew his associate pastor, knew him very well, and knew without a doubt that Marshall Pennington was a trustworthy man, not given to fantasy or foolish stories. As outlandish as this sounded, if Marshall said it had happened, then it had happened.

"Am I to understand, then, that you had a supernatural visitation from one claiming to be your guardian angel, and this visitor took you on some sort of spiritual journey, like what happened to Paul in Second Corinthians?"

"That's exactly right, Steven. Believe me, I would never have expected anything like it! I didn't really think things like that happened anymore, and I certainly never would have thought it would happen to me! But for whatever reason, God saw fit to extend to me this surreal, unbelievable privilege."

"Wow. That is remarkable. But I believe you. I have known you for a very long time, Marshall, and I trust you. If you say this happened, then it happened. Now please, share with me what God has told you."

Marshall smiled. True friendship was a wonderful thing. Amid a flurry of mixed emotions, he did his best to continue his account.

"It started with a trip to a worship service in heaven. Oh, Steven, you wouldn't believe it! I saw Lucifer before he fell. The most amazing thing I have ever seen. And the sound—the sound of his music was beyond description."

Marshall did his best to briefly touch on the high points of his journey while Steven sat spellbound, eagerly taking in everything Marshall said. He told of Lucifer's fall and his banishment to earth, the creation of mankind and its effect on Lucifer, or Satan by that time, how he felt betrayed and rejected, and how his mission became to seek his revenge by causing the humans to betray God as well. He relayed the peaceful unity of Adam, Eve, and God in the garden of Eden at their creation and then their terrible fall and the effects of that horrible choice on themselves and the rest of humanity for all time. He told him about Satan's attempts to kill Jesus followed by his intensive reconnaissance program against the humans after his final attempt to kill the man Jesus succeeded but then ultimately backfired altogether.

Steven just stared as Marshall opened up the passage in Romans about not conforming to the pattern of the world and shared a tear with him when he spoke of the Holy Spirit being a person whose feelings get hurt when people reject and betray him. He chuckled at the recollection of the training camp and the "Crispi" demonstrating the armor and weaponry of God from Paul's Ephesians passage. Marshall could see the illumination on Steven's face as he described the spiritual battle in terms of the infiltrator and the inside man and the wonder of the bank of screens and what it had allowed Marshall to see. But it was the wrap-up that really got to Steven. Marshall finished his recollection with a description of why people fail to come to Jesus and remain faithful to him. The seven self attitudes. Even when people hear the truth about God, Jesus's sacrifice, his power, our authority, God's will, God's law, and our sin, they still refuse to submit to the lordship of Christ and overcome and defeat the devil. The seven selfish attitudes. Very simple, but not easy. Then finally, he explained how a simple lack of trust in God is the root cause of all of them. A simple lack of true faith.

When he finished, he snatched three cookies from the tray, leaned back in his chair and plopped a whole one into his mouth. Steven sat speechless, his eyes still moist and his heart pounding. His imagination was running wild, trying to picture everything in his mind just as Marshall had described it. He thought he could almost feel some of the things Marshall had experienced although certainly not to the same degree. He sat silent for a moment, then let out a whoop and slapped his knee.

"Oh boy, Marshall! That is awesome! I can't believe you actually went through all that! Oh boy, how I wish I had been there with you! Oh Marshall, that is wonderful. Incredible. Oh how exhilarating that must have been!"

"Yes, Steven, it was really amazing. I am so thrilled that I was counted worthy of that experience. But now—the responsibility! Now I have to do right by God and do what he said. I have to teach the people. He said I have to tell them what I saw and heard and make them understand."

"Well then, what is our next move?"

"*Our* next move?" Marshall asked, taken aback.

"Yes, Marshall, what is our next move? If God told you to tell them and make them understand, then that is what you shall do. So what is our next move?"

Marshall smiled. Of course Steven would see it that way. He wouldn't need to convince him of anything. He could just relate the story, and Steven would be on board for anything God had instructed Marshall to do.

"I'm not exactly sure, Steven. I guess that's what I was hoping you would be able to help me with."

"Whatever you believe God is telling you to do, I'm in. We will do it together. Community Gospel Church and your old friend Steven Morrow are at your disposal. I suggest we begin praying about it now, and as the Lord leads, so shall we follow."

"Praise the Lord, Steven. God is still on the throne, and he still speaks to his people!"

"He does, indeed, Marshall."

The old friends got up, stretched their legs, and tended to the necessities of nature. Evidently the shelf life of a whole pot of coffee inside the human body is not really very long. Back in the office again, Steven started another pot of coffee brewing while Marshall downed three more of those wonderful little chocolate chip cookies Steven's wife always kept his office supplied with. Well, she did make them practically bite-size after all. They spent a several minutes in prayer, thanking God for the amazing adventure Marshall had experienced and asking him to guide their steps as they committed to diligently fulfill the commands associated with it.

"Now," Steven said with a more somber tone, "about the funeral."

"You know, Steven, as horrible as this is, as devastating the loss, as unfair and cruel, as unacceptable and as infuriating as this is, this funeral will be a celebration. Mel was a soldier. She loved Jesus, and she wasn't afraid to let it show. I firmly believe she was taken out as much because she was a threat as because I might be. She died a hero's death, and she will have a hero's memorial service. And I need to officiate the funeral myself."

"Marshall, are you sure that's a good idea?" Steven asked, knowing how difficult it was going to be.

"Remember how I said the two events were tied together?" Marshall asked.

"Yes…" Steven said tentatively.

Once again, Marshall leaned forward in his chair and launched into an explanation. He recounted the events of the whole night of Melanie's death as well as he understood them from the telephone conversation he had had earlier that afternoon with Stacy, the last human being to ever see Mel alive. He told of Melanie's attempts to reach out to Anna, their meetings after school, and particularly the meeting that night when the girls had foolishly crossed over from innocent fun into the dangerous and deadly world of the occult. Then he recounted the words of warning Gudan had given at the end of his own journey into the spiritual realm. Finally, he concluded by expressing his deep conviction that the two events must have been connected. Steven sat spellbound, again clinging to every word. By the time they sat back in their chairs to let the moment linger, they had put a hurting on the second pot of coffee and, yes, bid a fond farewell to several more of those wonderful little chocolate chip cookies. Seriously, she did make them basically bite-size. They probably really didn't even count as cookies.

"Wow, Marshall! That is another amazing story. Or another part of an amazing story. And you are convinced that the death of Melanie is a direct result of your journey?"

"Absolutely," Marshall said. "I would have thought so anyway, but after Gudan specifically warned me about that danger, I am certain. He killed my daughter to dissuade me from further engaging in this battle armed with the new information I have received and especially from teaching what I have learned to my family, my friends, to you and the rest of our congregation, and so forth. This was no small journey, Steven. This was no small privilege. And it comes with no small responsibility. It cannot stop with me. It cannot die with Mel. Her death will be for nothing if I am crushed under the weight of it and fail in my calling. She can die as collateral damage in the destruction of a pastor, or she can die a soldier in the army of God, fighting the good fight, giving all to further the kingdom of heaven on this earth. As long as there is breath in me, I will not let her death be in vain. I will fight. And that fight begins with this funeral service. I want you on the stage with me and my family, but I must be the one to recognize Mel's fight and her sacrifice. I must be the one to pass on encouragement, admonition, and resolve to the rest of my potential soldiers. I may have picked the fight, but the enemy has drawn first blood, and I will not take this sitting down. I will not sit and weep while somebody else continues the battle or worse, while the battle is forgotten altogether, overshadowed by grief and disillusionment. I will not be sidelined, and I will not be stopped."

"As you wish, Marshall," Steven said. "I will stand beside you. We will fight this fight together. Anything you need, you just let me know."

"Thank you, Steven. I knew I could count on you. But you must also be aware, this will not go over well. You will be bringing trouble on yourself too. No one is safe. Nothing is off-limits. They killed my little girl, Steven. They killed her. Nothing is sacred to them."

"Then may your daughter's death be avenged a hundred times over by all the good that will be brought forth because of it. Let the battle rage on. As the Lord wills, so be it to all of us."

And so it was resolved that what the enemy had intended to be not merely a terrible, pointless loss of life but more pointedly a demoralizing, crippling blow to the heart of Marshall J. Pennington and the whole of Community Gospel Church would instead be the catapult used to launch an offensive against that very same enemy.

Marshall sat at home in his living room trying to prepare for his daughter's funeral. Seeing was difficult for the tears that seemed to endlessly fall from his eyes. *His daughter. His precious Melanie.* He was reminded of Job, who lost seven sons and three daughters all in the same day. His crime? Being too obedient to God and ticking off the devil. Not that he would presume to compare himself to Job, but his "crime" was similar—asking for God's help, being found worthy of a great honor, accepting the mission, and in turn, ticking off the devil. But that was little comfort with his daughter being dead as a result. How many emotions can one man feel at the same time? Elation from the amazing journey Gudan had taken him not twenty-four hours ago—still so fresh in his mind—extreme sorrow and loss from losing Mel—also not twenty-four hours ago and still very fresh in his mind—extreme anger and fury at the devil for killing her, humility and gratefulness for being counted worthy to suffer for Christ, the weight of the responsibility to be strong for Reggie and Sandy, duty to tell his story and make them understand the grief and mourning of a father who has just outlived one of his children. The list goes on.

Marshall closed his eyes, and in his mind, he looked at the blankness of the sky as he had so many times during his journey. The word of God once again filled the sky in his mind. He heard God tell Joshua:

> Have I not commanded you? Be strong and courageous. Do not be terrified; do not be discouraged, for the Lord your God will be with you wherever you go."
>
> Joshua 1:9 (NIV)

And he heard King David apply those same words to his son in reference to the building of the temple:

> David also said to Solomon his son, "Be strong and courageous, and do the work. Do not be afraid or discouraged, for the Lord God, my God, is with you. He will not fail you or forsake you until all the work for the service of the temple of the Lord is finished.

1 Chronicles 28:20 (NIV)

Finally, the words of Paul, first to the Philippians and then to the Romans brought the message home to give Marshall strength:

> I can do everything through him who gives me strength.
>
> Philippians 4:13 (NIV)

> May the God of hope fill you with all joy and peace as you trust in him, so that you may overflow with hope by the power of the Holy Spirit.
>
> Romans 15:13 (NIV)

Marshall smiled. How, in the midst of all this, he could smile was beyond him, but somehow, he smiled. *Be strong and courageous. Be strong and courageous and do the work. My God is with me. He will not forsake until the work for the service of the temple is finished. I can do everything through him who gives me strength. And God will fill me with all joy and peace so that I overflow with hope.*

He lowered his head and looked down at his laptop sitting open on the coffee table. And yes, he smiled. As the power of the Holy Spirit washed over him, not removing the pain, but assuaging it with joy and peace, he began to type.

⇾ ✟ ⇽

There had never been a bigger funeral procession in the history of Stanhope County. Not when the last Stanhope had died. Not when the former mayor, after eighteen years in office, had died six months into retirement. Not even when the young police officer had been killed in the line of duty and officers from all across the state had come out to show support. The funeral, procession, and burial of Melanie K. Pennington, daughter of Rev. Dr. Marshall J. and Sandra K. Pennington of Community Gospel Church, graduating senior of Stanhope High School, beloved sister and friend, drew a crowd the likes of which had never been seen in Stanhope before. The building of Community Gospel Church was filled beyond capacity. The service was piped into the old sanctuary, which the youth used for their meeting place, and the fellowship hall, which was used for overflow on Christmas and Easter if the crowds deemed it necessary. It was displayed on large flat-screen televisions mounted on the walls in such a manner that allowed a decent view from any seat in either room. There was standing room only in all three rooms, and people indeed were standing along the side and back walls in order to participate in the service in all three rooms. The foyer and hallways never did seem to empty out since there really wasn't anyplace else for the remaining people to go. Nearly every one of the three thousand strong members and regular attendees of Community Gospel Church was there. Most churches within a fifty-mile radius were represented by either the pastor or some other senior staff contingent. The senior class of Stanhope High School officially moved their Senior Skip Day to the day of Melanie's funeral, and a surprising number of them were in attendance as were many members of the band, the drama club, and various other school groups of which Mel had been a part. It seemed like everyone in town was there, and in reality, they pretty much were.

Mel's MP3 player had been plugged into the church's sound system, set to shuffle, and piped throughout the building. Mostly Christian songs, with a few others thrown in, set the mood for the occasion. A handful of the church ladies, showing their support of their pastor in the best way they knew how to, had decorated the church for the funeral. In accordance with Marshall's wishes, it was not a dismal, somber occasion. There were small, tasteful fresh-cut fall bouquets fastened to the end of each pew, with much larger versions of the same arranged on either side of the platform. Bows, ribbons, and candles—lots and lots of candles— made it look almost like a wedding instead of a funeral, which was just fine with Marshall. Mel would have loved it. There were pictures of Mel from birth to those taken just the previous weekend arranged around the casket. Her head lay on the soft satin pillow, eyes closed in peaceful rest, a slight smile on her face. Marshall didn't know why more families of Christians who had made the passage home to be with God didn't insist that their loved one's body be memorialized with a smiling face. Her Bible lay across her belly, opened to her favorite passage, with her hands crossed and resting reverently on top of it.

The music stopped promptly at one o'clock. At three minutes after one, Dr. Steven Morrow walked to the pulpit and stood silently as the crowd quickly shushed and hushed until the only sound that could be heard was that of a barking dog somewhere in the distance as it penetrated the slightly cracked open windows. The scene was so unusual. The people didn't know what to expect. It was a funeral, but it was decorated like a fall wedding. The upbeat music of a variety of styles from smooth jazz to rock and roll to pop with a spattering of Christian rap and funky blues sounded like a party or a dance, but instead of a disco ball and a buffet table, there was a casket and a wall of a few hundred plants and floral arrangements adorning the front of the sanctuary. The family of the decedent was not crying softly in the front row. They were tearfully smiling from seats on the stage. And all around the building, out of view of the people, were thousands upon thousands of irate demons, their own celebration being thwarted by the ridiculous levity of the event.

"Ladies and gentlemen, welcome to Community Gospel Church. And welcome to the transition celebration for young Ms. Melanie K. Pennington, beloved daughter of our own Marshall and Sandra Pennington, sister of Reggie Pennington. You may have noticed that things are a bit different than your typical funeral here today." He smiled. "Let us pray."

Following the opening prayer, Steven introduced the family and yielded the floor to Marshall, who walked up to the pulpit and looked out over the crowd.

"First, I want to thank you all for coming, in behalf of Melanie and our whole family. We are touched and moved by the presence of such a huge crowd here today, which in and of itself is a testimony to our daughter and to the life she lived while she was here with us. I don't have to tell any of you what a wonderful child Mel was. In fact, I would prefer that all of us tell each other and offer up praise to God for it. So in that spirit, I would like to open up the microphones, which have been placed on either side of the casket, for people to come forward and share thoughts or stories about Mel, how she affected your life, or what she meant to you. Any who wish to, please step forward at this time."

Instantly, both outside aisles were flooded with people—classmates, Sunday schoolteachers, friends, family members. The music was turned back on quietly, and the party was underway. The sharing went on for nearly an hour before the lines dwindled down to the last two or three who wished to share. There was laughter as people shared funny stories about Mel, and there were tears as others shared how Mel had prayed for them or comforted them or simply stood beside them when they needed someone. Marshall and Sandra wept and wept as their friends, coworkers, colleagues, and associates praised their daughter and told how much her life had meant to them. Finally, Marshall reclaimed the microphone at the pulpit.

"So it isn't just us then?" he asked with a chuckle. "She really was that great, huh?" The people smiled back at him, and there was a low murmur of assent.

"Defiance of the Most High by the placing of self on the throne above him," Marshall stated. "A good friend once told me that that is how the majority of the human race lives, and that is how we treat God. Let me say that again because it is worth remembering. *Defiance of the Most High by the placing of self on the throne above him.* Well, that's not how my daughter lived. And that's not how I want to live. You see, my friends, we are all given two things by our Creator: life and the choice of how to use it.

The best way I know to pay tribute to my daughter, who loved Jesus and wanted to devote her whole life to serving him and furthering his kingdom here on earth, is by sharing what was happening the moment she died, and by challenging all of us to find what she found, to have the drive that she had to pursue God, and to serve him selflessly like she did. She had a young person's grasp of God and of serving him and of living for him, for which most of us adults would pat her sweetly on the head and think, 'Well, how nice for her that she doesn't have the pressures and responsibilities of adulthood so that she can think and believe and feel that way and devote her time and efforts to serving God like that.' Shame on us who would say that and who would have that attitude. Let me refer you to the words of the very Jesus we serve as recorded by Matthew." Marshall quoted Matthew 18:2-4, "He called a little child and had him stand among them. And he said: "I tell you the truth, unless you change and become like little children, you will never enter the kingdom of heaven. Therefore, whoever humbles himself like this child is the greatest in the kingdom of heaven."

"Who can tell me what they were talking about when Jesus said this?" A few people throughout the crowd murmured a response. "Yes, the disciples had just asked Jesus who was greatest in the kingdom of God. Let me submit to you that this type of childlike devotion to God, regardless of the rest of life, is exactly what Jesus was talking about. Unfortunately, very few of us are honestly willing to devote ourselves to serving Jesus and living for him as the Bible tells us to do."

Marshall paused and let that statement hang in the room. He felt the air change. The mood was like a living organism whose pulse he could now feel.

"Do I offend?" he continued. "I hope so! My Melanie understood it. She got it better than I did, even though I have been well trained by university and seminary in ministry and biblical studies, have several degrees, and have been actively employed and serving in professional ministry for eighteen years—twelve of it at this very church. It took a real live vision from God to get through to me. But he got through, and I will not fail him again.

"When Melanie died, I was in my office at the church. Mostly. I was having the most amazing, wonderful experience of my life, a vision from God. We don't talk a lot about visions today, but they are a very real thing. Consider the words of Peter as he explained the coming of the Holy Spirit at the Pentecost celebration. In response to people who had accused them of being drunk, he said in Acts 2:16-18, 'No, this is what was spoken by the prophet Joel: "In the last days, God says, I will pour out my Spirit on all people. Your sons and daughters will prophesy, your young men will see visions, your old men will dream dreams. Even on my servants, both men and women, I will pour out my Spirit in those days, and they will prophesy.

"I guess that makes me a young man instead of an old one since I saw a vision and didn't dream a dream. I think Dr. Morrow would probably have had the dream." There was a spattering of laughter at the friendly jibe to their senior pastor.

"I was studying in my office when I received this vision. It has already changed my life, and I believe that through this vision, God also wants to change your lives. In this vision, I saw myself. I don't mean that I was in it—I mean I saw myself. I *really* saw myself. I saw myself as God sees me, and I have to admit I did not like what I saw. It shamed me. I saw my failures. I saw how far away I live on a daily basis from the heart and will of Almighty God. I saw how my puny, pathetic human attempts to please God are useless. I saw how I try to do things my own way and in my own power instead of emptying myself of myself and allowing God to really, truly reign supreme in my life. Even if the things I do are good, noble, righteous, godly things, if I do them in my own strength and not in the power and with the leading of the Holy Spirit, I will miss the mark every time. Paul said it this way to the Romans. Wait—before I read it, I want you all to do something for me."

Marshall paused for a moment. "Are you ready? I want you to forget. Forget what you think you know about God. Forget what you think you understand about the Holy Spirit and his work in the lives of men. Forget what you have been taught and what you have lived your whole life. I dare you. Just forget it. And listen—listen with your heart—to these words. I challenge every one of you—I dare you—oh yes, I double-dog dare you!—to forget what you know and listen to the voice of the Holy Spirit speaking to your heart. And do not allow yourself to pass by this passage by thinking that when it says, 'Those who live according to the sinful nature,' it is only speaking of serial killers or death-row prison inmates. If you are a good person by the standards of the world but are not completely sold out and living every minute of every day of your life for Jesus, the Christ who died for you, and in obedience to the word of God, then this passage is talking about you. If you are a Christian—if you are a pastor or a missionary, I don't care—but you are living as a selfish person who does not yield to the Lord in every aspect of life every day, to your own personal loss and detriment if that is what is required, then this passage is talking about you. I implore you—every one of you—to humble yourself and approach this passage with the thought that it was written by God specifically for you. Specifically to you. The Holy Spirit will either convict your heart and offer you forgiveness or he will bless you for already having a handle on this concept. Either way, his will will be done.

"Please close your eyes, every one of you. Close your eyes and listen the voice of God speaking to you as I read his words to you." Marshall whispered a prayer and began to slowly read from Romans 8.

> Those who live according to the sinful nature have their minds set on what that nature desires; but those who live in accordance with the Spirit have their minds set on what

the Spirit desires. The mind of sinful man is death, but the mind controlled by the Spirit is life and peace; the sinful mind is hostile to God. It does not submit to God's law, nor can it do so. Those controlled by the sinful nature cannot please God. You, however, are controlled not by the sinful nature but by the Spirit, if the Spirit of God lives in you. And if anyone does not have the Spirit of Christ, he does not belong to Christ. But if Christ is in you, your body is dead because of sin, yet your spirit is alive because of righteousness. And if the Spirit of him who raised Jesus from the dead is living in you, he who raised Christ from the dead will also give life to your mortal bodies through his Spirit, who lives in you. Therefore, brothers, we have an obligation—but it is not to the sinful nature, to live according to it. For if you live according to the sinful nature, you will die; but if by the Spirit you put to death the misdeeds of the body, you will live, because those who are led by the Spirit of God are sons of God. For you did not receive a spirit that makes you a slave again to fear, but you received the Spirit of sonship. And by him we cry, *"Abba,* Father." The Spirit himself testifies with our spirit that we are God's children. Now if we are children, then we are heirs—heirs of God and co-heirs with Christ, if indeed we share in his sufferings in order that we may also share in his glory.

Romans 8:5–17 (NIV)

After he had finished reading, Marshall allowed the Holy Spirit to work through the silence that followed. There was no sound in the building, from one end to the other, except the quiet, reverent weeping and sniffling of those whose hearts were being broken by God, those whose will was being turned over to God, those who were admitting that they, like Marshall, had not truly been surrendered to the lordship of Christ in every area of their lives.

Suddenly, a voice broke the silence. Marshall looked up to see that a man from about three-quarters of the way back on his right side was standing up. Tears smeared his face.

"Pastor Marshall," he said again. "May I?" he asked as he gestured to the microphone standing to the side of Mel's casket. Marshall nodded.

Heads turned, but no one spoke as Ted Windworth stepped up to the mike. "That's talking about me, Pastor," he began, his voice choking off as the tears resumed. "I am Ted Windworth. I taught Mel's Sunday school class when she was in elementary school. But I never really understood it until just now. I have not been led by the Spirit of God. I have done the best I could but always in my own power. I prayed, read my Bible, served in the church, but I have never completely yielded every area of my life to the lordship of Jesus. I always made sure my own needs were taken care of first and served with whatever time or resources I had left over. I gave my God, my Creator, the one who gave his only Son to die for me—I gave him the leftovers of my life!" Ted fell to his knees, overcome by sobbing.

People rose to their feet from one end of the sanctuary to the other, falling in line to make their way back to the microphones. But this time, it wasn't about Mel. It was about Jesus. For the next hour and forty minutes, people from every walk of life and from every level of maturity in their faith made their way to the microphones to confess how they had failed their God and to offer praises for how that same God had come through for them in spite of it. Praise songs broke out from time to time. Some shared verses that had led them to a deeper relationship with God. Person after person humbled themselves in front of a crowd of thousands to admit their shortcomings and failures and to ask for God's forgiveness and the church's support. People knelt all along the altar, most deep in prayer for themselves, many interceding in prayer for others. Hearts were regenerated, minds purified, relationships between people healed, and new life infused into countless individuals as well as into Community Gospel Church as a body.

Marshall looked out over the crowd, again amazed at the work God was doing. So many people had been moved to bare their souls in front of a large crowd, wanting only to be closer to God, not at all worried about how they might look to their friends, peers, family, or anyone else. It was an outpouring of the Holy Spirit like Marshall had never seen before. Eventually, he made his way back to his own microphone, wiping his eyes with the back of his hand. A hush slowly fell over the crowd as people noticed Marshall standing at the podium. Many returned to their seats, some sat on the floor where they were, and some remained standing or kneeling. A few scattered groups continued praying. Steven looked at Marshall and nodded, smiling and dabbing at his own tears of peaceful joy.

"Friends," he began, then stopped and chuckled. "You know what, I'm not even going to try to recap this for you. We have just seen the personal presence of Almighty God in our midst. If anyone missed that or doesn't understand it, any words of explanation I might have for them would be meaningless. God speaks for himself.

"One thing I will caution you about, however, the spiritual realm is populated just like our world, and things work there much the same as they do here. Life is a battle. For as long as man has existed on this earth, there has been a battle raging, but what makes it really unfair is that the battle isn't even between humanity and the devil. The battle is between God and the devil. I have recently come to understand how it really works. God and Satan are engaged in a war that has been going on long before humans were even created. Unfortunately for us, as I will explain in more intimate detail in a different sermon, the war changed when we came on the scene. Satan understood right away how much God loves us and how much we mean to him, and that is why he changed his battle plan. He knew that the best way he could hurt God and get back at him was to take his most prized possession—human beings—and corrupt them to the point that they would betray and abandon God just like Satan felt like God betrayed and abandoned him. Even though Satan was the one to betray God and go against him, his twisted mind remembers it differently. He believes God somehow wronged him and that his rebellion was justified. Well, that is for the other sermon. What I am getting at today is that it is Satan's mission to destroy us, each and every one of us, to get back at God and to hurt him. It would be like one of us hurting the child of someone we had a vendetta against because we knew that (a) we could never really directly inflict much pain on our enemy and (b) hurting what is most important to our enemy would do so much more damage to him anyway. Therefore, even by simply refusing to acknowledge God or to give our lives to him and live for him, we are aiding the devil in his mission of hurting God.

"Friends, there are no spectators in this war. There is no Switzerland. Nobody gets to be neutral. Every single one of us is either actively on the side of God or actively or passively on the side of the devil. Doing nothing is not actually doing nothing—well, I should say that doing nothing is not actually *accomplishing* nothing. Doing nothing is giving success to the devil and his cause. Satan would like nothing better than to deceive every human being into simply doing nothing. Absence of a choice for God is in reality a choice against him. Again, it just isn't fair. To be on God's side requires diligence, effort, work, sacrifice, and action. To be on Satan's side, one simply has to do *nothing*. Nothing at all. The terrible result of the fall of man, or Adam and Eve choosing to follow the ways of Satan rather than remaining obedient to the commands of God, was that every one of us is born into sin. We are born separated from God. What once was and would always have been a perfect, sinless, holy nature bent on and perfectly capable of pleasing God became a damaged, sinful, evil nature that not only has no desire to please God but is not even capable of pleasing him. Therefore, Satan has merely to keep us from being saved from our sinful state to keep us separated from God. He doesn't have to steal us away from God or separate us from him. We are born separated! All Satan and his minions have to do is to keep us from choosing to run to God and from having him create in us a pure heart and renew a right spirit within us, Psalm 51:10.

"God stands ready to forgive and to regenerate us, but we must make the choice ourselves. Only that choice to live for God and to renounce our life of sin and selfishness will bridge the gap between us and God and put us on the side of righteousness rather than on the side of sin and rebellion. God says that if we confess our sins, he is faithful and just and will forgive us our sins and cleanse us from all unrighteousness, 1 John 1:9. I believe many of us have experienced just that today during this service. God gave his Son to pay the price for our sin, and redemption is ours for free. It is the free gift of God for all mankind. All we have to do is accept it, and change our lives.

"But do not accept it lightly. This is something many pastors and Christians won't tell you. Don't accept it lightly. If you are only looking to assuage your guilt and feel better about yourself, don't bother. That is a heart still steeped in selfishness. The whole point is, God is a person. He is our heavenly Father. He loves us, and he gave his Son to save us. He wants a relationship with us. He wants us to live for him. He wants us to live with him. He wants us to abandon our selfish ways and submit ourselves completely and totally to him and to his lordship. If you are not willing to abandon your self-centered life and become the person God wants you to be, then don't cheapen his gift of love by pretending to repent and give your life to him. God wants serious applicants only. He wants all of you. I don't mean you all. I mean all of you as in every bit of each one of you—your whole person. He wants to save you, regenerate you, guide you, direct you, be everything to you. He wants your total submission and devotion in every aspect of your life. He created you for total submission to himself so that he can live with you and in you and through you. Run to him. Run to him with reckless abandon. Nothing you can ever accomplish on this earth will compare to the joy and the peace and the thrill of living you will get by living completely for Jesus. Your plans will never be as good as his plans for you. Your accomplishments will never be as meaningful as those accomplished in the power and will of the Lord Almighty. His thoughts are above our thoughts, and his ways above our ways, Isaiah 55:8–9.

"But know this—living for Jesus requires sacrifice. Make no mistake, it is a battle. It is a battle, and there are casualties of war. Mel ran to him. She lived for him. And she died for him. Melanie was a casualty of war.

"Do you know what I was doing when Mel died? The very moment the life breath was escaping my beautiful daughter's mouth for the very last time? I was in the Spirit, with God, experiencing the vision I have just been telling you about. Do you think this is just a bunch of mumbo jumbo Jesus talk? That God's not real? That Satan's not real? That there isn't any more to life than what we can see and feel and touch? Tell that to Mel. Tell that to my beautiful baby girl, whose lifeless corpse adorns the front of our sanctuary this afternoon. Do you know what she was doing while I was having this vision? She was leaving a small gathering where some foolish girls got involved with dark supernatural things. They were mimicking a séance, and what people commonly call an apparition appeared to them. An apparition? Let's just call it what it was—a demon! We all know it was a demon. *Apparition* sounds so harmless and so imaginary. No, this was a demon, plain and simple. Well, one of the girls was intrigued by the whole thing and wanted more. Two of them were terrified, and Mel was just plain angry. She had known better than to let the evening's activities go that far, but she had been trying to build a relationship with that girl for a several weeks, and she was trying to show her God's love in her own world. Mel was on her way home that night to talk to me and her mother about what had happened and about how to proceed next and how to appropriately deal with the situation. Only she never got home. Are you connecting the dots here? I was having the most intense spiritual experience of my life in the very presence of God, Mel was on her way home to talk to me after breaking up an intense spiritual experience with the devil, and she never made it home. Coincidence? Oh, come now. Not a chance. I will tell you what happened. They killed her. I know, it sounds ridiculous. I sound like some kind of crazy fool to even suggest that demons would interfere that way in our world, but they do every day. We just don't see it for what it is. I will tell you one thing I know. When you pick a fight with the devil, he will not shy away from it. You will have your fight! And he does not fight fair. This vision I had is like nothing I have ever experienced before or even read about. The angel even said it was a once-only human experience, then he gave me strict orders. I will never forget this. He said, 'You have been granted a rare and terrifying opportunity, the acceptance of which presents you with an equally rare and terrifying responsibility. You must teach the people of the Most High. Teach them what you see, and make them understand.'"

Marshall paused for a moment. "Mel died because she obeyed God. And she died because I obeyed God. She was killed by the enemy because she was becoming a threat and because I was becoming a threat. Well, I will tell you this, and then we will adjourn to the cemetery. I will not back down. Her death will not be in vain. I can celebrate today through the most intense, gut-wrenching pain I have ever experienced because I know that God is still on the throne, that Jesus is still alive, and that all things work for the good of those who love God and are called according to his purpose, Romans 8:28. Melanie is with Jesus right now. Her assignment on this earth is finished, and she is now hanging out in glory with her God and Savior. And I know he is saying to her, 'Well done, good and faithful servant, enter into your master's rest,' Matthew 25:21. What will he say to you when it is your time? Will he say, 'Depart from me. I never knew you'? Or will you stand with Mel and hear him say, 'Well done?'

"I have been given a rare and terrifying responsibility to teach the people of the Most High and to make them understand," Marshall concluded. "Beginning this Sunday, we will be starting a new series. We will be starting a new way of life. We will be starting a new way of doing church. We will just be starting new.

"I challenge you all to show up. I dare you. If you have the courage to face your own failings and shortcomings, to swallow your pride, to yield your will to the lordship of Christ, and to enter in to a relationship with the Lord of Hosts, then I will see you Sunday morning. If you are willing to humble yourself, deny yourself, and become what Jesus wants you to be, then I will see you Sunday morning. If you are tired of living your life on your own terms and are ready to submit completely to Jesus and live for him—not like we have been doing, but like he actually commands us to do in his word—then I will see you Sunday morning. If you don't, then the rest of us will be praying for you Sunday morning." He grinned as muted laughter rippled through the crowd.

"Now, friends," he said somberly, "let's go lay to rest an honorable soldier of the army of God, whose death has started a revolution. Someone who, had she known she was about to die, would have and could have said as Paul did in 2 Timothy 4:6-8, 'For I am already being poured out like a drink offering, and the time has come for my departure. I have fought the good fight, I have finished the race, I have kept the faith. Now there is in store for me the crown of righteousness, which the Lord, the righteous Judge, will award to me on that day—and not only to me, but also to all who have longed for his appearing.'

"Mel's day was Monday. I don't know when my day will be, but I will tell you this: I will be able to stand with Mel and say that verse. I will fight the good fight. I will finish the race. I will keep the faith. I will be able to humbly bow before my King, knowing that I held nothing back from him. Say this verse with me from Ephesians 3:20-21, 'Now to him who is able to do immeasurably more than all we ask or imagine, according to his power that is at work within us, to him be glory in the church and in Christ Jesus throughout all generations, for ever and ever! Amen.'

"May God have mercy on us all. Now, come friends, brothers, sisters. Let's go lay to rest a fallen soldier who has made the ultimate sacrifice and has given all in the service of her King. Let's go bury my daughter."